THE BODY IN THE BIRD STORE

"Murderer!"

The lightbulb blinked to life. My pupils shrank back to human dimensions. I could now see the string from the chain dangling in Esther Pester's clawlike grip.

I looked at my feet. After all, that's where Esther Pester was looking.

I could now see the body of a medium-sized man lying on his back on the floor, his face twisted. He looked like he could practically reach out and touch my toes. Then again, judging by appearances, unless he had some zombie blood in him, I didn't think he'd be touching anything.

Die, Die Birdie

J.R. Ripley

Kensington Publishing Corp.
www.kensingtonbooks.com

KENSINGTON BOOKS are published by

Kensington Publishing Corp.
119 West 40th Street
New York, NY 10018

All Kensington Titles, Imprints, and Distributed Lines are available at special quantity discounts for bulk purchases for sales promotions, premiums, fund-raising, and educational or institutional use. Special book excerpts or customized printings can also be created to fit specific needs. For details, write or phone the office of the Kensington special sales manager: Kensington Publishing Corp., 119 West 40th Street, New York, NY 10018, attn: Special Sales Department, Phone: 1-800-221-2647.

Kensington and the K logo Reg. U.S. Pat & TM Off.

ISBN-13: 978-1-4967-1854-9
ISBN-10: 1-4967-1854-2
First Kensington Trade Edition: August 2016
First Kensington Mass Market Edition: September 2018

ISBN-13: 978-1-4967-1855-6 (e-book)
ISBN-10: 1-4967-1855-0 (e-book)

10 9 8 7 6 5 4 3 2 1

Printed in the United States of America

ACKNOWLEDGMENTS

As always, many thanks to my family, friends, and fans, and to my editor, John Scognamiglio, and the entire crew at Kensington for all their efforts, and my agent, Priya Doraswamy, for her patience and dedication.

1

"Welcome to Ruby Lake. Relax . . . Enjoy!" read the sign at the edge of the road.

Two perfectly nice sentiments, but I was perfectly unable to indulge in either of them at the moment.

I whizzed by the sign into town and kept on driving. It was late and the night was falling down on me like the final curtain of a closing Broadway musical. There was so much to do—too much to do. This couldn't be happening. I was two days from opening my new and first business, Birds & Bees. And, so far, it seemed like all I had was a hornet's nest of troubles.

Relax and *enjoy* were mere dreams at this point. The stuff of fantasies. Like imagining myself starring in a big Broadway musical when I can't even carry a tune.

Why couldn't I relax? Why couldn't I enjoy?

First, my major birdseed supplier hadn't shown up. When I'd called the distributor down in Charlotte, I was told the driver's truck had broken down somewhere between here and there. It may as well have been Timbuktu and Sri Lanka for all the good that bit of information was doing me. How do you sell bird food and birding supplies when you have an insufficient amount of one and none of the other?

Second, my best friend and partner in this little enterprise, Kim, had had to leave suddenly for Florida to attend to her mother, who'd broken her hip in a spill outside the swimming pool of her retirement complex. Kim had been gone a week and I wasn't sure if she'd be back in time for our pending grand opening. My last voicemails and texts to her had gone unanswered. Not a good sign.

At least the rain had stopped.

I shot a glance in the rearview mirror. I took comfort in the fact that I at least had a batch of brand-new handcrafted bluebird houses to add to my understocked shelves. I'd purchased them from Aaron Maddley, a local farmer who was a woodworker on the side. He did good work too. The darling houses had gingerbread roofs, copper trim, and were each hand-painted pale blue. The birdhouses ought to sell well. I couldn't wait to get to the shop and set them up. Finding Aaron had been a prize.

I'd had a pair of bluebirds hanging around an old birdhouse at the edge of my front porch. The pine house was rotted and warped. I vowed to replace it with one of Aaron's new cedar ones as soon as I had the chance. Not only were they far more aesthetically pleasing, it would be good advertising. What customer wouldn't want one once they got a look at it? Especially if my bluebirds decided to create a nest.

As I pulled up to the curb outside my fledgling shop, I caught sight of Gertie Hammer walking past. She had wrapped herself up in a puffy, lime-green, plus-size, three-quarter-length down jacket that made her look like a big green shrub with a cold, holly-berry-red face. Her lips were pulled tight and her mitten-covered fists were balled up even tighter. She wasn't my biggest fan. She'd sold me the rundown old three-story Victorian Queen Anne–style house thinking she'd gotten the best of me.

Now I was turning the place into a store for bird lovers, bee lovers, and all things nature. If I was lucky, business would thrive, my love life would spark to life, and I'd be getting the best of Gertie Hammer. Our families have a long history. Think Thirty Years' War, western North Carolina style.

I wiggled my fingers in her direction. I knew that would get her goat. And it did. The woman practically bleated as she turned on her heel and headed across the street to Ruby's Diner, whose slogan was Eat Here, Get Gas. It was an old joke, but then Moire Leora Breeder, the café's owner, is an old jokester—well, older than me by a few years anyway.

Besides, the diner really had been a gas station originally, so it made sense. Moire had added the slogan to the old diner once she'd bought it from the retiring owner. Other than that, things hadn't changed much. The sign with the big green dinosaur on it still stood proudly in the parking lot at the edge of the street. Moire Leora did serve up her own take on a bronto burger as an homage to the corporate apatosaurus.

Moire Leora wouldn't be too happy about Gertie showing up at the diner. When Gertie ate in Moire's place, everybody else got indigestion.

I parked and opened the back door of the minivan. She's a white Kia Sedona with tan upholstery, what little there is left of it. The minivan's a bit of a dinosaur herself. The old girl's got 117,000-plus miles on her, but I'm sure she'd be good for plenty more—like 118,000, fingers crossed. The aging Sedona may not be the sweetest-looking vehicle on the road, but it suited my requirements, with plenty of room for everything I needed to haul, both in and out.

I glanced up toward the second floor of Birds & Bees. Sure enough, Esther Pilaster, Esther Pester, as I liked to call her—in private, of course—was peeking out her window.

Typical. Esther was my renter, at least for another nine months. She'd unfortunately come with the property and her lease wouldn't be up till the end of the year. I couldn't wait. The woman could teach a class in Busybody 101.

I walked up the short, uneven pink brick path and climbed the broad steps to the porch leading to the double French doors. I wasn't surprised to find one of them unlocked. With so many distractions, I'd been forgetting that a lot lately. Besides, Esther Pester sometimes used the front door, though I'd told her time and time again to stick to the rear entrance. Front for customers, rear for renters. I preached it over and over to the woman like a mantra. But it had always been in vain. You'd think she'd learn to listen. You'd think I'd learn to save my breath.

Maybe the Pester needed new hearing aid batteries. Maybe she needed a whole new hearing aid. Maybe I'd take up a collection for her.

The scent of fresh gardenias met me. I'd set two vases full of the flowers in the front window just that morning. I had purchased the gardenias from Francoise Early. Mrs. Early is a seventy-five-year-old widow with the greenest thumb I've ever seen. She's a prim woman with silvery hair, a fleshy nose on whose tip a pair of glasses is normally perched, a ruddy complexion, and a pleasantly plump figure. For all I know, she's secretly married to Santa Claus, because she looks exactly like I'd pictured Mrs. Claus when I was growing up.

Francoise Early lives at the edge of town on a large piece of property with its own greenhouse. We'd worked out an arrangement where I'd carry some of her plants in Birds & Bees. Francoise had even agreed to cultivate some of the specialty plants I wanted to make available to my customers, plants to attract and support various species of birds and bees throughout the seasons.

I sighed with contentment as I hit the light switch near the door, but nothing happened. Oh great. I could feel my contentment leaving like the tide. Did I have any spare lightbulbs? No. I did have some spare daffodil bulbs, but I wasn't sure what wattage they were. They sure would be eco-friendly if they worked though, wouldn't they?

I silently cursed my bad luck and went back to the minivan for the Aaron Maddley houses. It took me three trips, but I hauled all twelve of the bluebird houses in through the front door, dropped them on the counter next to the register, then paused to catch a breath. I know, twelve lightweight red cedar birdhouses shouldn't have tired me out, but it had been a long day.

It had been a very long two months. I was looking forward to opening the doors of Birds & Bees and watching all the customers fly in and the products fly out.

A girl could dream, couldn't she? Like Dorothy in *The Wiz*, I just wanted to "Ease On Down the Road" to happiness and success.

I'd heard some of the comments around town in my daily rounds since coming back home after so many years away. Some folks thought it was crazy to open a bird lover's shop in Ruby Lake. Well, let them eat crow when I succeed, that's all I have to say!

I locked the front door behind me and worked my way through the back. Getting farther and farther from the yellow light cast by the street lamp out front. Not for the first time, I realized just how spooky this old house could be in the dark.

As a girl growing up in Ruby Lake, I'd heard all the stories too, about the ghost that supposedly dwelt in this old place. I shooed the memory away before I scared myself any further. If I let my thoughts run in that direction any longer, no doubt I'd be hearing ethereal oohs, aahs, and clanking ghostly chains.

I have a vivid imagination. Sometimes a blessing but sometimes a curse.

Maybe I could find an extra lightbulb in the storage closet, or unscrew one from somewhere else for the time being. As I made my way awkwardly across

the sales floor, feeling like a bat that'd lost its sense
of echolocation, my shin banged against the sharp
rim of a low-profile, hand-chiseled granite birdbath.
The bowl wobbled. I grabbed it with both hands to
prevent it from falling and felt one of my fingernails break against the coarse stone. I started to
curse whoever had put the darn birdbath there in
the first place, then realized it had been me.

Rubbing my throbbing shin and cursing some
more, I felt around in the dark for the light switch
to the small room in back that did double duty as a
storeroom-slash-office. The office portion, at this
point, consisted of a composition notebook resting atop two cases of berry blast suet cakes stacked
on top of each other.

The light in back wasn't working either. For the
first time, I wondered if the power was out in the
entire house. But no, there had been a light on in
Esther Pester's upstairs apartment, so that couldn't
be the problem. Life should be so easy. I hoped the
house wasn't having electrical troubles now. I had
problems aplenty as it was. I didn't need more
problems or more expenses. And if the house was
having electrical issues, the solution would, no
doubt, be expensive. It seemed everything in an
old house needs fixing at one time or another and
that such fixes are, as a rule, pricey.

I breathed a sigh of relief at the thought that
whatever was wrong with the electrical system was
likely limited to the first floor. Mom and I shared
an apartment upstairs too, but not on the same
floor as Esther. We had the entire third floor to
ourselves. Well, there might have been some squirrels roosting between the ceiling and the roof. I

hadn't quite made up my mind yet about those weird scratching noises coming from the rafters. If the noises were animal in nature, I preferred to think they'd emanated from squirrels rather than mice. Squirrels I could live with, at least temporarily. Mice creep me out.

Anyway, I was glad we weren't without power. Things were hard enough on Mom.

"That's it," I muttered to no one, "I'm calling it a day." It was nearly 9:00 p.m. I'd been up since five. Definitely quitting time. I had half a bottle of white zinfandel in the fridge. A glass of wine and a Lean Cuisine followed by a quick shower. That was all I needed. Plus, I was in the middle of a recently published tome on the birds of Western North Carolina. If you're going to own a store for bird lovers, you've got to stay current. I'd promised myself I'd read a chapter each night. Unfortunately, being alone—except for Mom—and single, I didn't have anything better to do. There, I've said it: I'm single.

As I set my foot on the stairs, I felt a thump and thought I might have heard a cry. In fact, the treads themselves seemed to shake ever so slightly. Like a train passing. But the nearest train track was miles from here.

What the heck was that? I hoped Mom hadn't fallen.

The stairs led up to the second-floor landing where Esther's compact one-bedroom apartment and a now empty two-bedroom unit sat separated by a small storeroom. I hesitated. Maybe I'd gone too far. Maybe my overactive imagination was playing tricks on me.

Maybe.

I steeled my nerves, or at least tried to, and slowly climbed the stairs. I was swallowed in darkness here. Not a beam of light penetrated this far back. I didn't hear anything now but the beating of my heart. The air grew chill. For a moment I considered turning back. "Mom? Ms. Pilaster?" No answer. The storeroom door stood open. The room was empty and unused, but I planned to store extra stock up there eventually. Right now, I didn't have enough stock for my shelves, let alone extra. A musty odor spilled into the foyer, tickling my nose.

"Hello?" I strained my ears. Nothing. "Anybody here?"

It was pitch-black inside. There were no windows in the storeroom or on the door leading to the outside stairs. The metal stairs on the outside of the house had been added to the house later, when the rooms on the second and third floors had been converted for use as separate apartments.

A bare bulb hung from the ceiling of the empty room. That is, I knew there was a bulb—I just couldn't see it. It was screwed into one of those light fixtures that you pull on and off with a string. Now, if only I could find that string. I fished around in the darkness, my hands swimming around like tentacles. Not that I'm saying I have a head like an octopus. Even if Jerry Kennedy did say I did back in third grade. Real mature, Jerry. Of course, the only thing dumber than being told you have a head that resembles an octopus is remembering that dumb comment decades later.

"Ouch!" My feet bumped into something on the floor and my juvenile thoughts jumped forward to the present. The mysterious something I'd hit clattered as it skidded away along the hardwood. I sank to my knees and groped around. My fingers found metal. Wrought iron, by the feel of it. My hands worked their way up and down the invisible object's length. Hmmm, it felt like one of the hooks I'd be selling. The kind you attach a birdfeeder to in order to keep the squirrels and raccoons at bay. What was it doing up here?

A light shot at my face and I was momentarily blinded. I held the hook out, not so much as a weapon, but to defend myself from whatever was trying to spotlight me to death.

"Murderer!"

The lightbulb blinked to life. My pupils shrank back to human dimensions. I could now see the string from the chain, dangling in Esther Pester's clawlike grip.

I looked at my feet. After all, that's where Esther Pester was looking.

I could now see the body of a medium-sized man lying on his back on the floor, his face twisted. He looked like he could practically reach out and touch my toes. Then again, judging by appearances, unless he had some zombie blood in him, I didn't think he'd be touching anything.

"Amy Simms, you're a murderer!" repeated Esther, aiming her free hand at me.

Esther took a step back.

I jumped and screamed.

Then Esther screamed too, exposing her long,

uneven teeth, aiming her finger at me like a death ray.

I dropped the feeder hook—it landed on my big toe—and threw my hands in front of my face. "Please," I cried, "turn that thing off!" My foot throbbed smartly.

Esther, bless her pestering heart, complied. I was going to have to give the dear a tenth month's rent. Free. Plus, she was smart enough to own a flashlight. A darn good one too. I could have used a flashlight like that when I slammed into the bird-bath downstairs.

Click. I was now in the dark. With Esther standing there accusing me of murder. With a dead body practically licking my toes. A chill shot up and down my spine. The hairs on my arms shot to attention. I really needed a better depilatory.

"No!" I cried. That's it. I was kicking the woman out just as soon as I got this dead body thing sorted out.

"Turn the lights back on! Turn the lights back on!" Geesh, I'd only wanted her to turn off that lighthouse-like LED flashlight of hers. That thing could burn holes through solid steel. I rubbed my eyes with my fists. What damage had that thing done to my retinas?

I looked down through watery eyes. The dead man seemed to be looking up at me out of one eye like it was my fault. But I swear, it wasn't.

That was when I noticed the sticky red substance clinging to my fingers.

2

A sudden pounding on the back door below set both of us off and we screamed in unison. It was nothing to make the church choir proud. But it sure would have set the cat's hair on end, if I had a cat.

We looked at each other in wide-eyed fear. Was it the boogeyman? Had Death come knocking on my back door? I struggled to calm my nerves. I cleared my throat. "Maybe you should go see who's at the door, Esther," I suggested.

Esther shook her head adamantly. "Not me, young lady. This is your house. You answer the door." Esther Pilaster is a small, narrow-shouldered, elflike woman with a hawkish nose, sagging eyelids, and silver hair normally pulled tightly to the back of her head in a four-inch ponytail held in place with an elastic black velvet hair tie. Her gray-blue eyes, topped with wispy white eyebrows, dared me to challenge her.

The banging picked up again, harder, louder.

I sighed heavily and pushed the birdfeeder hook out of my path, nudging it closer to the body with my shoe. I shuddered as I looked at the man's lifeless form. He was slumped on his side, his pale face toward the wall. He wore baggy blue jeans and a long-sleeve black T-shirt with an unbuttoned brown flannel jacket over top. His wavy black hair was matted on the side facing toward the ceiling, no doubt indicating where he'd been struck. Who was he? Why was he here?

Why was he dead?

The banging continued.

"Don't touch anything!" I hollered at Esther as I scurried down the dark stairs.

"Don't you worry," Esther shot back. "Wouldn't touch a thing if you paid me."

I tromped down the steps and struggled for the doorknob in the dark. The light from the sliver of moon in the sky did little to help. Finally, I managed to find the doorknob. I twisted and pulled, realizing a moment after I'd opened the door that I just might be letting a murderer back into the store.

I impulsively swung the door shut again, but a big black boot got in my way.

"Ouch!"

I hesitated, squinting into the darkness. "Wh-who are you?" A large, brooding hulk of a man stood on the stoop, clutching something in his left hand. A flash of lightning appeared in the far distance. That meant a storm moving in from the mountains. Bringing snow, or maybe more rain.

He looked at the dark object in his gloved hand. "I've got a delivery for a—" He paused. He pulled

one of his brown leather work gloves off using his
teeth. He must have done it a hundred times because he did it rather adeptly, like a titmouse nim-
bly breaking open the shell of a sunflower seed to
get to the nut inside.

His free hand rummaged around in his trouser
pockets. A small flashlight attached to a keychain
blinked on. "Amy Simms?" I recognized the dark
object now as one of those electronic clipboards
that drivers carry nowadays.

I heaved a sigh, felt my trembling subside. I
nodded. "That's me."

"Sorry I'm late," he said lazily. "Accident out on
the interstate." He traced the weak light across my
chest and face. "You okay, miss?"

"What's going on down there?" shrieked Esther
Pilaster. "How long you expect me to stand around
up here all alone with a dead guy?"

Despite the dimness, I noticed the deliveryman's bushy eyebrows jerk upwards.

I forced a weak smile. "We have a bit of a problem."

He glanced at the bloodstains on my hand and
took a step back, and I didn't blame him. "Maybe I
should come back another time."

"No, wait!" I pleaded. I pointed toward the stairs.
"There's been an accident. I think a man is dead."
And the businessperson in me needed those store
goods.

I grabbed him by his jacket. "Follow me." He
had no choice but to trail me up the stairs.

Esther stood hunched in the corner of the
room, as far from the body as she could possibly
get. Her nose wrinkled up. "Who's he?" A billowy,

pale yellow cable-knit sweater hung loosely to her hips. A black and red tartan skirt hung just as loosely to her feet. The sweater might have been white once. The entire outfit looked a million years old.

"Deliveryman," I said quickly to Esther. I turned to the beefy trucker. There was now a dab of blood on his jacket where I'd grabbed him. I'd have some explaining to do both to him and the police. He wore blue trousers, a matching blue shirt with the name *Dwayne* stitched above the pocket, and a baggy tan jacket.

I felt safer just having him there in the room with us. His presence would certainly discourage any murderers who might be lurking in some dark corner of the house, weapon in hand.

"You see?" I waved to the body on the floor, not that it needed pointing out.

The driver nodded nervously. "Have you called the police?" He had a white-knuckled grip on his electronic clipboard.

I shook my head. "I was going to do that when we heard you banging on the door."

Dwayne wasn't looking so good. A bead of sweat ran along his hairline. He backed out of the room and pulled out his cell phone. "I'm calling 9-1-1."

"Good idea," I said. We trooped back down the stairs and waited for the authorities to arrive.

A small kitchenette, nothing more than a single stainless-steel sink, a compact microwave, and a coffeepot, was set into an alcove in the back right corner. Years ago, the original kitchen had no doubt occupied this space and more, but previous tenants had removed the house's kitchen to make room for the various businesses that had come and gone in the space before the old house finally came to an ignoble end, sitting mostly vacant and ignored for several months before Mom and I purchased it from Gertrude Hammer.

I lit a handful of scented beeswax candles and washed my hands in the sink, then filled the glass carafe from the tap. The water ran icy cold this time of year, with spring still several weeks away. I dumped in several scoops of ground coffee, frowned, then dumped in a few more. It looked to be a long, dreary night and I figured we could all use an extra jolt of caffeine.

Esther took her coffee with two cream packs and three sugars. Dwayne the trucker declined and stood gazing silently out one of the side windows in what had originally been the formal living room.

I heard what sounded like a car alarm in the distance but knew it was nothing more than a northern mockingbird. As proof of my theory, the car alarm tune morphed into the pleasant *what-cheer*, *what-cheer* sound of a northern cardinal, North Carolina's state bird. The mockingbird is famous for its ability to imitate other birds. The mockingbird is the Rich Little of the bird world.

The front door rattled with the force of knuckles on wood. "Thank goodness," I said to no one in particular. "It looks like the police are here." Flashing blue light from the sedan parked out front illuminated Lake Shore Drive. Through the glass, I noticed the glint of a badge on the brown uniform of the man at the door and quickly opened it. Another officer hung a step back to his left, one foot off the path and in my new flowerbed. Trampling the bulbs I'd so lovingly planted there two weeks ago. I decided to let it go. After all, murder trumps mashed daffodil bulbs.

"Thank heavens you're here." I stepped aside and let the two men in. The burning candles filled the room with a scent reminiscent of wildflower honey.

The first removed his hat and bounced it nervously against his thigh. Underneath his cap, his crew-cut blond hair stood up in front. He must have been the last man on earth rubbing Brylcreem in his hair and styling it like it was 1960. He was rather boyish looking, with a fleshy, squat nose, an uneven smattering of freckles, and dark jade eyes.

And I knew him.

William Gerald Kennedy.

I closed my eyes for a moment to collect myself. Third grade was a long time ago. High school was not. Jerry and I had gone out a few times and it had ended badly.

He squinted and the beginnings of a smile came to his lips. "Amy? Is that you? I heard you were back in town." He folded his arms across his chest and looked around. "So what exactly have you got going on here?"

"Hello, Jerry," I said, trying to keep the bad taste in my mouth that I got when I said his name from spilling out in the tone of my voice. I looked him up and down. Even in uniform, he still looked like the annoying boy I'd grown up with. "I'm opening a new business, Birds and Bees."

"Cute. Birds and bees, huh?" he quipped. "What are you selling, sex ed books for twelve-year-olds?"

His companion snorted.

My lips turned down. "More like birding supplies, gardening and apiary supplies to support bee colonies and butterfly populations as well as birds." I quirked up my eyebrow. "But if you need a book on sex ed, I'm sure I could order one for you."

The officer shadowing him laughed again and Jerry Kennedy shut him up with an icy look.

Jerry cleared his throat and I noticed, with satisfaction, quarter-sized red blotches on his cheeks. "You do this all on your own?"

What was he asking me? Whether I was married or not? Not that he stood a chance with me.

"With my mother's and Kim's help." Actually, Mom's twin sister, Betty, had also contributed. Aunt Betty's a little goofy, kindhearted and thrice married. Her current husband is a retired developer who likes to tell people that the only thing he's trying to develop these days is his golf game.

A lopsided grin crossed his face. "Kimberly Christy?"

I nodded.

"You two were joined at the hip in high school. Some of us were surprised she didn't go off to college in Chapel Hill like you did."

Kimberly was sharp but not the studying type, and had stuck with the local community college. I'd opted for the University of North Carolina at Chapel Hill. "So, you're a police officer now?"

His smile bloomed. "I'm chief of police," he boasted. "Been so for going on four years."

I suppressed a grimace. There must have been a lack of candidates.

Jerry rested a hand on my shoulder. "So what's

going on here?" He glanced at his companion, a younger but beefier-looking police officer whose brown eyes darted around the room like a woodpecker watching for a lurking red-shouldered hawk. "A call came in about a dead body?"

I nodded. "That's right." I jerked my head toward the rear of the store. "Upstairs."

He smirked. "Not a dead bird, I hope."

"A dead man," I replied stiffly.

"She killed him," Esther said ever so helpfully, shaking her coffee cup at me like she was Lady Justice waving her sword in judgment. She had commandeered one of the two walnut rockers in the alcove. Her feet didn't reach the ground and her lace-up white orthopedic shoes bobbed up and down as she swayed, revealing thin white socks bunched around her ankles. "I found her standing right over him. Then she washed her hands in the sink." Esther's eyes bulged out.

"I had to!" I shot back. "I had blood on them—" I clammed up.

"See?" Esther's sharp jaw jutted out. Esther had helped herself to the orchid throw I'd picked up at the American Orchid Society's former headquarters and botanical garden in Delray Beach, Florida, some years before, draping it tightly over her shoulders. I couldn't help hoping she didn't spill coffee all over it.

I frowned at her and rolled my eyes for Jerry's benefit. "I did not kill anybody." I explained my actions. "I don't even know who the man is, Jerry."

"Chief Kennedy," he said out of the side of his mouth, tapping his badge with his finger.

"Somebody killed him, all right." Dwayne stood

near the window, his hands stuffed in his pockets. "There's a poker with blood all over it lying right there beside him."

"It's not a poker, it's a—"

"Who are you, exactly?" demanded Chief Kennedy, cutting me off and looking past me.

"Dwayne Rogers. I work for Cole's Trucking." He picked up the electronic clipboard he'd set atop one of the near-empty shelves. "I was making a delivery." He sighed. "Wish I'd stayed home now." He twisted toward the window—like a rooster seeking freedom—the fingertips of his gloves sticking out of his jacket pockets like chicken combs.

"What's with all the candles?" Chief Kennedy inquired. "This is a criminal investigation, not some romantic soirée. Can't we get some lights on?"

"There seems to be a problem with the electric," I replied.

"Officer Sutton will check out your fuse box while we go check out this body of yours."

"It isn't *my* body."

"Well, let's go see just whose body it is." Jerry extended his hand toward the stairs. He glanced at my boarder. "Ms. Pilaster, correct?"

"That's right," Esther answered. "I'm innocent, Chief." She turned her eyes on me. Gee, could she be more obvious?

With introductions and pleasantries finished, we marched upstairs, me in the lead, Jerry Kennedy close behind. He stood in the open doorway and took in the scene, then approached the body slowly, crouching beside it.

I joined him, much as I loathed squatting so close to a dead man. Or Jerry.

"Don't touch anything," cautioned the chief. The birdfeeder hook and prime candidate for murder weapon lay at his feet.

"Not in a million years," I grumbled.

"Her fingerprints are all over it!"

I looked over Jerry Kennedy's shoulder to see Esther peering accusingly at me. She was in full Esther the Pester mode.

I pursed my lips. "Of course my fingerprints are all over it." I rose. "It's my hook. Plus, like I said before we came upstairs, I kicked the hook with my foot in the dark and picked it up."

I glared at my renter. "I didn't know what it was." I folded my arms across my chest. "And I did not swing it at anybody." Not that I wasn't in the mood to just then.

Esther's gray-blue eyes honed in on me. "She was standing right here in this room, in the dark, with that thing in her hand when I came in."

"You already said that, Esther," I said sourly. "Where's my mother, by the way?" I was surprised all the commotion hadn't brought her down. Was she asleep?

"Went to the movies with that friend of hers, Cheryl Harper." Esther coughed uncontrollably. Esther was a reformed smoker. At least that's what she told me. There were times I swear I could smell cigarette smoke coming from behind her apartment door. "I saw them when they were heading out."

I'll bet she saw. Esther saw everything. So why didn't she see who killed this stranger in my house? Or had she?

Maybe she murdered him herself. A crazed lone spinster who lures unsuspecting men up to her apartment, then clobbers them when they try in vain to leave as they realize she doesn't have the beautiful young daughter she'd no doubt enticed them with . . .

If Esther went to jail, I wouldn't have to evict her.

The good news was that with Mom at the movies, at least she didn't have to deal with all this. And if she'd been home at the time of the murder, she might have been a victim too. A frisson ran up my spine as the thought struck my heart.

Jerry's fingers played a march along the textured grip of his pistol. He stood and I heard his knees crackle. "I'm afraid you're going to have to come down to the station, Ms. Simms."

"Ms. Simms?" I blubbered, wiping my sweaty palms against my slacks. When had I started sweating? "What are you talking about? You know me, Jerry. I didn't kill anybody!" Though I might later, after he was gone.

He held out a fleshy palm. "Now, now. You may not want to say anything until you've had a chance to speak with your attorney."

Officer Sutton appeared in the doorway. "I found the circuit breaker box in a downstairs closet in the back room. Breaker was tripped."

Tripped or turned off on purpose? I wondered.

Chief Kennedy scratched the side of his nose. "Any sign of a break-in?"

Sutton shook his head. "Nope."

"I found the front door unlocked when I arrived," I explained.

Jerry Kennedy looked bemused. "You always leave your front door unlocked when you're away from the premises, Amy? I mean, I know this is a small town and all, but still . . ."

I frowned. "I'm pretty sure I locked it." I shook my head. "Or at least I think I did." I looked at my tenant. "Esther might have come in through the front, though I've told her a thousand times not to, and forgotten to lock it."

"Did not!" Esther snapped.

"Might have!" I snapped back.

Chief Kennedy stuck his hand up like a stop sign and nodded to his companion. "Officer Sutton, you'd better read Ms. Simms her rights."

"But, Jerry—Chief Kennedy—" I began.

He held up his hand once again. "Not another word." He turned to Officer Sutton. "Take Ms. Simms down to the squad car and see she gets to the station, Dan. I'll be along as soon as I can. Sure hope the ME gets here soon." He pulled at his watch. "Looks like it's going to be a long night. Got any more of that coffee?"

"Please, help yourself," I said, hoping he caught the unveiled sarcasm, as Officer Sutton took me by the elbow and led me from the storeroom. "And help yourself to the Girl Scout cookies too!"

I heard him thank me even as we disappeared down the stairs. The joke was on Jerry; I didn't have any cookies.

3

I stared glumly at my reflection in the restroom mirror. My just beyond shoulder-length chestnut brown hair was frizzled and flat. My baby blues were ringed with dark circles that made me look like a raccoon, and my face was pale as an albino ghost's. Most of my lipstick had been wiped away because I have a nervous habit of licking my lips repeatedly when nervous. I pulled a tube of Parisian Passion from my purse and made a halfhearted attempt to freshen up.

I pursed my lips in the mirror, doing my best to imitate a haughty French woman, and frowned.

Let's face it. I was a wreck. And no amount of lip gloss was going to help the situation.

I yanked down on the sleeves of my faux-wrap blue jersey V-neck blouse in a vain attempt to combat the cold. I'd left the store without even thinking to ask Officer Sutton to let me grab my coat. March in Ruby Lake was not the time of year to be running around in a flimsy shirt, especially after dark.

I yawned for the umpteenth time. Then again, it was no wonder I looked and felt the way I did. I'd been up half the night here at the police station while Ruby Lake's finest did their best to confound and confuse me.

I frowned at myself. They'd managed to do a pretty good job of it so far, too. Maybe it was the sleep deprivation. Maybe it was knowing a man had been murdered in my house-slash-business. Maybe it was wondering if I was going to end up charged with murder and, if I wasn't, if I'd be allowed to open Birds & Bees as scheduled.

Would the police keep the store locked up and off-limits as a murder scene? If so, all my business plans would go up in smoke.

And where would Mom and I sleep? We lived in that same house. Esther the Pester lived in that same house. Would we all be out on the street? Would Mom and I be sharing a Dumpster with Esther? Could I keep collecting her rent?

The prison guard assigned to make sure I didn't make a daring escape from the ladies' room was waiting for me when I came out. Okay, so she wasn't a mean-eyed, mean-faced prison guard with an itchy trigger finger. She was Anita Brown, the department's middle-aged nighttime dispatcher and part-time home-based pastry chef. She could be pretty mean if you beat her at pinochle. At least, that's what Mom told me.

Mom loves her pinochle. I didn't understand the game at all, though my mother tried to explain the ins and outs of the card game to me on multiple occasions. I didn't get it and I couldn't help it. Every time she starts describing something called *melds* my mind turns to images of Mr. Spock and his Vulcan mind-melds, and everything else just turns to mush and gibberish after that.

Mom was waiting for me too, dressed for a night on the town in a pair of wide-legged black slacks with a black-and-white, horizontal stripe wool sweater. There was no sign of her friend Cheryl Harper, the woman Esther claimed she'd gone to the movies with. Instead, a sixtyish man, black-and-silver hair swept regally back over his head, stood at her side. One hand rested on her elbow. Had Mom been out on a date? Without telling me? His nose looked like it belonged on an old Roman coin.

He wore a brown suit and he extracted a business card from the inside pocket of the loose-fitting jacket. Chief Kennedy took one look at the card and dropped it on his desk. "I know who you are, Mr. Harlan."

It was a small office, no more than a couple hundred square feet with several desks scattered about, and with absolutely no sense of style at all. These guys could use a feng shui session. They could also use a vacuum cleaner. The view looking out on Barwick Street was barely visible because there were filing cabinets blocking half the windows. The dented and rust-pitted file cabinets were themselves topped with stacks of sun-yellowed and dust-covered folders and drooping potted plants.

Officer Dan Sutton sat back in a simple wood chair propped against the side wall with his hat down over his eyes. I didn't know if he was simply bored or snoozing.

Mom shoved past Jerry Kennedy's desk and raced to my side. "Amy!" she cried, pulling on my arms. "Are you all right, dear? I came as soon as I heard." She looked over her shoulder. "Well, as soon as I heard and could get hold of Mr. Harlan." She wiggled her fingers at the gentleman.

My brow wrinkled and I whispered close to her ear, "Just who exactly is Mr. Harlan?"

"He's your attorney, dear." Mom fluffed her blond bob. She was a brunette like me, but had been dyeing her locks for a number of years in an attempt to hide the gray that she says she caught from me. I'm not convinced mothers can "catch" gray hair from their teenage daughters, but I wasn't about to argue the point with her. She'd only accuse me of giving her yet another strand or two of gray hair. And I thought the hair color and style made her look more like I imagined actress Jenny McCarthy's mom would look than mine.

I stiffened. "My attorney?" My eyes bounced from the elegant-looking Mr. Harlan to the inelegant-looking Jerry Kennedy. "Do I need an attorney?" I confess I was somewhat relieved he wasn't her date, but less happy to think I actually needed an attorney.

There was a lone cell in the far corner, currently occupied by one forlorn and disheveled young man with an acne-scarred face who watched us dejectedly. I couldn't blame him since the cell had no TV. I prayed I wasn't about to become his roommate.

Heck, I'd rather room outside in the Dumpster with Esther the Pester.

I noticed a hint of trouble in Mom's blue eyes. Had I missed something while I was freshening up in the restroom?

"Jerry here—"

"Chief Kennedy," Jerry said rather wearily, and I sensed a tone of defeat in his voice. Maybe that was because he'd suffered through two years of school with Mom as his high school science teacher. Mom's retired now, but she'd seen his grades, knew his study habits and at least some of the secrets in his teenage closet. He'd get no respect from her.

Mom rolled her eyes dramatically and continued. "*Jerry* seems to think you had something to do with the murder of that poor man at our house." Mom dragged me past Chief Kennedy's desk toward Mr. Harlan. "Mr. Harlan is here to protect you from getting arrested."

Jerry scowled and his cheeks puffed up like a chipmunk's, as they always did in such circumstances—like when I'd rebuffed his teenage hormone-induced urges back in eleventh grade. "I never said Amy was under arrest, Mrs. Simms."

Mr. Harlan stuck out a brown and weathered hand. "Ben Harlan. Pleased to meet you, Ms. Simms."

He handed me a business card. Mr. Harlan seemed to have a never-ending supply. I rolled it over in my hand and slid it into the pocket of my butterscotch corduroys.

"Are you saying Ms. Simms is free to leave, Chief?"

Chief Kennedy nodded. His chin rested on his fists. His elbows were anchored to his desk. "Yeah, but I'm going to want to have a word with you in the morning. There are still a lot of unanswered questions."

"Are we free to return to Birds and Bees?" I asked with trepidation.

Chief Kennedy thought for a moment, then shrugged. "Just so long as you stay away from the crime scene. We might have missed something. I may have to call in the boys from state and have them take a look too."

"I have no intention of going anywhere near the crime scene, Jer—Chief Kennedy," I replied.

"Where's your coat?" Mom asked, hustling me toward the door. Maybe she was afraid Jerry would change his mind and lock me up.

"At the house." On the counter where I draped it while waiting for the cops to arrive.

Mom grabbed her charcoal peacoat from the hook and threw it over my shoulders. "See you Sunday, Anita?" Sunday's their standing pinochle game.

"Wouldn't miss it," Anita Brown answered with a smile and a wave. "I count on beating you for my weekly lunch money."

Mr. Harlan held the door. "I trust you will keep me informed over the course of your investigation, Chief Kennedy."

Jerry waved his hand halfheartedly. I didn't know if that meant yes or no, and I didn't care. Surely, I couldn't need a lawyer. I hadn't done anything wrong. He pointed a finger at me. "I mean it, Amy. Stay out of that storeroom until I give you the all clear."

I nodded. Boswell may have been mistaken when he quoted Samuel Johnson as saying the road to hell is paved with good intentions, but that didn't make the aphorism any less true.

4

There was no telltale light leaking from the crack between Esther Pilaster's door and the floor. She was probably sleeping. I turned on the hall light and stared at the crime scene tape that did its best to block entry to the storeroom.

Now a crime scene.

Mom had already gone upstairs to bed. I knew I'd told the police I'd stay far away from the storeroom, but I wanted to see the scene of the crime one last time. It was mere hours till morning anyway, and I didn't think I'd be able to sleep a wink. There was black powder all over the floor and a darker stain where I suspected the dead man's head had lain. Recognizing what that stain represented, I instantly regretted my decision to revisit the scene.

Funny to think a man had been murdered here in this quaint Victorian house. It seemed such an uncivilized thing to do. We should be drinking tea and talking about flowers and birds. Not knocking each other in the head with birdfeeder hooks. After which, the only talk of flowers would be what floral arrangement to lay atop the deceased's grave.

I yawned and trudged up to our private apartment. Mom's door was closed. In a few minutes, my eyes were too.

I woke to the smell of coffee. There's no better way to wake up. I sucked in the life-giving aroma, then remembered the horror of the night before. I glanced at my bedside clock. Somehow I'd managed to get a solid four hours' sleep.

Thankfully, the rats or mice or squirrels or whatever critters were partying in the attic had taken the night off for once. I'd hire a critter wrangler to rid me of them if I had the money to spare, but the business was taking all I had and more. Soon, the weather would be warm enough that whatever had found shelter in my attic would return to a life out of doors. Hopefully, I could get the attic checked out and sealed properly before next winter's infestation.

I found Mom in our small yet well-appointed kitchen.

"Jerry's waiting for you downstairs," she said.

I grabbed a mug and poured a cup of coffee. My hand was shaking, which only made me mad. Mad at myself. "What do I care," I snapped, "if Jerry Kennedy's waiting for me?"

From the small kitchen I could see the edge of Ruby Lake; a very light chop kept the surface churning. That meant a cold wind was sweeping across the lake from the mountains to the west. A Carolina chickadee scrabbled along the gnarled limbs of a red oak in the yard, probably in search of insects.

Mom twisted her head to look at me. One hand clutched the spatula she was using to push eggs around the cast-iron skillet. "What?" She was still in her pale blue housecoat and slippers. I was in my flannel pj's with the pink piglets on them.

"Sorry." I blew my lips over the coffee. "Guess I'd better go see what he wants and get this over with." I gave her a kiss on the cheek.

"What about breakfast?"

"It'll have to wait," I said, though my stomach disagreed with the decision.

"Maybe you should wait until I call Ben Harlan." Mom wiped her hands on her frilly apron and reached for the phone on the wall. Mom had to be just about the last person on the planet who insisted on a landline.

I rested my hand atop hers. "That won't be necessary. I can handle Jerry Kennedy." Though I still couldn't get used to the idea of seeing him in an official law enforcement uniform. I would never have expected to see him dressed like a policeman unless it was for Halloween. Even then, he'd have been more likely perpetrating tricks rather than gathering treats.

I returned to my room and pulled on a pair of jeans and threw a navy blue cable-knit sweater over my head, then headed downstairs feeling a lot less confident than I talked. Besides, as a kid, Jerry had had a habit of sticking his fingers where they didn't belong. I didn't want him making a shambles of my business before I'd even had the chance to open my doors to customers.

"Got any more of that?" Jerry stood behind my sales counter peering at my register. I noticed he was wearing latex gloves.

"What?"

Jerry gestured in my direction. It took a second for it to sink in that he was talking about the coffee mug in my left hand. "There's none in the pot."

I frowned. Maybe I should be opening a coffee shop rather than a bird store. "I'll put some on." I went to the corner and grudgingly rinsed out the pot. The remains of last night's brew had stuck to the bottom of the carafe. I'd probably forgotten to turn the pot off last night. I'd had more important things to think about, like a dead man on the second floor and my own possible incarceration. Thankfully, the machine was on a timer and had turned itself off eventually, leaving nothing but a sticky coffee residue.

A few minutes later, I set a mug of fresh coffee on the sales counter.

"You sure nothing's missing from the till?"

I shook my head. "We aren't even open yet. There wasn't anything in the till to take."

Jerry, Chief Kennedy—it was going to be hard to think of him as representing the law—looked around the room. There was no sign of a break-in. "You said the front door was unlocked?"

"That's right." I'd explained all this the night before. Though the more I thought about it, the more I was convinced that I had locked up before I left. That meant either Esther had unlocked it and not locked up afterward or somebody else had picked the lock.

Jerry Kennedy nodded between sips of coffee. "And nothing else was stolen?"

I nodded once more. Again, we'd been over this a hundred times. "Look around," I said, waving a hand. "There's not a whole lot here to steal."

Jerry grinned. "Yeah, who'd bust into a store to steal a bunch of birdseed, let alone murder a man over it?"

I ignored the insult that I was sure was buried in that sentence. "Did you get any fingerprints off the door?" Like maybe matching those of the dead man.

"Only yours."

Great. "Any idea who the dead man is—was—yet?"

Jerry pulled in his lips. "We're working on it." He helped himself to a refill. "You sure you'd never seen him before?"

"Never." Though the way he was lying there, I'd only seen half his face. I grabbed a few of the Aaron Maddley bluebird houses off the counter and arranged them on a shelf facing the front door. I forced myself to think about something more pleasant. The best way to take my mind off something I didn't like was to keep busy.

So I did.

I tapped my fingernail against my teeth. I'd have to make up a sign to hang from the shelf explaining that the birdhouses were locally handcrafted. Tourists love to buy things local to the area they are visiting. I'm that way myself—like the orchid throw or the cheesy kitchen magnet I'd brought back from Dollywood in Pigeon Forge. And with the mountains and the lake, the town of

Ruby Lake gets its fair share of tourists, winter, spring, summer, and fall.

I dragged a forty-pound sack of black oil sunflower seeds toward the bins that lined the bottom half of the side wall between the sales counter and the front of the shop.

"So who was this guy then?" Chief Kennedy peeled off his gloves and scratched his forehead. "And what was he doing in your house?"

By *guy*, I supposed he meant *dead man*. I looked up from my chore. I was scooping sunflower seeds into one of the glass-fronted bins. I'd always enjoyed the soft rustling noise that falling unshelled sunflower seeds make. "Aren't you supposed to be telling me that?" I pushed the big green scoop into the bag. "It is your job."

"I have my theories." Jerry Kennedy sounded rather cryptic.

"Such as?" I grunted as I lugged the twenty-five-pound bag of shelled peanuts over to the bins. Manhandling all these heavy sacks was a bother but buying in bulk saved me a bundle. Chief Kennedy hadn't offered to help, but that was okay by me. I would have refused anyway. I began filling another bin with peanuts.

Chief Kennedy hitched up his pants. "A crime of opportunity would be my guess."

I arched an eyebrow. "Crime of opportunity?"

"Yep." Jerry reached into the bin and helped himself to a handful of peanuts. "You said yourself the front door was open. Our victim walks in, probably intent on robbing the place, and ends up dead."

"Yeah," I said, snapping the lid of the bin down

before he ate up all the profits, "but how do you explain the dead part? Did he turn despondent on discovering I have nothing worth stealing and whack himself in the head with a wrought-iron birdfeeder pole?"

"Or you caught him, grabbed the first thing handy," speculated Chief Kennedy, "and whacked him in the head with said birdfeeder pole." He blinked. "As I recall, you were on the girls' softball team all through middle school and high school."

"Oh, please, you know I never could hit anything." I was a terrible hitter with a team record-low batting average. I had been a pretty good outfielder though.

Chief Kennedy shrugged.

I felt a head of steam rising behind my eyes. "I wasn't even here."

His eyes danced. "So you say."

"Like I told you before, I was picking up birdhouses. These birdhouses," I said, grabbing one off the shelf and shaking it. "Ask Aaron Maddley." Like I'd demanded last night.

"I plan on it," Chief Kennedy replied.

"Shouldn't you have done it already?" Then he'd know I was innocent. "It's not like there are a lot of crimes to go investigating in Ruby Lake." Especially outside of peak tourist season when we had a few more minor offenses due to the influx of people. Nothing too serious: public intoxication, speeding on the lake—small stuff for a top lawman like our Jerry Kennedy.

The chief hitched up his trousers. "Had a break-in at the hardware store a few nights back. Caught the perp quick too. If I do say so myself." He wriggled his jawbone. "Though he disposed of the stolen goods before we caught up with him. Probably stashed them someplace around here."

"Congratulations," I said as drily as possible. "I still don't see what's stopping you or one of your men from talking to Mr. Maddley."

"I couldn't go waking him in the middle of the night, could I?" He lifted the lid of the peanut bin and stuck his paw inside.

"Peanuts are three ninety-nine a pound." I crossed my arms over my chest. A handful of peanuts fell from Jerry's fingers.

I was enjoying watching Jerry pout when the front door was thrown open with a jarring blast that rattled the windows and set the wind chimes, hanging from a carousel to the right of the door, ringing. The tubular sounds of Pachelbel's Canon filled the air. "Kim!"

I ran to the door and embraced my partner. As she'd loaned me money to help set up shop, making Kim partner seemed the right thing to do. Though neither had insisted on it, and Mom had been vociferous in her objections, I'd made her and Aunt Betty both partners in Birds & Bees, too. Minority partners, but partners nonetheless.

Kim had even decided to turn her investment into a working partnership and I was glad she had. I was also glad she was back in Ruby Lake. Now more than ever.

I took a step back, my hands on Kim's shoulders. "What's going on? You didn't return my texts or my calls. I thought you were still in Tampa. When did you get back? How's your mother?"

Kimberly laughed, a tinkle that blended well

with the wind chimes. Kimberly is a long-legged blonde with devilish blue eyes. She has set more than one young man's heart afire. But so far none had been able to hold her—at least for long. Kimberly is thirty-four, like me, but likes to brag that she's younger. Three months, big deal. I'm taller.

She uncinched the belt of her charcoal wool jacket and pulled off her gloves. "Slow down," she said with a laugh. "That's too many questions, too fast and too early."

It was well after eight, but that was Kim. I was planning on opening the store daily at nine and staying till five. Kim would come in at noon and stay till closing.

My partner—and longtime friend—was rocking a pair of tight blue jeans and a raspberry plaid shirt. Kim's head swung around the room. Her little gold hoop earrings swayed like tiny bird perches. She looked pleased. "Hey, you've made some progress." She nodded appreciatively. "Coffee on?"

Chief Kennedy cleared his throat.

"Hi ya, Jerry," Kim said rather abruptly. I noticed he didn't bother trying to correct her and insist she call him chief. I think Jerry's a little afraid of her.

"Pleased to see you, Kimberly. I hear you and Amy are partners in this little shop."

Had I just seen Jerry suck in his gut? Not that it was going to do him any good. There was just too much gut to contain and nowhere for it to go. If Jerry had been paying attention when Mom the high school science teacher had tried to explain physics to him, he'd have known better than to even bother trying.

I ignored Jerry's not-so-buried "little" jibe and headed to the coffeepot. The police chief arrived right behind me, his cup extended. I passed over his arm and filled a cup for Kim—one cream, two sugars—before topping off his mug.

"What are you doing here, Jerry?" Kim blew across the top of her mug. "Don't tell me you and Sandra have taken up backyard bird watching?" Sandra is Jerry's saint of a wife.

Chief Kennedy pulled himself upright. He'd always been a sloucher, figuratively and literally. "Haven't you heard?"

Kim's eyes went from me to the police chief. "Heard what?"

"There's been a little accident," I began softly.

Chief Kennedy barked out a laugh. "A little accident," he scoffed. "A murder is what there's been."

"Murder!?" Kimberly set her coffee down on the small table between the rockers. "Who?" She grabbed my hand. "Not your mother!"

"No, no." I stroked her arm. "Nothing like that."

"Who then?" Kimberly furrowed her brow. "The Pester?"

It was Chief Kennedy's turn to raise brows, and he did. "The Pester?"

"Kim means Esther Pilaster," I explained.

"But she said—" Jerry pointed a finger at my business partner.

"You know how Kim is, Jer—I mean, Chief Kennedy. She gets names mixed up." I shot a warning look at my friend. No point sharing our not-so-friendly nickname for my renter. What good could come of it? "No," I said, turning to Kim, "not Esther."

"Then who?"

I shrugged. "That's just it. I don't know." Kim paled as I explained how I'd gone to fetch my order of birdhouses from Aaron Maddley and returned to find the front door unlocked and a dead man waiting for me in the upstairs storeroom.

"You must have been horrified!" gasped Kim.

"Worse," I quipped.

"Worse?" Kim looked confused. "What could be worse than finding a dead guy in your storeroom?"

The corner of my mouth quirked up. "Being accused of murdering him."

5

"I'm just afraid that what with all the bad publicity we're bound to get that we may be better off putting off the grand opening," I replied to Kim after Chief Kennedy had departed and we'd gotten around to discussing the future of Birds & Bees.

Kimberly was shaking her head in a scolding fashion. "Nonsense, Amy." She was sitting atop the sales counter and banged her fist against the butcher-block slab. "You've got too much riding on this. We've all got too much riding on this."

I chewed my lip a minute. "Maybe you're right."

"Right about what?"

I turned. Mom stood at the bottom of the stairs. She'd suited up in her violet and charcoal color-blocked jacket and matching bottoms. I suspected she was planning a walk. That's the only time I saw her in her L.L. Bean Pathfinders. Mom seemed to have served out her high school teaching career in Naturalizers.

"Hi ya, Mrs. Simms." Kim slid off the counter and gave my mother a hug.

"How's your mother, dear?" Mom pushed a stray lock of hair behind Kim's ear. "Back on her feet?"

"No, but I'm sure she'll be line dancing in no time. The doctor says she's healing well."

"That's nice." Mom sidled up beside me. "So?"

I quirked a brow. "Sooo?"

"So what is Kim right about?"

Kim giggled. "About opening Birds and Bees."

Mom frowned. "I don't understand. Were you considering not opening?"

I explained how the thought had crossed my mind that we'd be better off delaying things until the whole murder situation was either resolved or subsided. "Hopefully, sooner rather than later."

"What did Jerry want?" Mom asked. "Did he come to tell you that you *couldn't* open Birds and Bees?"

"No." I thought about everything the chief had said last night and this morning. A million questions and a lot of snide remarks, but nothing about needing to keep the doors to the business shuttered. "He was just poking around. He didn't say anything about not opening."

"There you go!" Kimberly clapped her hands. "We open tomorrow!"

"Tomorrow?" I gasped. "But we were scheduled to open Saturday."

Kimberly shrugged. "So we open a day or two early. What's the big deal?"

"What's the big deal?" I anchored my hands on my hips. "Number one, a man was murdered upstairs. Number two, we are not ready. Number three,

I paid a hundred dollars to place an ad announcing our big grand opening Saturday morning. Number—"

"Enough with the numbers, Amy." Kimberly stopped my rant. "Your mom and I know you can count. I say ready or not, here we come!" She turned to my mother. "Are you with me, Mrs. Simms?"

Mom nodded. The traitor. "It's your decision, Amy, but I agree with Kimberly." She looked out the window. "Open the doors, let people in." She turned back to me. "Smiling, happy shoppers. That's what you need. It will help flush out all this negative energy." Mom patted the top of the cash register. "And fill this thing."

I felt a chill run up my arms and my eyes lifted toward the ceiling. Negative energy was right. I couldn't get the picture of that dead man upstairs out of my head. "Maybe you're both right," I said. "But take a look around. Even if we wanted to open, we're only half-stocked."

I had explained to Kim how the delivery driver had shown up after the murder and how that had put yet another kink in our plans because the truck had never been unloaded.

Kim pursed her lips. "I noticed the shelves looked a little bare."

"The place does look rather anemic," Mom added. "More like we're going out of business than starting."

"No problem," Kimberly replied. "Cole's Trucking, right?"

I nodded.

Kim grinned. "I saw a Cole's Trucking semi parked outside the Ruby Lake Motor Inn."

"You think it's the same truck?" Mom asked. "Cole's is a pretty big regional company."

"It's got to be the same guy," Kim said. "I mean, what are the odds that it's not?"

I agreed. "I'll call the trucking company." I searched for the company's number on my phone and dialed.

"Well?" Kim asked.

I frowned. "It's a recording." I held the phone up so they could hear. "I'm heading down to the motel. Kim, would you mind staying and unpacking the rest of the suet that's out in the storeroom?"

"Natch." Kim pointed a finger at me. My mother agreed to lend her a hand.

The minivan was frigid as an icebox. I cranked up the dial on the heater as I headed the mile or so down the winding Lake Shore Drive toward the historic Ruby Lake Motor Inn.

Built in the so-called neon era, the Ruby Lake Motor Inn was an L-shaped building with the office and a small diner in the shorter line of the L. There were also several small, rustic cabins with kitchenettes behind the motel—like studio apartments for those wanting a few more home comforts or spending an extended stay.

I parked beside the rust-pitted thirty-foot-tall steel posts that held up the giant red-ruby neon sign. A smaller amber sign braced high up between the posts proclaimed that, yes, there were vacancies.

Kim was right. The big white semitrailer truck, with Cole's Trucking stenciled on the trailer's side and cab door, was parked along the west-side lot along with two other trucks, a pickup with a boat trailer, and two motorhomes, one pulling a smaller U-Haul.

I shut off the Kia's engine. I'd have loved to have let it idle—to preserve warmth—but it was a waste of fuel and polluting too. Not good for people, birds, or the environment. I spent a minute adjusting my hair and makeup. It never hurts to look your best when trying to get someone, especially a man, to do you a favor.

Not that delivering goods for my store, merchandise I'd bought and paid for in advance, was so much a favor as an obligation. Still, after last night, I wouldn't blame the guy if he refused to ever step foot in Birds & Bees again.

I had no idea what room Dwayne was staying in. I also had no idea what his last name was. I was sure he'd mentioned it last night, but I couldn't for the life of me remember what he'd said. I'd had a lot more important things on my mind.

I pulled my collar tight and hiked to the office. A blast of moist, warm air greeted me—so did a thin man with a head of receding dirty brown hair, resting on a stool behind the counter.

He settled his mug of coffee down atop the newspaper he was reading and looked up. "Good morning." He smiled. "Can I help you? Diner's through there"—he pointed to his left—"if you're interested in breakfast."

His Southern drawl was as strong as cold molasses. I pegged him at about forty and his accent as South Carolina. "Five ninety-five, all-you-can-eat buffet for guests." He wore a long-sleeved white dress shirt with thin gray and brown stripes and a pair of cuffed dark brown trousers. "Just show the hostess your room key."

"Actually"—I cleared my throat—"I'm not a guest at all." I pushed out my hand. "I'm Amy Simms. I own Birds and Bees on upper Lake Shore Drive." Upper Lake Shore Drive is the local, though unofficially named, part of Lake Shore Drive that diverges up from the lake and intersects with Airport Road. I had no proof, but I'm pretty sure the name Airport Road was some long-ago town official's idea of a joke. The town of Ruby Lake has no airport. Never did. Probably never will.

Maybe whoever had come up with the moniker had been optimistic. Overly optimistic.

Airport Road extends into the mountains at a steep thirty-five degree incline in places. I avoid it, if at all possible. Its banks are precipitous and the town has no money for such frills as guardrails.

Ruby Lake Motor Inn is located on what we locals consider lower Lake Shore Drive, which is also where the big marina is located.

"Dick Feller. I'm the front desk manager." He shook my hand and furrowed his brow. "Sorry, I'm afraid I've never heard of your store." He yawned and took a sip from his steaming mug.

I smiled. "Nobody has. I mean, that's because we aren't open yet." I looked over my shoulder and out the window. "That's sort of why I'm here."

"Oh?" He blinked and laced his fingers together atop the open newspaper. There was a coffee ring where his mug had lain previously. His espresso-brown eyes were a strong contrast to his pasty white skin.

I took a moment before replying. What should I

say? How much should I tell? It wasn't like the murder was any kind of secret I'd been asked not to reveal—but did I want to tell all that to this man?

What would he think? I might even scare him off, and then what good would he do me? I'd never find out what room Dwayne with-no-last-name was staying in. If it even was Dwayne who was driving the truck in the motor inn's parking lot.

An elderly gentleman in a long trench coat came through the door and dropped off his room key. The front desk manager slid off his stool and printed out the guest's receipt and wished him a good day.

"Can you tell me what room the guy is in who's driving that truck?" I pointed out the window to my left. "It's the one with Cole's Trucking written on the side." Dick Feller looked at me blankly. "His first name is Dwayne. I'm not sure of his last name."

Dick Feller pressed his hands against the counter and leaned forward. He frowned. "I suppose I could cross-check the license plate number on the computer and get a name."

"Great." I rubbed my hands together.

"But that would be against regulations."

"I won't tell if you won't." I wriggled my brow conspiratorially.

The front desk manager was shaking his head even as the words spilled out of my mouth. "Sorry, no can do, Ms. Simms." Not so great. I'd run into a desk clerk who was averse to conspiring.

"But I really need to talk to him," I pleaded. "You see, my store is opening soon and I need the merchandise that's on that truck."

Dick Feller refilled his coffee mug from a stained pot behind the desk. "If that truck does have your merch, I'm sure it will get delivered."

I didn't need placating, I needed my stuff. I needed Dwayne. I was contemplating jumping over the counter and seizing Dick's computer when the front door opened, bringing with it a burst of cold air.

"Good morning," said Dick, putting on his meet-the-guests grin.

"Mornin'," came the reply.

I spun around. "Dwayne!"

Dwayne didn't look too happy to see me. In fact, he looked decidedly displeased. Was this what they called guilt by association? He'd seen me with blood on my hands and a dead man in my shop-slash-house and made up his mind that I was some sort of homicidal maniac? A homicidal maniac with a bird supply store?

His gaze jumped from the front desk manager to me and back again. "What's she doing here?"

I hurried over. "Looking for you. I'm so glad you haven't left town."

His face soured. "Police wouldn't let me. Said they had some more questions."

"Police?" Dick Feller said worriedly.

"This lady murdered somebody," explained Dwayne.

Thanks, Dwayne. "I did not!" I cried indignantly.

"That old lady said you did," Dwayne shot back.

I bit my cheek. Esther the Pester. What a loudmouth. "Look, it's all just a big misunderstanding." I spread my arms wide. "A really big misunderstanding."

"So, there is no dead body?" The front desk manager's eyes darted from Dwayne to me.

"Well . . ."

"And now I'm stuck here," Dwayne whined.

"Maybe it would be better if you left now, Ms. Simms." Dick motioned toward the door.

I ignored him and focused on the trucker. "Great. I mean, it's too bad that you got mixed up in all this and had to stay over." I'd win Dwayne over with my charm. "But that means you can deliver my stock." I smiled and grabbed the sleeve of his coat. I'd haul him out the door physically if I had to.

He jerked his arm away. "Haven't had my breakfast yet."

"Oh, of course. I'll join you."

Dwayne shrugged and headed toward the diner. I trailed, uninvited, after him. He helped himself to the buffet and took a seat at a small two-top. While his plate was piled high, I'd settled for toast and scrambled eggs.

He scowled as I slid into the chair across from his but perked up when I said that breakfast was on me. How much was breakfast for non-guests?

Dwayne wasn't much of a talker. I watched in amazed silence as he shoveled food down his gullet. Once in a while he made eye contact, then went back to grazing.

"So," I said, catching Dwayne between mouthfuls, "terrible about last night, isn't it?"

Dwayne grabbed a strip of bacon and pushed it around in a puddle of maple syrup on his yellow plate.

"I'm Amy Simms, by the way." The fatty bacon

slid across his tongue and disappeared. "You're Dwayne, right?"

I was awarded with a bob of the head. "Rogers."

Okay, we were making progress, Dwayne Rogers. "Pleased to meet you, Dwayne Rogers." I smiled and motioned to the waitress that our cups needed refilling.

"I didn't even have a change of clothes." Dwayne pouted. "Not a toothbrush. Nuthin.'"

Huh? "Excuse me?"

"I wasn't expecting to spend the night, just get in, get out."

Now I understood. That explained the rumpled blue shirt and trousers. He'd been wearing the same outfit last night. "Sorry," I said. "I'm sure none of us wanted last night to end the way it did." Certainly not the dead guy taking up floor space in my upstairs storeroom. "So you're not from around here."

"Live in Huntersville."

I knew Huntersville. It's a little north of Charlotte. "I'm sure the police will let you leave soon."

"My supervisor was none too happy. I'm supposed to make a run to Myrtle Beach today." He twisted the band of his watch around his left wrist. "Now I'm stuck here."

I grabbed the bill the waitress had dropped between us and opened my wallet. She had charged us each the guest rate. I wasn't about to correct her. I was sort of a guest of a guest, after all. What did it matter that I was paying? Besides, I'd hardly eaten a thing. "What do you say I take care of this and then you follow me over to Birds and Bees?"

I slid a twenty atop the check and signaled for

our waitress. "I'll even help you unload the truck. As a matter of fact, I've got a couple of friends there now who will be glad to pitch in too."

Glad might not be the exact term to use in Kimberly's case, but she'd help. She'd grouse, but she'd help. Mom would pitch in without question. Though her health isn't the best and I didn't want her overexerting.

Dwayne headed for the door and I followed after him like a young doe. "Sorry," he said, stamping his feet outside. "But I've got to be at the police station at ten."

My heart sank. I couldn't let Dwayne leave Ruby Lake with my desperately needed stock still packed away in his truck. Not to mention Kim would never let me live the defeat down. "Great," I said. "I'll head over to Birds and Bees now, and we'll be all set to help you unload when you get there."

"I don't know . . ." Dwayne rubbed his thumb and forefinger along the underside of his chin. "After what happened last night . . ."

I clapped him on the shoulder. "Not to worry. I promise." I held up my free hand. "Nothing like that's going to happen today. Besides," I said, "I called your office this morning. The impression I got was that they were expecting you to complete yesterday's delivery today." I mean, I'd only talked to an answering machine, but Dwayne didn't need to know that.

"Well . . ."

"Terrific," I said, without giving Dwayne a chance to back out. "You go down to the station, make your statement to the police, and we'll see you soon."

Back at the store, I gave Kimberly and my mother the good news.

"Perfect," replied Kim. Her sleeves were rolled up to her elbows. She was distributing bird-themed greeting cards along a tiny shelf in front of the register. They were the creation of a local watercolorist.

Mom handed her another card from a box on the floor. She looked troubled.

Kim blew a strand of hair from her eyes. "Now do you want to hear the bad news?"

6

Kim glanced at my mother, then said, "Matt Kowalski."

"Matt Kowalski. Wow." I cocked my head to the left. "That's a name I haven't heard in a long time." And could die happy if I never heard it again.

Kim smiled but it wasn't a happy smile. "Well, you better get used to hearing it because I have a feeling you're going to be hearing a lot more of it."

"Why?" I said, planting my hands on my hips. "What's that jerk done now?"

Mom gasped and brought her fingers to her lips. "Amy!"

"What?!" I demanded. "What is wrong with you two? What's going on?" I glared at Kim, then Mom. Neither spoke. "Somebody tell me what's going on here!"

Esther Pilaster bounded down the back stairs. She was grinning ear to ear. She was either feeling smugly triumphant or she'd found the bottle of

Jack Daniel's I keep in the cupboard above the fridge. "It doesn't look good for you now, does it?" She tugged down the sleeves of her baggy navy sweater, first one sleeve, then the other.

I lowered my eyes at her. "Are you going to tell me what's going on here? Or do I have to raise your rent?"

"Hey," she blurted. "You can't do that! I have a lease." She marched up to Kim. "You didn't tell her yet?" There was mischief in the Pester's eyes.

I pushed between them. "Tell me what?"

"About Matt Kowalski." Her eyes twinkled malevolently.

"They mentioned his name," I said, sternly looking from Mom to Kim and back again. "They just won't tell me what he's done."

Esther cackled. "What he's done is get himself killed."

"What?" I cried.

"In *your* storeroom!" Esther's eyes rose to the ceiling.

"What?" I cried again, higher-pitched this time. I'm versatile that way. "You're telling me the dead man last night was Matthew Kowalski?" I shook my head, trying to remove the words I'd heard. "No. No, that can't be." I turned to Kim and Mom for support. For comfort. Neither provided any. Kim busied herself with the greeting cards. Mom wrung her hands.

"Come on, guys. It just can't be." I forced a smile. I wondered at what precise moment Birds & Bees had become *Little Shop of Horrors*.

"We all know what Matt Kowalski looks like. The man who was murdered had black hair. Matt's a blond. And with all the time he spent out of doors hunting and fishing," I argued, "he was a very sun-bleached blond." I could have added "and drinking." Matt liked his beer.

Mom and Kim silently nodded their heads.

"The man upstairs was thin." The Matthew Kowalski I knew had always been a good sixty pounds overweight. Most of it beer gut—and he was still in high school at the time. It was no wonder it had taken him two years to finish the twelfth grade. He liked to drink his lunches.

More bobbing of heads.

"It wasn't him," I said forcefully.

"It was him all right," Esther was only too happy to reply.

"The police called while you were out," Kim said.

Mom nodded. "They identified him through his fingerprints."

"They say he was even wearing blue contact lenses." Kim wrung her hands.

"It seems he didn't want anybody to recognize him," added my mother. I remembered that Matt's real eye color was green. I recalled how the dead man's eyes seemed to be looking at me. I wouldn't have thought it could get any spookier than that, but now they were telling me the dead man was a man from my past?

My heart thumped in my chest. I think it would have fallen to my feet if it were physically possible. Fortunately, my knotted intestines obstructed its fall. "No," I said. I felt myself visibly blanching. "It can't be." I looked to Mom for support. Good old Mom. She'd supported me through thick and thin.

Through my awkward teenage years. Through my
first kiss and my first breakup.

Her brow rose. "Sorry, dear. I'm afraid there is
no doubt."

Great. A lifetime history of support out the window like so much dirty dishwater. This didn't bode
well.

No doubt Matt Kowalski being the dead man
was going to prove troublesome for me.

For all of us.

The door banged open and Dwayne Rogers
stood in the open doorway dripping water and
mud. When had it started raining? "Dwayne!" I
said. "You're early. I wasn't expecting you until
later." Truth be told, I wasn't certain he'd even
show up. But I was sure glad he had.

I frowned at his muddy boots. He'd already left
footprints all over the all-weather lovebirds doormat that I'd ordered special for the entrance. The
two lovebirds even chirp adorably when stepped
on. Though I really liked the mat, Kim worried
that the constantly cooing lovebirds would soon
become annoying. I disagreed and told her she
was just sensitive because her own love life seemed
to be in the doldrums.

Then again, she could take solace in the fact
that my love life was in the very same position as
hers and could keep hers company on these cold,
end-of-winter nights.

Dwayne shrugged his burly shoulders, sending a
light rainfall from his jacket to the original hardwood floors. The guy seemed to create his own
weather. "The police let me go pretty quick. Chief

Kennedy said he all but had the case wrapped up and didn't need much help from me anyways."

I shivered, more from this latest bit of news than the mess the trucker was making of my reasonably clean floors. There had been a fair amount of black fingerprinting powder on most of the horizontal surfaces, but Mom and Kim seemed to have done a good job of wiping most of it away. "How about if you meet me around back?"

"Sure thing," the deliveryman said amiably. He seemed in a much better mood now that he could get on with his job. He turned for the door.

"Wait," my mother said. Her index finger bounced over her lower lip. "Dwayne Rogers." He narrowed his eyes. "Aren't you Chris and Alexandra Rogers's boy?"

Dwayne grinned. "Mrs. Simms. Is that you?"

I did a double take. Mom knew my Cole's Trucking deliveryman? The guy who said he was from Huntersville? Wait, he said he *lived* in Huntersville.

"Wow." Dwayne scratched the top of his head. "Sure has been a long time."

Mom beamed. "It's good to see you again, Dwayne."

"So," I said, "you two know one another?"

Mom smiled. "Dwayne was one of my students." She thought a moment. "Ninth grade, wasn't it?"

Dwayne nodded. "Yes, ma'am."

She patted his arm. "And tell me, how is your uncle?"

Dwayne shook his head. "Not so good. But I do what I can for him. Stop in and visit whenever I'm in town."

Mom turned to the rest of us. "Dwayne's parents

died when he was only seven. His uncle raised him, the poor dear."

"I'm surprised you didn't stay with him last night," I couldn't help saying.

Dwayne blinked at me. "It was late. The company put me up in the motel. I didn't want to disturb him."

Mom shot me a look to let me know I'd spoken out of turn. Mom is a guardian of the social graces. I am not. Dwayne left to pull the truck around.

"I'm glad to see he's doing well," Mom said as we watched the big semi round the corner to the alley. Esther had followed him out the door and taken cover under the bus shelter up the street.

"I'd better go unlock the back door so we can finally get those goods unloaded and on the shelves."

Kim snatched a towel from under the counter. "You go ahead, Amy. I'll wipe up this mess at the door and join you."

I glanced outdoors. "I hope nothing gets ruined in this rain."

"Don't worry," assured Dwayne, "I've got plastic tarps in the truck to cover the pallets." He headed out to his truck and climbed up into the cab.

"Who knows?" I said to Mom. "With luck, we just might be able to open tomorrow after all."

"Count on it!" Kim shouted encouragingly. "Lucky is my middle name!"

Unfortunately, my middle name isn't Lucky, it's Hester—after my mother's mother, Sarah Hester Hopkins. It could have been worse, my middle name could have been Sarah.

And yes, that was Chief Jerry Kennedy standing there at my back door, rain dripping from his wide-brimmed brown hat, looking all ugly eyed and official.

Dwayne hovered behind him, looking unsure of what to do.

7

And yes, I was under arrest.

Again.

Okay, so maybe technically I hadn't been under arrest last night when I'd been escorted to the police station and maybe I hadn't technically been read my Miranda rights yet. But there was no doubt about it this time.

I was in trouble.

"Look, Jerry," I said from my chair. I was both tired and angry and in no mood to call this former high school loser *chief*. "Just because I once chased Matt out of my house with a baseball bat and across the lawn to his car does not mean that I smashed his head in with a birdfeeder hook. Besides, that was something like fifteen years ago."

I paused for a gulp of stale air. "More." I folded my arms over my chest. I wasn't good at doing math in my head. Especially when upset and facing the firing squad. Well, okay, so maybe it was premature to start worrying about the firing squad, but I knew trouble when I was looking at it.

And Chief Jerry Kennedy was IT.

He'd been holding a grudge ever since eleventh grade when we'd gone out on a date that I regretted almost before it had started and refused to let him get to second base. The only reason he'd even made it to first base was because he grabbed me before I had a chance to react. Giving me a hard time now was probably his puerile way of exacting revenge.

The chief tilted back in his chair, the heels of his boots smooshing the papers on his desk. "Yeah, I know, I know. And you had a lousy batting average." His eyes hardened. "But all it took to kill Matt was one solid blow." He shrugged. "Maybe two or three. Haven't got the results from the coroner yet."

"Good luck with that," I said. The coroner in Ruby Lake is about ninety years old. It probably takes him an hour simply to tie his shoes. And that was after first spending another hour trying to remember where he'd last put them after taking them off. How long would he need to discover the exact cause of death of Matthew Kowalski?

"Tell me again," the chief began, his voice tired, "when was the last time you saw Matt Kowalski?"

I groaned. "Like I told you the first hundred times, I don't know when I last saw Matt." I pressed my hands against his desktop. "Matt Kowalski isn't exactly the kind of guy a girl keeps a record of in her diary." My hand flew through the air. I paused, took a deep breath of calming air, and tried one last time. "Look, Jerry—Chief Kennedy—Matt and

I went our separate ways after high school. Heck, I was away at college for four years, then worked in Chapel Hill, and only moved back to town in the last few months."

He blinked but said nothing, so I continued. "The last I heard, and I don't even remember when, was that Matt Kowalski had moved away from Ruby Lake." I shook my head as if sifting through the data banks for a small memory. "South Carolina, I think." I shrugged. "I could be wrong." After a pause, I added, "I didn't really care, you know?"

Jerry's hands were tucked behind his head. "I don't know, Amy. What do you want me to do? All signs point to you." He shook his head like this whole thing was my fault.

"I want you to let me go and start looking for Matt Kowalski's real killer!"

I jumped from my chair and Officer Sutton leapt up and dogged me. I turned on him. "Really?" I said indignantly. "You have to stick to me? Even here? Inside the police station?" I locked my hands on my hips. "What are you afraid I'm going to do?"

Officer Sutton looked nervously at Chief Kennedy but kept his mouth shut.

I snorted. "Are you afraid I'm going to steal your gun, hotwire a car, and make a break for the border?"

Officer Dan Sutton's right hand went protectively to the holster locked to his side.

I rolled my eyes. "Oh brother . . ." I sank back into my chair before the trigger-happy cop took a potshot at me.

We all turned to look when the front door to

the police station opened. It was Mom's friend, Ben Harlan. I hadn't been too happy to see him last night, but right now he was looking just as good as Santa Claus, or Robert Redford in his prime.

He unbuttoned his long beige trench coat and hung it over the hook at the door. "Ms. Simms, Chief." Mr. Harlan ran a slim hand through his silver locks and ambled over to Jerry's desk. Ben Harlan turned his smile on me. That smile must have charmed the ladies in his youth—probably still did for the over-fifty crowd. "They treating you all right, Ms. Simms?"

I nodded. "They haven't resorted to sticking needles under my fingernails, beating me with a roll of nickels, or waterboarding yet."

Chief Kennedy shot me a dirty look. Good grief. The man acted so high school.

I made a face back when the lawyer wasn't looking.

Ben Harlan pulled a chair up to the chief's desk and sat. "A bit premature to be charging my client with murder, don't you think?"

Chief Kennedy fell forward and, I swear, I felt the floor shake. Maybe the man ought to jump on a treadmill once in a while. "I didn't charge her with murder. That's not my job. You know that, Ben." He made a face at me again. "I simply asked Ms. Simms to come down to the station and answer a few more questions."

Mr. Harlan's bushy brows shot up. "And has she answered your questions satisfactorily?"

"Answered them, yes," replied Chief Kennedy. He glared at me. "Satisfactorily, no." He grabbed a packet of papers and banged them on the desktop. "Her fingerprints are all over the murder weapon."

I rose. "My fingerprints are all over everything in my store—that birdfeeder hook and every other one included!"

"The only fingerprints we found on that thing," boomed Jerry Kennedy, "were yours and yours alone!"

Mr. Harper waved me back down. The door flew open once again. It had stopped raining and the sun was peeking out from behind the gray clouds scuttling slowly past from the east.

The tall man at the door was ruggedly handsome despite the conservative charcoal suit that he filled to perfection. He was clean shaven and his blue eyes sparkled even from across the room. He wiped his feet at the door, though the condition this place was in, there was no need. He looked over at Ben Harlan and smiled warmly. "Sorry it took so long, Dad." He unbuttoned his overcoat. "I had to wait for the school bus."

Dad? Sure, and he probably stopped to let the baby duckies cross the road too. I self-consciously ran a hand quickly through my straggly hair. Rain was my hair's natural enemy. That and cheap shampoo from the dollar store.

Ben Harper made the introductions. "Derek is joining me in my practice."

His son's name was Derek. I rose and he shook my hand. "I'm Amy Simms," I practically stammered. "Ruby Lake's most wanted."

Derek Harper chuckled and I immediately liked him for it. What woman doesn't like a man who will forgive her being on her town's most-wanted list? "A pleasure."

His warm fingers sent a tingle up my arm. Strains of "At Long Last Love," a Cole Porter tune from the musical *You Never Know*, ran through my head. This hunk of handsome even had a young Robert Redford beat.

"My granddaughter get off to school okay?" Ben Harper asked.

His son nodded. "Her mom's picking her up afterward."

So, Derek Harper was married. My dreams of a Jamaica beach wedding, my bare toes luxuriating in the warm Caribbean sand as I walked to the shoreline in my billowy single-shoulder gown with ruching and floral beaded appliqués, with family and friends in attendance, were shattered. The saccharine strains of "I'm All Alone" from *Monty Python's Spamalot* crashed over me like a rogue wave.

"What's the situation here?" Derek Harper asked, suddenly becoming all professional. I discreetly noticed the simple gold band on his ring finger.

Ben Harper turned to Jerry. "Anything further here, Chief?"

Chief Kennedy blew out a breath. "All of you get out of my office. But don't go anywhere, Amy. I'm going to want to talk to you again."

"Not without me present, you're not," Ben Harper shot back.

"I'm going to be needing a ride back to Birds and Bees," I said, reaching for my coat.

Derek Harper helped me into it. I could have gotten used to that. "I can give you a ride."

I looked up at him. At five-eight, I estimated Ben Harper's son at six-one. Perfect. Except that he was married. Derek told his dad he'd catch up with him later and we parted ways on the sidewalk.

"Was it rough in there?" Derek Harper asked, once we were in the car and moving. We were heading away from the station.

"I guess it could have been worse." I paused and considered the many worse options. "I could be locked up right now, for instance."

He laughed. "It's nice that you can keep your spirits up like that."

My brow rose. "Really? Because if you could see my insides, Mr. Harper, well, they're a mess."

His hands pressed the button on the Civic's heater. "Warm enough?"

I gulped. I was getting there.

"How about we stop for coffee and go over the case?"

"Case?" Was that what I was now, a case? That was a scary thought. The stuff of TV and newspapers. Not something I ever thought would be used in context with myself.

"Huh?"

"Sorry, I guess I hadn't realized until just now that that's just what I am." He blinked. "A case," I said.

"Sorry, Ms. Simms," he replied. "I didn't mean to imply or insinuate any guilt on your part."

"Please, call me Amy."

He smiled. "Only if you'll call me Derek."

I agreed and suggested we try the Coffee and

Tea House on the square. It's run by a friend of mine, Susan Terwilliger. Though I'm convinced she and her husband, Tom, could afford to live on his income alone—he's a dentist—Susan hangs out at the shop on a regular basis. I think it's her escape from what she lovingly calls "the brood." Her four children—three boys, one girl, and as she liked to say with a smile, albeit a slightly weary one, all trouble.

Better still, the Coffee and Tea House is an intimate establishment. No point in nosy locals seeing me conferencing with a lawyer. I'd be getting enough unwanted scrutiny as news of Matt Kowalski's demise in my home-slash-store spread around town. Mom, Kim, and I had had our personal run-ins with Matt. Not enough to kill him over, but no doubt enough to make some folks think that we might have.

"You know, I really can't afford an attorney." I blew across the top of my mug and watched the tiny rings pulse outward.

"Not to scare you," Derek said with a small smile, "but I don't think you can afford not to have counsel in your current situation."

I sucked in a deep breath. "Those aren't exactly words of comfort."

"Sorry, again." He chuckled. "Sorry, I seem to be apologizing a lot. Oops. Sorry."

Derek stopped and reached for his coffee, apparently before he could embarrass himself further. But I didn't find him embarrassing at all; I found him alarmingly charming. And I didn't need that right now. I needed a lawyer. Besides, the guy was married.

"Look, Dad said your mom paid him a small retainer and I'm sure we won't be charging you anything more until we see how this whole thing plays out." He laid his palms open. "Okay?"

I nodded.

"So," Derek Harper said, "how well did you know the deceased, this Matthew . . ." It was like being interrogated by the police all over again.

"Matthew Kowalski," I finished. "And I didn't know him well at all. Besides, he looked so different. I don't think I would have recognized him even if I had seen him walking around town."

"Different how?"

I explained how the Matt Kowalski I'd known had been thinner. And blonder. "And younger," I quipped.

"The police told me he'd even been wearing tinted contacts."

I still couldn't get over it. Wonders never ceased. Why was Matt in disguise? "That's what I heard too. I don't think I'd even seen Matt since high school." And that had been more than enough. "And I didn't want to. I mean, it wasn't like I'd been avoiding him or anything—like crossing to the other side of the street if I saw him coming." I paused. "But still . . . a little Matt Kowalski goes—I should say, went—a long way."

Derek Harper nodded his understanding. "I guess I know what you mean. We all have people like that in our life."

"Oh?" My brow raised in question.

He didn't rise to the bait. "Any idea how Matt Kowalski ended up dead in your upstairs storage room?"

I frowned. "None. None at all." I leaned back as Susan refilled our coffees for free. I wasn't surprised to see her in so early. She was usually in the shop until noon, then resumed her child-raising duties as the kids got out of their respective day cares and schools. Susan gave me a good-natured wink and departed. "This may sound callous, but I wish he'd found someplace else to die."

We chatted some more about the murder. I glanced at my watch and gasped. "I'd better be getting back to Birds and Bees."

Derek Harper slid a ten-dollar bill under the check and stood. "Don't worry. I'm sure the police will find out what really happened to Matthew Kowalski."

"You're not from around here, are you?"

"Just moved up from Charlotte." He held the door open as we prepared to leave. A lawyer and a gentleman.

"That explains it. You don't know Chief Kennedy like I do."

Derek Harper laughed deeply and deposited me at the curb out front of Birds & Bees. As my hand reached for the door handle, he turned my way, one hand on the steering wheel, the other resting on the side of the passenger seat. "In the meantime"—he spoke hesitantly—"how about dinner tonight?"

I flinched. "Tonight?" I ran my fingers through my hair. "Sorry." I shook my head. "I can't. I have tons to do. We're planning on opening tomorrow. Grand opening. A pre–grand opening, actually."

Geesh, what a complete and total jerk. If I wasn't in potentially dire need of legal help I'd have told this guy where to get off—like the Gates of Adultery Hell.

"Oh. Sure." His hands fell to his lap. "How about Saturday?"

I gulped. My throat felt suddenly parched despite the two large coffees I'd just consumed. I shook my head more firmly. "Look, Derek, Mr. Harper," I stammered. What was with this jerk? "That's very kind of you, but I'm afraid I'm seeing someone." If that didn't send the message maybe I'd have to deliver it to his wife.

He tilted his head back. A small smile appeared on his face. "Is it serious?"

"I'm afraid so." I cleared my throat. "I mean, yes. Very." I had to nip this in the bud. "Goodbye, Mr. Harper." I made my exit as gracefully and quickly as I could—before the lecherous lawyer could say or do anything else.

Okay, I may have slammed the car door. Hard.

What a creep.

I couldn't believe I'd earlier spent an entire fake wedding on the beach with him in Montego Bay, Jamaica. What a waste of a perfectly good daydream. The man was a sleaze.

I might have been lonely, but I could do way better than that guy.

8

"Remind me." I sighed, gazing out the window at the dark gray sky above. Sheets of driving rain obscured the street, giving it the look of an Impressionist painting. "Whose idea was it to have our grand opening today?" So far, the Birds & Bees grand opening was anything but grand.

"Don't worry," cooed Kim, who'd come in early to help with the anticipated first-day crowd. "I'm sure things will pick up. Especially once this weather clears." Dainty gold hoops dangled from her earlobes and she'd pulled her hair back in a loose ponytail that spilled over the collar of a buttery-yellow silk blouse.

"If it clears," I replied. I'd settled for a practical pair of jeans and my cornflower-blue cardigan.

"Weather Channel promises it will." Kim could be annoyingly optimistic—anticipating sunshine even in the irrefutable onslaught of showers.

I turned and busied myself rearranging stock

on the shelves. I had plenty to sell. Now all I needed were some customers to buy.

The lovebirds started singing. I turned with a smile. "Good morning," I said, waving. "Welcome to Birds and Bees!"

"See?" Kim mouthed.

I waved for her to keep quiet. "How can I help you today?" I approached and caught a whiff of spicy cologne. He was a slightly overweight middle-aged gentleman with a receding hairline and a nose that bent to the left. He wore a lumpy black parka over a pair of beige corduroys and cowboy boots with mud stained heels.

"Just looking," he replied. A trace of a smile appeared on his face and his eyes darted around the store.

"Sure." I gestured him to come in. "Please, take your time, and if there's anything I can help you with—"

He cut me off with a shake of his head. "That's okay." He headed for a display of birdhouses, running his fingers idly over their sides.

Kim and I shrugged at one another. Fortunately, the lovebirds started cooing once again and a young couple pushing a stroller entered. The young man pulled his black umbrella shut. I noticed him looking around for someplace to put it and made a note to myself to add an umbrella stand. He settled for tucking the damp umbrella awkwardly under one arm.

The couple also had a child of maybe four with them, wrapped in bright pink leggings and a waterproof pink jacket. A white scarf was wrapped around her face, covering her mouth and nose.

The young girl started jumping up and down on the doormat and I was beginning to see what Kim had meant about coming to rue having singing lovebirds start up every time somebody came in our door. I might have to rethink the idea. Maybe I'd remove it to the back room and buy a simple coir mat for up front.

Then again, if I'd had the doormat down the previous night, maybe those chirping lovebirds would have scared off Matt Kowalski and he wouldn't have ended up dead in my house.

As if on cue, Kim mouthed, "Told you so." Kim's also big on use of the "told you so"—and mouthing like a campy twenties movie siren.

"Good morning!" the young mother called out to us before I could even open my lips. "Nice place you've got here." She angled the stroller to one side and I found myself facing a cherubic smiling boy swathed in light blue from head to toe.

"Thank you."

Her husband nodded agreement and gently pulled his daughter away from the doormat. I liked him already. It didn't hurt that he was wearing a beanie from my alma mater, UNC-Chapel Hill.

Kim headed for the coffeepot warming in the corner. Probably to escape the noise. I'd laid out fresh coffee, tea, and cookies for our customers as part of our grand opening welcome. Between us, so far, Kim and I had managed to eat half a tray of butter cookies. I vowed to power walk around the lake tomorrow. Twice. Maybe.

"Welcome to Birds and Bees." I wiggled my fingers at the toddler.

The young woman quickly unbuttoned her knee-length gray coat. Raindrops spilled to the ground. I gritted my teeth but reminded myself that now that Birds & Bees was open, I couldn't expect the place to remain pristine.

"We just moved into a house with a big yard over on Sycamore and I thought it would be nice to add a birdfeeder or two."

I grinned. "Then you've come to the right place." I motioned for her to follow me over to the side of the shop where I'd placed a variety of feeders. "We carry a full selection," I explained to the young woman, as her husband and older daughter wandered off. "What types of birds were you hoping to attract?"

The young woman laughed nervously and glanced over her shoulder at her husband. "To tell you the truth," she admitted, "I don't know." She shrugged apologetically. "I didn't even know it made a difference."

I smiled. "No problem." I pulled a tube feeder from a hanging display. "Do you have squirrels?"

"Sure, why?" Her son leaned forward and pulled a red-breasted grosbeak plush toy from the low shelf. His mother gently took it from his hand and pulled a small stuffed bear from a zippered pouch on the stroller.

"Then you may want to consider a squirrel-proof feeder." I pulled down on the feeder. "It has a spring mechanism that prevents any animal heavier than a bird from accessing the seed." She nodded. I grabbed a tray feeder from the shelf. "Of course, you could go with a platform or hopper feeder. You can mount these on a pole. And if you add a baffle"—I pointed to a stacked selection of black and white baffles at the end of the aisle—"it will prevent squirrels, raccoons, and other furry critters from stealing all the bird food. You'll also attract larger birds." I winked at the blue-eyed toddler in the stroller. "Like that grosbeak your boy was playing with."

The young woman nodded. "I never realized there was so much to this." She glanced over her shoulder for her husband again, but there was no sign of him. "I guess I always thought a bird was a bird and a feeder was a feeder."

"Don't worry," I replied. "Birding can be as simple or as complicated as you want it to be." I beckoned her to follow me. Birds & Bees is laid out with the front counter and register to the left of the entrance and, while the area in front of the counter and register is fairly open, perpendicular rows of shelving plus wall shelves, racks, and carousels filled the space to the right and going back. A TV monitor playing birding videos was mounted on a supporting column in the center of the store. Two rows of bins flowed along the outer wall. Customers could buy their seed by the pound if they didn't want to buy the prepackaged stuff. I'd even made up some Birds & Bees custom blends.

Another section of the store held more items of a gifting nature, like towels, mugs, gardening tools, and other odds and ends for nature lovers. These largely featured bird and butterfly themes. Once the weather was better, I'd move some merchandise out onto the porch during the day and, of course, offer plant varieties popular for attracting wild birds, butterflies, and bees in the front garden.

"As you can see"—I swept my hand along a shoulder-high book-rack—"we have a collection of books and DVDs on birding, from beginner guides to detailed references. Of course, Ruby Lake Town Library also has a fair collection of titles. And though they tend to be older publication dates, most information about birds doesn't go out of date too fast."

She giggled. "No, I don't suppose it's like computers or something."

I agreed. I was still holding on to a laptop running Windows 2007. It ran like a dinosaur in a bog, but it ran.

The woman peppered me with questions, then settled on one of the squirrel-proof tube feeders I'd first shown her. She fished out a fat blue wallet from her purse. "You take Visa?" I nodded. She slipped out a card and looked at it. "Oops." She smiled and slid it back in its slot. "Library card." She thumbed through her cards some more. "Got it." She handed over the plastic.

I rang up the woman's purchase as several more customers spilled through the door. Once the weather warmed and the spring tourist season kicked in, I was hoping things would really pick up. "What happened to that guy who came in earlier?" I wondered aloud. The rain had eased up though the sky was still dirty gray. Sometimes it stayed that way for days.

Kim shrugged, coffee mug at her lips. "Beats me. One minute he was here, the next he was gone."

"Weird."

"By the way, you ought to keep the door to the back room closed during the day."

"Oh?"

"Yeah, that guy with the little girl wandered back there by mistake. In fact, I had to stop his daughter from climbing the stairs. You might want to put some sort of rope or chain across the newels during store hours."

I agreed. We didn't need customers wandering around in our supply room or upstairs in the apartments. More and more I could see that running a business was all about the details. I just hoped I could keep up with them all.

"Excuse me," interrupted an elderly woman in a red felt pillbox hat. "Where do you keep the bags for these bins?" She pointed a bent finger toward the Buy-The-Pound sign hanging over the rows of seed bins. I'd made the sign myself with an inexpensive wood-burning tool I'd picked up at Olde Towne Hardware and a piece of scrap oak I'd found lying around downstairs. The previous occupants had left plenty of junk when they'd moved out, and while I'd tried to reuse as much as I could in an effort to keep my start-up expenses down, I'd had to pay to have a good portion of it hauled to the dump. It would have been nice if Gertie Hammer had cleaned the place up before selling it, but then Gertie Hammer wasn't nice. Still, the long piece of inch-thick white oak had been perfect for my first woodworking project and I was proud of the result.

"Oh, sorry!" I'd forgotten to fill the wooden slot at the end of the row with paper bags. "Give me a moment and I'll get you one." I ran to the storeroom. The bags were in a packet on a metal rack near the floor safe. Running back to the front, I spotted the owner of the diner across the street climbing down from her large white pickup truck. "Moire Leora!"

"So?" Kim glanced toward the window.

Lights, bells, and whistles went off in my head. "Of course," I muttered. I thrust the packet of bags at Kim. "Take over for me, would you?"

I didn't give her a chance to answer. I threw on my down jacket and ran across the street, dodging cars and angry, startled drivers as I zigzagged my way to the diner.

"Wait! Amy!" I heard Kim cry. "I don't even know how to work the register!"

9

It was lunchtime and Ruby's Diner was practically standing room only. All the sixties-era red vinyl booths along the window were full, and the one table that wasn't occupied was littered with the remains of somebody's lunch.

I took a lone swivel stool at the counter between a couple of men, the man on my right in a suit, the man on my left in the gray-and-red pinstriped uniform of a local HVAC company. He said hello. The man in the blue suit ignored me and focused on his *Wall Street Journal.*

When the waitress, Tiffany LaChance, popped up across from me, I ordered the baby bronto—the full bronto burger's too much for me, but I did go with the onion rings. Usually I opt for the house salad instead, but stress does things to people. Me? It makes me crave fat, the kind of comfort-inducing fat that you can only get in fried foods, like the delicious greasy grams of fat found in things like

French fries and fried donuts. Or in my case, onion rings.

Try as I might, I couldn't for the life of me figure out why Matthew Kowalski would wind up dead in my shop. It was probably wrong to think it, but it made me mad to think that the lowlife had really screwed things up for me. Why couldn't he have died somewhere else? Like Gertie Hammer's house.

Scarfing another five-hundred-calorie onion ring, I knew I had to solve this murder because it was, among other things, making me gain weight. I shrugged and grabbed another golden ring. I'd burn off all the extra calories on the walk around the lake I'd vowed to take tomorrow. Though at this point, I'd have to lap the darn lake about a hundred times just to break even on today's lunch.

No matter, the food here was worth breaking any diet or dietary restrictions for. I kept chiding Moire Leora Breeder, the owner, that she should expect Guy Fieri to pop up any day in his flashy red Camaro convertible to do a segment on her and her diner. She said she wasn't holding her breath. Still, I like to look my best whenever I'm in the place—just in case the camera crew shows up.

Sitting at the counter also gave me a better chance of catching a few minutes with Moire Leora. She's a hands-on owner, and when it's busy she can be found doing anything from running the register, cooking on the line, or busing a table. Moire, she'd once told me, means *star of the sea* and Leora means *shining light*. Her Scottish and Italian parents had named her well. Considering she'd lost her U.S. Marine husband in a training accident half a dozen years ago, she was remarkably optimistic.

"Thanks, Tiff." I arched my back and inhaled the savory aroma of prime ground beef and hot fries.

"No problem." All the diner's employees, including the owner, wore khaki pants and Kelly green shirts with white name patches, stylishly reminiscent of those worn by old-school gas station attendants. I almost expected Tiff to offer to clean my windshield for me.

I took a look around the bustling and noisy diner. "Is Moire Leora around?"

Tiffany nodded and slid a bottle of ketchup my way. If you're looking for Heinz or Hunt's in this diner, keep looking. Moire Leora makes her own, and it's phenomenal. Folks keep telling her she should go commercial, but she isn't interested. "Saw her a minute ago."

She joined me in the search. Tiffany's a green-eyed buxom blonde a few years my senior. If the guys didn't come here for the food, they came here because of her. She is very easy on the eyes.

Tiffany used to be married to the man who owns the biggest car lot in town. Now she and her son were living in a small condo in Lakeside Village and she was adding to what I'd heard through the rumor mill was a pittance of a divorce settlement by pulling shifts in the diner. "There she is." She pointed toward a table in the corner with her ballpoint pen.

I nodded. Moire Leora was sharing a laugh with

Mac MacDonald, our town's laid-back new mayor, and some of his friends. I caught her eye and waved.

Moire Leora headed back my way, swinging a stainless steel coffee carafe. "Hi, Amy." She held out the carafe and I shook my head. I was sticking with ice water. I had to balance out all those burger and onion ring calories somehow. I know coffee contains no calories, but not the way I drink it. Plenty of cream and too much sugar.

"How are you holding up?" She flopped down on the stool that Mr. Blue Suit had relinquished.

"Okay." I swirled a fat onion ring around in a puddle of ketchup.

"Really?" She looked bemused. "I don't think I'd be doing okay if I'd found a dead body here in the diner."

"You heard, huh?"

Hearing Moire Leora's laugh was like being doused in warm sunshine. She laid a soft hand on my shoulder. "Honey, everybody in Ruby Lake has heard. The whole county, I expect." She shook her head. "The whole state maybe."

I groaned. I could just picture the headlines spreading out across the land: "Birds & Bees or Birds & Bodies? Dead Man Found in Ruby Lake Shop. Shopkeeper Under Suspicion of Murder."

Strains of the prologue to *Little Shop of Horrors* ran through my mind. Moire Leora must have been reading my thoughts. She certainly couldn't have misread my body language: sloping shoulders, sagging chin, sad-sack expression, and skittish eyes.

"I just can't believe Matt Kowalski, of all people,

Matt Kowalski, was murdered in my house." I bit my lip. "I mean, why was he there in the first place?" I sighed heavily. "And how did he get in?"

"Beats me," Moire Leora replied.

"I'm sure the back door had been locked. I unlocked it to let Dwayne in." And with no broken windows or other signs of illicit entry, that left only the front door.

"Dwayne?"

"The deliveryman." I explained how the truck driver had arrived late with my merchandise for the store and I'd let him in after finding the body and being accosted by Esther Pilaster. "Did you see anybody else?" I asked hopefully. She followed my gaze across the street to Birds & Bees. "You do have a perfect view from here."

"No." Moire Leora shook her head. "Sorry. I keep an eye on what's going on inside more than outside." Moire Leora looks like a slightly older, slightly plumper version of Jennifer Anniston, with blue eyes and natural blond shoulder-length hair, which was also a little grayer and which she normally kept parted over her left eye. While the actress did commercials for hair color, Moire Leora doesn't believe in hair dye. At about five-four, she's a few inches shorter than me.

"Of course." I stuffed the last onion ring in my mouth and took a swig of water.

"I do remember seeing a few people, couples mostly, taking a stroll, walking their dogs. That sort of thing. Oh, I did see Gertie go by a couple of times."

"A couple of times?"

"Yeah."

"I wonder why."

Moire Leora shrugged. "Who knows why Gertie Hammer does any of the things she does? You know how Gertie is." I grunted as the proprietress continued. "Nobody around here has ever been able to make any sense of her."

"Tell me about it," I commiserated. Gertie was pretty much the town grouch. I almost regretted buying the old place from her.

"Oh, and I did see Mac MacDonald."

I straightened. "The mayor?"

Moire Leora nodded. "Yeah, he went to the door, knocked, looked in the windows, then drove off."

"What was that all about?" I wondered aloud. Could be nothing; then again could be something. I'd never even met the man. I only knew him from his picture when it popped up occasionally in the *Ruby Lake Weekender,* the town's local newspaper.

"Why don't you ask him yourself?"

We both looked around the diner, but Mac Mac-Donald was gone and the booth the mayor had been occupying was empty.

A shout from the kitchen caught Moire Leora's ear. "Sorry," she said, patting my shoulder. "Sounds like I'm needed to put out another fire, literal or otherwise."

Tiffany slid the check under the rim of my plate. "Anything else, Amy? There's still some apple-rhubarb pie left."

"Please," I said, patting my bloated stomach, "don't even tempt me." Moire Leora's pastry chef adds a dash of fresh ground cinnamon to the filling, which gives the pies that extra something that

I find practically irresistible. I was about to give in to temptation when I noticed Tiffany's eyes were a little red around the edges. "Everything okay with you, Tiff?"

She forced a small smile. "Oh sure."

"How's Jimmy?" Jimmy is her eleven-year-old son.

"He's good." Her sigh seemed to say otherwise.

I arched my brow and waited her out.

"It's Robert," she confessed a moment later. Robert is her ex. "He's been giving me a hard time."

I furrowed my brow. "What sort of a hard time?"

She shrugged. "Calling, following me." Her eyes jumped to the window. "Watching me."

"Watching you?"

Tiffany nodded. "Just yesterday I caught him spying on me from across the street."

I threw some money down on the counter and told her to keep the change. "Why would he be doing that?"

"Because he thinks I'm seeing another man," she whispered. The HVAC man lifted from his stool and headed for the door.

"Are you?" I asked. "Wait"—I held up my hand— "it's none of his business or mine if you are. After all, didn't Robert leave you?"

She pursed her lips. "Uh-huh."

For a woman nearly half his age and barely legal to boot, as I remembered.

"If you catch him stalking you again, call the police."

"I don't know." She sighed. "He is Jimmy's dad, after all. I don't want to make trouble."

I don't know, it seemed to me that Robert

LaChance was the one making all the trouble. But I didn't want to get involved in any family squabble, especially when it wasn't even my family. That could only lead to trouble—I'd taken sides in such disputes in the past and it had always backfired.

There's nothing worse than taking sides and then having the two sides reconcile and end up hating you for what one previously thought was helpful advice and that they've now jointly decided was unwelcome interference.

Do I sound sensitive? You bet I'm sensitive.

Besides, I had troubles of my own. Like figuring out who wanted Matt Kowalski dead and why they chose to do it in Birds & Bees, before I OD'd on onion rings.

10

"We need to talk." I locked the front door and turned over the Closed sign. It was after six, and while I expected to stay open evenings once tourist season kicked in, this time of year the streets were fairly deserted once the sun went down. Most businesses, except places like the diner and other establishments offering food or souvenirs, closed by five these days, and that meant dwindling traffic. Even some of the more touristy shops closed early through the winter and only began extending their hours once school was out.

Not to mention it was raining cats and dogs. I expected the only shoppers on the streets to be umbrella- and galoshes-seekers.

"Sure," chirped Kim. "About what?" She looked completely worn-out. Kim's last job had been working as a Realtor. I guess working on her feet all day in a wild bird supply store had proven to be a little more taxing than she'd anticipated.

"About Matt Kowalski." I looked Kim in the eye.

She's my best friend, but that didn't mean I couldn't ask her the hard questions.

A heartfelt sigh spilled over Kim's lips. "Buy a girl a drink first?"

I agreed and Kim followed me upstairs to the apartment I shared with Mom.

"Do we have to talk about this?" Kim had slumped into the dark green easy chair, balancing a glass of cabernet in one hand while I folded my legs under me on the brown leather sofa. Both pieces had been fixtures in my parents' house for as long as I could remember. Now they'd come to rest here in the top-floor apartment along with my mother and me. I didn't mind at all. There was a certain comfort in having them with us. The sagging chair cushion was a constant and pleasant reminder of my father.

I took a long sip and nodded. "You knew we'd have to sooner or later." Mom was in her bedroom with the door closed, probably resting. Mom's been diagnosed with adult onset muscular dystrophy—myotonic muscular dystrophy 1, or MMD1, to be precise. It seems to be only affecting her distal extremities, mostly her legs, but her hands a little too. The specialist over in Raleigh said this might be as bad as it gets. We could only hope.

Kim frowned and I spotted a tear at the corner of her left eye. "It's just been so long, you know?" I nodded. "You wouldn't think it would hurt this much." She swatted away the tear, finished her glass of wine, and poured a refill. She held the bottle out to me and topped off my glass as well.

We both knew the story. Her high school sweetheart, Tommy Regan, had been the passenger in an automobile that Matt Kowalski had been driving and smashed headfirst into a utility pole. Matt survived with injuries; Tommy died of his. Both boys had been seventeen and, while most folks agreed Matt must have been drinking, a sobriety test had never been performed and Matt had never been charged with a crime.

Not everybody was happy with that decision. Not Kim and not Tommy's family. The Regans had sold their home and moved away within a year of the accident, unable to live so close to the accident or Matt Kowalski.

"Can you think of anybody who'd want Matt dead?"

Kim smiled grimly. "Besides me?"

"I know you didn't kill him."

She shrugged. "There were times I wanted to."

"Do you ever hear from Tommy's parents?"

Kim shook her head. "Last I heard they'd retired to wherever they were from in Ohio." She tapped the side of her glass. "Matt's mother is still around though."

I perked up. "Oh?" It might be worth having a talk with her. "Maybe she can tell me what Matt might have been doing at my place."

Kim shrugged again. "Maybe."

I decided to change the subject. Kim was looking more morose by the minute. "What can you tell me about Mac MacDonald?"

"Mac?" Kim set her glass on the coffee table between us. "Nothing special. Why?"

I explained how Moire Leora had seen the mayor outside Birds & Bees the night of the murder. "You used to work for him in his real estate office. Can you think of any reason he might have been coming here?"

Kim pursed her lips.

I kept on. "I mean, I know he wasn't coming to see me. I don't even know the man."

"He's a politician now." Kim leaned back and rubbed her bare toes. "You know how it is. Maybe he came to wish you luck and drum up your support for some initiative or something. Maybe he was looking for a campaign donation."

"Maybe." I gave the suggestion some thought. He'd just recently been elected. But like most politicians, he was probably looking to fill the reelection-campaign war chest already. Though if he wanted money, he was in for a long and ultimately futile wait. "If he knew you were my partner, he might have been coming to see you." I shook my head. "But you were out of town."

Kim's eyes jumped. "Well . . ."

I leaned forward and set my empty glass next to hers. "Well?" I waited expectantly.

Kim opened her mouth to speak, but the sound we heard was the rattling of the apartment door. "Now what?" I grumbled. I pulled open the door. "Esther." The old woman stood in the doorway wrapped in a yellowed shawl and a long black woolen skirt. She looked up her cragged nose at me. "What do you want?"

"There's a lot of banging downstairs." She folded her arms across her chest.

"So you decided to do some banging of your own?"

She tilted her head to the side. "The banging is Chief Kennedy banging on your front door wanting to be let in, smart aleck." Esther the Pester turned on her orthopedic heels. "If I was you, I'd let him in before he breaks down your door."

My heart skipped a beat. I slipped on my shoes and headed down the back stairs to open the front door. "What is it now, Jerry?" I was in no mood for formalities.

Jerry's visor hung low over his brow and rivulets of rainwater spattered the tops of his black leather shoes. "I'm going to have to ask you to come down to the station and answer a few questions."

I puffed out my chest. "Are you kidding? Now?" I started to close the door. He stuck his toe against the door. "Can't this wait till tomorrow? Besides, I've told you everything I know."

But Jerry wasn't even looking at me. I swiveled my head to see just what the guy was looking at.

Kim stood several steps behind.

And she looked like a rabbit caught in a trap.

11

"I got here as soon as I could." Derek Harlan laid a firm hand on my shoulder.

Some comfort. I hadn't even wanted him to come at all. In fact, I'd pleaded with Mom not to call him last night. If anything, I'd said, call his dad, Ben. But Mom had informed me that Ben was out of town and unavailable. And when she'd heard that the police had requested Kim come down to the station for questioning, she'd insisted we do something. That something was Derek.

And he was something, all right. A jerk. I couldn't wait to get Matt's murder behind me and get Derek out of my life.

"Thanks," I said, sliding out from under his hand. The man was slimier than a state fair deep-fried stick of butter. "How's Kim?" Derek Harlan had gone down to the station to look after Kim at my and my mother's request.

Derek unbuttoned his peacoat. "She's fine. Chief

Kennedy harangued her for an hour or more, then let her go."

"That's good." I offered Mr. Harlan some coffee and helped myself to a cup. "I tried telephoning Kim several times last night and all my calls went to her voicemail."

Derek fell into one of the rockers and rested his cup on his knee. "Guess she wanted some alone time. I've got to say, it doesn't look good that she lied about not being in town the night of the murder." He scraped his lower lip. "Especially in light of her history with the guy."

"Wait a minute." I gasped, nearly spilling my mug. This was expensive stuff, too. I buy organic, shade-grown, bird- and earth-friendly coffee. The Smithsonian Migratory Bird Center created the Bird Friendly seal of approval to encourage production of shade-grown coffee and biodiversity. Besides being better for us all, it's better tasting. "You're saying Kim lied about not being in Ruby Lake when Matt Kowalski was murdered?"

Derek paused, maddeningly, to take a sip, then nodded. "You didn't know?"

"No! Why would she do that?" Kim's my best friend. Why would she lie to me? Was that what she was about to get into last night when Esther pounded on my door and Chief Kennedy showed up? It did explain how she'd noticed the Cole's Trucking semi parked outside the Ruby Lake Motor Inn the morning she'd claimed to return. It was on the opposite side of town from where she would have been coming had she driven straight up from Florida.

I had been wondering about that, but not enough to give it any serious thought. I mean, she could have headed out that way to stop at some particular store or a gas station she favored before coming by Birds & Bees. I'd had no reason to think she'd been lying to me about being back in Ruby Lake.

The lawyer shrugged. "It took some badgering," he said, "and I think a little fear of maybe ending up behind bars, but your friend Kim told the chief that she was with a guy named Randy Vincent."

"Randy Vincent?" My mouth went dry. This wasn't good.

He nodded. "Spent the night, apparently." Derek's brow jiggled.

The lovebirds at the front door cooed and I rose to greet what I hoped would be a customer. We'd had a number of looky-loos the day before, more interested in asking questions about the murder and exactly where the body had been found than about birds and birdseed.

The whole time, I couldn't help thinking about what Derek had just said. Kim had been with Randy Vincent. And she had spent the night? Randy's a local property manager. He owns a string of cabins around the lake and several vacation rental properties around town as well. He's also married. Though I had heard, from Kim come to think of it, that he was separated.

I pasted a smile on my face as a wizened gentleman in a rumpled tan wool suit and overcoat held a weathered and worn cylindrical Plexiglas birdfeeder up by two fingers. "Can you help me?" he asked.

"Certainly," I replied. "What do you need?"

Although he appeared to be in his seventies, his blue eyes shone brightly. He looked at the feeder. "Can't figure out how to get the darn thing loaded."

"Loaded?" He was holding a birdfeeder, not a shotgun.

He cleared his phlegmy throat, handed the feeder off to me, and rummaged in his coat pockets. He pulled out a plastic grocery bag filled with mixed birdseed. There were a couple of tiny holes in the bottom of the bag and a fine rain composed of bits of millet, cracked corn, sunflower seed pieces, and oat groats spilled over his shoes and onto my floor. It was your typical universal blend of birdseed. I recognized the brand as one generally sold in the big box stores.

He ran a wrinkled hand through his thinning white hair and frowned as he looked at his brown leather loafers. He kicked his toes against the hardwood to clear his shoe tops. Okay, so now the mess was just all over my floor.

I gently relieved him of the plastic bag. "No problem. Follow me." I dropped both bag and feeder on the sales counter. The feeder looked quite old. It was covered with dirt and bird poop. I grabbed a pair of disposable nitrile gloves and got to work.

"I tried pouring that stupid food in the holes, but every time I did it seemed like half spilled back out." He jabbed his thumb at one of the feeder holes. "They oughta make the holes bigger."

I grinned. "Like I said, no problem. The top comes off." His brows drew together as I grabbed the tethered lid and turned. It was frozen. I huffed, tapped it gently against the counter, and tried again. This time the lid turned with a squeak, then popped off in my hand. "Why don't I hold it open while you pour?"

The old man nodded and slowly poured seed from his bag into the feeder. I didn't know if it was his age or his natural motor skills, or lack thereof, but there was just as much seed spilling over the counter as there was down the barrel of the feeder.

I twisted the lid back on tight and placed the birdfeeder back in his now empty grocery bag. There was bound to be some food spilling out the feeder holes as he carried it home. At least this way, he'd recover it. "You might want to consider one of these," I said, tossing the soiled disposable gloves in the trash can at the end of the counter and gesturing for him to follow me across the aisle.

"What is it?" he said, scratching the top of his head.

I handed him the red plastic device. "It's a combo birdseed scoop and funnel. You pour the seed in the top, place this narrow end in your feeder, then twist this little damper with your thumb, and voilà!" I explained. "The seed pours into your feeder tube." And not onto your shoes or my floor.

He grunted and turned it over in his hand, playing with the doodad on the bottom—open, closed, open. "Looks like it could work."

"It does," I assured him.

"How much?" He toyed with his moustache using the thumb and index finger of his right hand.

"Four ninety-five."

"Sold." He fished out his wallet and handed me a credit card. "Used to work here, you know."

I swiped his card. "Oh?"

"Yep. Used to be a bank."

"I'm afraid that's before my time." The old place had started life as a boarding house as far as I knew, and over time been home to countless business enterprises.

He barked out a surprisingly loud laugh. "Everything's before your time. Now me, I'm ancient. I remember everything."

"You're not that old." I handed him back his card. "Would you like a bag for that?"

"Toss it in with the feeder." He opened his rumpled grocery bag. "So if I'm not that old," he said with a mischievous twinkle in his eyes, "how's about going out with me sometime?"

My tongue clicked. "Sorry," I replied. "I wish I could, but we have a strict rule against dating our customers."

He shrugged. "Your loss." He headed for the door.

"Come again, Mr. Withers."

He paused and turned around. "How'd you know my name?"

"Your credit card."

Dwayne Rogers opened the door and brushed past the old man. "You looking for me?" The two men nodded at one another.

I waved. "I was hoping you could remove the pallets from the back room." I'd called his boss earlier and learned he was still in town. We'd emptied all the store goods from the wooden pallets and now the things were simply in the way.

Dwayne scowled and thrust his hands in his pockets. "Removing pallets isn't part of my job."

"I understand. I don't mean to be any trouble. But I'm glad you haven't left yet." I described how the pallets were too large for me to haul off and the trash pickup service wouldn't take them.

He shook his head. "Thought I'd spend a few days. I'm staying with my uncle." His lips twisted. "Besides, the police want me to stick around a little longer"—the driver looked pointedly in my direction—"in case they have any more questions. He paced up and down and I couldn't imagine why. "Fine," he said finally. "Where are they?"

"Storeroom. You want me to—"

The driver cut me off with a wave of his hand. "I know the way. Don't worry. I'll take care of it."

Apparently I wasn't Dwayne's favorite person. I guess his first impression of me, fear and surprise etched on my face, blood dripping from my hands, hadn't been a good one.

No, definitely not.

No matter, I saw Mom chatting it up with Derek Harlan over in the corner and was about to join them when a small crowd entered. At the tail end of the sudden and welcome crowd came Aaron Maddley, the farmer-slash-talented-woodworker who'd sold me the handcrafted bluebird houses. "Mr. Maddley, this is a pleasant surprise."

Aaron Maddley's a tall man about my age, with the rugged good looks of a man who spends a good deal of his time out of doors and has the calluses of a man who knows how to use his hands. He wore a brown leather jacket with a fleece collar, a pair of blue jeans, and heavy work boots. Though of a similar age, our paths hadn't crossed until he'd shown up at the store with his offer to supply me with the handcrafted bluebird houses—an offer I'd gladly and quickly accepted.

"Hello, Ms. Simms." He wiped his feet at the mat. "I thought I'd check out your new place."

I shook his hand.

"I see you gave the houses a good home." He beamed. "No pun intended."

"None taken," I replied. "And, please, call me Amy." I swept my hand along the shelf. "I gave them a place of honor." I picked one of his cedar birdhouses and told him how I planned on adding a small sign along the edge of the shelf with his name, a brief bio if he'd provide me with one, and an explanation of how he was one of Ruby Lake's local artists. He appeared very pleased. "They really are pieces of art."

"I'd be honored to give you a bio. Not much to tell though," he said modestly.

"In fact"—I'd had a sudden thought—"you ought to have your signature on them. Folks love that."

He seemed to give this some thought. "I suppose I could use a marker."

"Or a wood-burning tool," I suggested. "I've got one you can borrow."

"Thanks. I'll write it on the bottom," he said, turning the house upside down.

"That would be perfect."

"Sell any yet?" He looked at me shyly.

"Sorry." I shook my head and set the birdhouse back on the shelf. "Not yet. But then I've only been open a day. We're kind of off to a slow start."

Aaron did a turn around the store. "Yeah, I heard about Matt Kowalski."

"That's right, the police mentioned they'd be checking with you. I told them I'd been out to see you at the time of the murder." I smiled at him. "I hope you gave me a good alibi."

The farmer dipped his chin. "Yeah, told them how we'd had business. That officer they sent wanted to know exactly what time you came and exactly when you left."

I let out a breath. Thank goodness somebody could vouch for my whereabouts. "Did you know him? Matt Kowalski, I mean."

Aaron nodded and leaned idly against the front counter. "Went to school together. Had some classes together. Do the police have any idea who might have killed him?" Aaron had lowered his voice. He stepped aside as I rang up an order for a birding field guide to the Carolinas.

"Besides me, you mean?"

"Come on, you didn't kill anybody." He ran his fingers through a thick thatch of brown hair.

"Tell Chief Kennedy that."

Aaron rolled his hazel eyes. "I find it almost as hard to believe that somebody around here killed Matt in your store as I can that folks picked Jerry Kennedy to be their chief of police."

We laughed. Mom and Derek Harlan joined us. I made the introductions.

"New in town?" Aaron asked the lawyer as the two men shook hands.

"Yes, I've joined my father's practice." Derek's eyes seemed to be sizing up the other man. "That's quite a grip you've got there. What line of work are you in, if you don't mind my asking?"

"Got a place outside town. Do a little farming." The edges of his mouth cracked. "Took over my father's practice, you might say."

Derek nodded.

"Aaron also builds the most wonderful birdhouses." I pointed to the shelf across the way.

"Very nice," said Derek. "Listen, Amy"—I watched Derek's Adam's apple bob up and down—"if you aren't busy Saturday night—"

"Sorry," I said, already cutting the man off. "Like I said. I am. Aaron and I are having dinner at Lake House. Aren't we, dear?" Amy's eyes begged Aaron to play along. Lake House was a romantic, upscale restaurant in the Ruby Lake Marina. Probably the most romantic spot in town for food.

Aaron cleared his throat and his toes scuffed the floor. "Yeah, that's right. We've got a date Saturday night at Lake House." Aaron shot me a nervous look. "What time did you say I was supposed to pick you up, miss, I mean, Amy?"

"Seven thirty, darling."

He bobbed his head. His cheeks glowed strawberry red. "Yeah, that's right, seven thirty."

Mom followed the conversation like she was watching the world's strangest tennis match.

"I understand," the lawyer replied. "Hey, can't blame a guy for trying, right?" He'd directed his comment to Aaron, my make-believe boyfriend. The two men shook hands once again. "Oh." Derek stopped at the door. "You really should get that leak looked at. Could be some serious water damage."

"What leak?"

12

"Thanks for playing along." I stared dejectedly at the slow drip coming from the ceiling. A three-foot damp circle stained the ceiling and the wall all the way down to the windowsill. Derek had pointed it out to my mother before leaving. That's what they had been talking about while I'd been busy.

"You mean we don't really have a date?" Aaron feigned insult but his eyes and smile gave him away. "You're canceling on me? What is it? Is there another man in your life? You can tell me."

I smiled despite my latest woes. "Very funny." Aaron looked at the ugly stain on the wall. Was he actually upset? If so, was it because I'd made him lie to Derek or because I'd practically scoffed at the idea of the two of us going out to dinner together?

I guess I could see how that might come across as insulting. I swallowed. "I mean, do you want to?"

Aaron turned and faced me. Our eyes met. "Go on a date, I mean." I took a step back. Geesh! Now I was asking a man out on a date!

A man I barely knew.

I took another step back and banged into a chair. "I mean, we *could* go out to dinner." Why wasn't he saying anything? And why was he looking at me like that? I rolled my tongue over my teeth. "At the Lake House."

"Sure." Aaron stuffed his left hand in the back pocket of his jeans. A small smile played across his face. "We could talk business."

"Yes, I would like to talk"—I hesitated—"business. I mean, I did want to ask you if you might be interested in supplying other sorts of birdhouses."

"Watch out."

"Huh?"

Aaron pushed me gently to one side as a water-logged ceiling tile came crashing down. He clucked his tongue and shook his head.

"I guess I'd better make a phone call." I groaned, taking the opportunity to change the subject and relieve us both of an awkward situation.

A couple of hours later, I stood in the shadowy and damp basement beneath my old house with visions of dollar signs dancing in my eyes. Where were the sugar plums when you needed them?

"That's quite a mess you've got here," pronounced Cash as I joined him. Cassius Calderon was a local general contractor and owner of CC Construction. He'd done some work for Mom in the past—replacing the roof on Mom and Dad's old house—so I knew I could count on his expertise.

Cash had spent the better part of an hour inspecting the old Victorian from top to bottom. He'd discovered a leak that started at the roof and fell, apparently unhindered, to the basement floor. "I'm afraid we'll have to fix the roof and open up some walls to repair the damage." He fingered the crumbling basement wall. "There's a lot of wall damage." He turned his dark eyes on me. "And in these dark and wet conditions. . . ."

"Yes?"

He blinked. "You don't want mold. Trust me."

I nodded. I trusted him. Mold I didn't need. Money, on the other hand, I feared I could use a bundle of . . .

Cash is a big man with a barrel chest, dark blue eyes, and a bristly crew cut. There's a small brown mole just below his left earlobe, the size of a pencil eraser. Though I knew he was somewhere between fifty and sixty years old, he was as fit as any forty-year-old. Heck, he was probably as fit as most twenty-year-olds. Cash's brown bomber jacket with his company's name, CC Construction, stitched in red lettering on the front, was unzipped. Underneath he wore a comfortable gray sweatshirt and a pair of Wranglers.

"How much do you think this is going to cost?" I asked with trepidation.

Cash pursed his lips. The tip of his steel-toed boot bounced in a puddle of rain water. "Too bad you didn't get this place inspected before you bought it, Ms. Simms."

"I know." I waited. Cash is not a fast mover. Or talker.

The unfinished basement had a low ceiling and the contractor stooped as he paced up and down the cramped, dank space. "To tell you the truth, and I'm not criticizing or anything . . ."

"Yes?"

"Well"—he stopped and scratched his head—"it's just that I'm surprised you didn't notice the problems earlier. I mean, what with all the work you've been doing down here."

"Work?" What the devil was Cash Calderon talking about?

He must have noticed the confusion on my face because he pointed his big flashlight at the opposite wall.

I gasped. Large chunks of concrete were missing from the walls in several places and the floor was littered with mounds of wet dirt, assorted bits of debris, and gray dust. "What on earth?"

"I'm not sure what you're up to," Cash Calderon said, "but you've got to be careful of digging into your foundation like that." His head turned to the ceiling. "The whole place could come crashing down."

I couldn't help looking up too. I gulped, picturing the entire three-story Victorian house crashing down on our heads. I'd never been one for small spaces. I particularly didn't like small, dark spaces. I even more particularly didn't like small, dark, and dank spaces that harbored potentially deadly black mold. And I even more particularly didn't like small, dark, dank, potentially death-harboring black mold spaces that could come crashing down any minute and crush me to a wet pulp.

I ran.

Mr. Calderon caught up to me back on the ground floor.

"Sorry about that," I said, my hands braced against my knees as I forced myself to take slow, even breaths. "I don't know what came over me."

Mom patted my back. "Are you okay, dear? You look like the Devil himself has been chasing you."

I gulped and bobbed my head up and down. This was totally embarrassing. Thank goodness nobody else had been around to see my temporary breakdown. I straightened and pushed my hair behind my ears.

I saw Mr. Calderon wink at Mom. "No problem," he said. "Happens all the time."

I was sure it didn't, but it was nice of him to try to make me feel better.

"Oh dear," Mom cooed, "another customer." I watched as Mom hurried to greet the newcomer. I perked up. Good, I could use a thousand customers. So I hoped this one brought company. Unfortunately, he didn't. He was the mail carrier and he brought mail.

Probably bills.

I perked down.

Cash Calderon pulled out a calculator and rolled the edge of his tongue over his upper lip while his fingers punched the keypad. The more he punched, the more I worried. The contractor extracted a pad from inside his bomber jacket and tallied up his figures.

"Yikes!" I said as he handed me the estimate. "That's a lot of zeroes."

He shook his head. "I know. I gave you the best price I could. But between the materials and the labor—"

"Oh, I know," I said, patting his arm. "I didn't mean any offense." I giggled nervously. "It's just, well, I don't know how I'm ever going to afford this." I tapped the paper with my fingernail. At the same time, I couldn't afford not to get that leak repaired. "I don't suppose you have a layaway plan, by any chance?"

I'd only been half joking, so I was surprised when he answered, "Nope. I'm afraid not." He smiled as he spread a plastic sheet down in the spot where the ceiling tile had caved in earlier. "But I'll tell you what: You pay me a few hundred dollars a month. Interest free."

"Really? Do you mean it?"

He nodded. "We'll call it an installment plan."

"Oh, Mr. Calderon, that's so generous of you." I planted a kiss on his ruddy cheek. "And I promise, I'll pay you three hundred dollars first thing every month and quicker when business picks up."

The contractor vowed to get started right away. He'd even offered to patch the holes in the basement wall. Next time I bought a place, if there was a next time, I swore I'd get a complete building inspection. And I promised to give the job to Cash Calderon, who was also a licensed home inspector.

In the meantime, I had a few holes of my own to fill. Only these holes weren't letting in rain—and probably the furry, clawed critters I was sure I'd been hearing in the attic and walls. No, these holes concerned the mystery of who killed Matthew Kowalski, and why.

I'd start with a visit to his mother's house. If anybody had known he was in town and what he'd been up to, particularly on the night he was murdered in my own home and place of business, it would be her.

I shoved the soundtrack to *Oklahoma!* in the CD player and cruised up Lake Shore Drive. The Kowalskis lived in a small sub-division up the hill near the elementary school. It was a lower-middle-class neighborhood with smallish older homes; most had detached garages.

I parked at the curb and gazed at the house. The small patch of grass was brown, and in contrast to the well-kept yards of her neighbors, Mrs. Kowalski's yard, in particular the shrubbery, seemed to be suffering from years of neglect. I shut off the car stereo in the middle of Gordon MacRae belting out "Oh What a Beautiful Mornin'."

Everything might have been going his way, but they sure weren't going mine.

A petite woman with a stooped back and mousy features answered on the third knock. I hadn't seen Mrs. Kowalski in ages. The woman looked years older than the one I remembered. The skin around her large brown eyes sagged, and wrinkles spread to her hairline. "Yes?" She clutched the weathered doorknob for support.

The woman at the door wore a thick cotton check-pattern dress in shades of brown, beige, and gray. It was pleated at the waist and buttoned up the front. The sleeves covered her arms completely and the bottom extended to her ankles, revealing only white stockinged feet covered in simple green fuzzy slippers. "Mrs. Kowalski? It's me, Amy Simms. I went to school with Matt."

She stared vacantly for a moment. "Art and Barbara's girl?"

I nodded. "That's right." I looked past her to the dark formal living room. "Would it be all right if I came in for a moment?"

She pulled the door wide and I preceded her into the tiny, cramped space. She motioned for me to sit on the sofa. "Can I get you something?" Mrs. Kowalski fiddled with her thin gold wedding band. I remembered that her husband had passed years before. "Coffee? Tea?"

"Nothing, thanks." I folded my hands on my lap. A giant gray cat rubbed against my shins.

"Pay Dilbert no mind," Mrs. Kowalski said with obvious love. The big cat lumbered over to a table under the front window, hopped up and curled himself into a ball. Matt's mother leaned back in an old-fashioned walnut rocker with a pillowed back. Under the glare of the lamp beside her, I noticed that her face was heavily made up.

Silence filled the space between us as I wondered where to begin. She had to be aware of her son's death. She had to also know that he'd been found murdered in my house and that I was high up on the suspect list.

"You want to talk about Matt," Mrs. Kowalski said, rocking slowly. Her short gray-brown hair was pulled back sharply over her forehead with a simple brown plastic headband, giving her the appearance of a barred owl.

"First off, I want you to know that I had nothing to do with his death."

She shrugged and rocked faster. From the worn lines in the carpet, it was a habit of hers. "Never thought you did."

"Then who?" I said. "Who do you think would do such a thing?"

Mrs. Kowalski shook her head. "No idea." She grinned, revealing yellowed teeth. "May as well ask old Dilbert here."

I glanced at the cat. He didn't look eager to chat. "When was the last time you saw your son?"

"A couple of Christmases ago, I guess it was." Her feet touched the ground and she stopped rocking. "Yes, that sounds about right."

It didn't sound like mother and son had been terribly close. "Did he stay in touch? Do you know where he was living?"

"Down in Myrtle Beach last, I believe he said. Had a job working at one of those amusement parks or something."

"So you didn't know he was here in Ruby Lake?" She shook her head in the negative and I sighed. Matt's mother wasn't giving me much to go on. "Do you have any idea why he'd been wearing a disguise?"

"I guess he didn't want to get recognized," she said softly. "Not everybody around here was so fond of him."

I refrained from commenting. "Can you think of any reason that he might have been in Ruby

Lake? And what he might have been doing at my store, Birds and Bees?"

Mrs. Kowalski shook her head and rose stiffly. "If you don't mind," she said, "I'm feeling kind of tired now. I'm not used to talking so much these days. Old Dilbert's not much of a conversationalist."

"I understand," I said, following the old woman to the front door. I paused at the threshold. "Did Matt have a girlfriend? Somebody he might have confided in?"

"I don't have a clue, Ms. Simms. I'm afraid you'd have to ask Matt that." Her hand went to the doorknob. "But I'm afraid you can't, because he's dead." She grabbed a worn wooden cane beside the door and used it to gently block Dilbert from leaving. "No you don't, cat. You stay in here with me, where it's safe."

I hesitated once more on the front stoop, looking from Dilbert to Mrs. Kowalski. "If you can think of anything that could help—"

"Police already gave me that speech."

"Of course, it's just that if you could think of anything, come up with any information that could help uncover Matt's killer—" I took a step toward her.

She nodded. "I already told Chief Kennedy everything I could when he came by. He's like you. He asks lots of questions."

"We all want to find out who killed your son." I could understand how the poor woman felt. Even estranged, he was her flesh and blood.

A small smile passed her lips, then faded. "I know who killed Matt."

A frisson ran up my arms. "You do?"

"Sure," the old woman said, leaning on her cane. "Like I told Chief Kennedy, it was that girl that did it."

"That girl?" Could Mrs. Kowalski really know who killed her son? "That's wonderful!" I clapped my hands and Dilbert disappeared from sight. The big scaredy-cat. "Who? Who is she?"

"It was that Kimberly Christy," Mrs. Kowalski said firmly.

"K-Kim?"

"She always said she'd kill him. Blamed him for what happened to that boyfriend of hers. Even though it happened a million years ago." She banged the ground with the tip of her cane so hard I expected sparks to fly. "And my boy wasn't to blame at all!" She sniffed. "I guess she finally got up the nerve to do it."

The door swung shut in my face.

13

I raced down the road and headed for Kim's house. My best friend was harboring secrets, secrets that might have something to do with Matt Kowalski's murder. She was trying to avoid me, but I was not about to let her avoid me any longer.

I slammed on the brakes as a young woman darted into the road pushing a stroller. I recognized her as the woman who'd been in the shop with her family to buy her first feeder. I waved, but she ignored me. I guess she didn't recognize me all bundled up in my thick coat with my knitted blue skullcap pressed low over my forehead.

I lifted my foot from the accelerator, then hesitated. She had crossed the road now and was heading for the cabins behind the Ruby Lake Motor Inn. That was weird. I didn't know her name, but I did remember that she'd told me that she and her family had just moved into a house on Sycamore.

What was she doing here? Way across town? I admit, my first thoughts led to prurient notions.

Like, maybe a secret assignation. But who takes a baby stroller to an illicit rendezvous?

She rolled up to the third cabin in, hefted the stroller onto the narrow porch, and knocked. I recognized the youngster at the door. A moment later, the man who'd been with her at the store, her husband no doubt, folded up the stroller and carried it inside.

The driver of the car behind me blew its horn and I zoomed off. I hadn't gone far when a frenetic squirrel jumped out in the road, hopped several steps, then froze. I swerved to the left, veering into the oncoming lane. Fortunately, no one was coming.

Unfortunately, there was a police cruiser pulling out of the bank parking lot. I held my breath and prayed it was payday and the officer was in a good mood. I watched nervously as the police sedan eased into traffic. So far, so good.

Then the ominous sound of a police siren and the glare of its accompanying lights set my teeth on edge. I pulled over to the curb and rolled down my window. A rush of cold air hit my face.

I watched in the side-view mirror as the officer exited his vehicle and approached my van. "Is there a problem, miss?"

I turned to face him, offering up my prettiest smile.

"Oh, it's you." It was Officer Dan Sutton, the same cop who'd been with Jerry Kennedy the night Matt had been found. The same cop who seemed to prefer to find me guilty of murder first and ask questions later.

"Hello, Officer Sutton." I cleared my throat. "Sorry about that." I wiggled my finger toward the windshield. "Suicidal squirrel." He glared. I continued. "You know how they get this time of year." I rubbed the side of my neck. Stress does funny things to my neck muscles. "I think it's the stale acorns." Smile.

If Dan Sutton had a sense of humor he kept it well under wraps. "License and registration, please." He held out a beefy paw. If I'd had a dead squirrel to hand him, he just might have eaten it raw like some wild beast.

"Oh, come on," I said, reaching into the glove box. "You can't be serious."

He was. A few minutes later, I stuffed the forty-dollar reckless driving ticket in my purse and started dreaming about my retirement—someplace warm and sunny all the time—someplace not named Ruby Lake.

I also kept my eyes on the road and sent a mental warning to squirrels everywhere to stay out of my path.

Kim lived on the opposite side of town in a Craftsman-style bungalow with a full-width porch. Square posts rested atop chestnut redbrick piers rising to just slightly above the white porch railing. There was a red flower box beneath the triple attic window, though I'd never known it to hold any flowers or living things of any kind, other than the occasional rooting chipmunk.

She'd maintained the home's classic color scheme: stone colored weatherboard with white trim and a red door. Kim's driveway was empty, but she had a single-car garage behind the house, so I wasn't surprised or concerned that she might be out. Though if she wasn't home, I was going to try Randy Vincent's house.

I rang the bell and pounded on the door. This was no time for formalities. Besides, I was hungry. And cranky. And, yes, I needed a cookie. Unfortunately, I'd rooted around in my handbag and come up empty-handed. I try to keep a snack cookie or granola bar for just such emergencies.

"Kim!" I said. "It's me, Amy!" Like she didn't know who I was by the sound of my voice. We'd been best friends since middle school. "Open up." I banged again. "I know you're in there!" I pressed my ear to the door but heard nothing more than the sound of blood rushing through my veins.

I whipped out my cell phone and dialed her number. I was sent straight to voicemail. I stamped my feet on the porch. "This is ridiculous," I muttered. Her curtains were pulled tight, but it looked like a light was on inside. I glanced at the neighbors' houses. Nobody seemed to be watching.

I headed down the driveway and around the back. For as long as I could remember, Kim's always kept a spare key under a flowerpot off the back porch. It may be a dumb thing to do in this day and age, but Kim can be a bit of a ditz and is always losing things, like her house key.

Besides, in a small town like Ruby Lake, who'd break in? I mean, what are the odds?

I lifted the pot, scooped up the key, and let myself in.

"That's breaking and entering," Kim said, looking at me from the kitchen table with a sour expression. She was wearing the same clothes she'd had on yesterday, only now they looked rumpled and smelled of wine. So did Kim.

"I didn't break anything," I replied sharply, tossing the key at her. It bounced off her chest and landed on the tabletop. "But I can if you want me to." I grabbed the back of an empty chair and spun it around. "It's been one of those days."

Kim's eyebrows rose and a small smile played across her lips. "Uh-oh. Somebody needs a cookie." Her face was sallow and her eyes puffy and red rimmed.

"I do not," I huffed, "need a cookie!" I slammed my butt down in the chair and faced her. "What I need are answers!"

An awkward silence passed between us. The ticking of a big brass spoon clock on the wall seemed excruciating as I waited for my best friend in the whole world to tell me what was going on.

Was she seeing Randy Vincent? Was she an adulteress? Worse, had she swung a wrought-iron birdfeeder hook at Matt Kowalski's unsuspecting head? Was she a murderess?

After a moment, Kim pushed back from the table with a groan. She rose, crossed to the cabinet, and pulled out a bag of pecan sandies. She thumped the bag down in front of me. "Cookie first," she said, tapping her foot impatiently. "Answers second."

I opened my mouth to protest. But I do love pecan sandies. I hadn't eaten in hours. And these were Keebler. My favorite. I sighed and broke open the bag. The deliciously sweet odor of fresh pecan-and-shortbread cookie wafted upward. Nothing like the smell of a fresh bag of pecan sandies.

I helped myself to a cookie—okay, two—before resuming my attack. "I just came from Mrs. Kowalski's house." I filled a glass of water from the kitchen sink.

"Oh, what did she have to say?"

"She says you killed her son."

Kim snorted. "Matt killed himself."

I scrunched up my face. "Are you trying to make me believe that Matt hit himself in the back of the head with a birdfeeder hook?"

Kim scowled. "You know what I mean." But I didn't, so she continued. "The guy made bad choices in life. One of those bad choices killed him." Kim lifted her wineglass and took a sip.

I snatched the glass from her and put it in the sink with the rest of her dirty dishes. "We all make bad choices," I said. "What I want to hear about now are yours."

"What's that supposed to mean?"

"It means I know all about you and Randy Vincent." She opened her mouth to respond, but I held up my hand to stop her. "And I know that you were in town when Matt was killed."

Kim looked troubled, frightened.

"That explains how you'd seen the Cole's Trucking semi parked outside the Ruby Lake Motor Inn. The motel is nowhere near your place." Kim didn't deny it. She didn't deny anything, and that made me worry all the more. "Talk to me," I pleaded. "Tell me what's going on. I want to help you."

Kim remained intransigent. "I need a drink."

"You need a lawyer!" I barked. I'd reached the end of my patience, friend or no friend. "The police think you might have murdered Matt. And Mrs. Kowalski is convinced of it. You mind explaining to me what makes her so sure?"

Kim stared at the kitchen floor, old refinished red oak in a rich, dark stain. "I was sort of seen leaving Birds and Bees the evening Matt was killed."

My head snapped back as if I'd been hit in the face with a pile driver. I scrubbed my face with my hands as I fought to regain my equilibrium. This whole situation just kept getting worse and worse. I took a swig of water.

"And for the record," Kim said, her voice low, "the police don't think I murdered Matt."

I twisted my head to the side. "Oh?" I could feel the beginnings of relief, just a tickle, rising from my toes. But I'd take it. I could use some good news for a change.

Kim shook her disheveled head slowly, in time with the clock. "They think we're in on it together."

14

And things just got worse again. I fell into a hard kitchen chair. "What? Why?" This couldn't be happening. This really, truly, could not be happening. I'd led a good life, been a good girl. Helped my mother. Stopped for suicidal squirrels even if it meant getting a traffic ticket for reckless driving.

What had I done to deserve this?

I reached for the bottle of wine. Empty.

No matter. I knew where Kim kept her supply. Upper cabinet, third door on the right. Bingo!

"Who saw you?" I pulled down a bottle of sangria and dumped a generous portion into a relatively clean coffee mug.

"Gertie Hammer."

Great. Of all people, Kim had been seen by the Queen of Sour. Moire Leora had mentioned seeing the old woman pass by a couple of times. I drank and wondered what the old biddy had been up to, while Kim pouted.

"What about me?" she whined.

"You need coffee." I wrinkled my nose. "And a shower."

Kim thrust her tongue out.

"And a toothbrush."

While Kim steamed, I finished my wine. And had another cookie. "Okay," I said, laying my hands on the table, "tell me why Kennedy thinks we're a couple of killers." Though I wasn't sure I wanted to hear this.

"Well," stuttered Kim, taking a sudden interest in her hands.

I slapped her hand. "Spill it."

Kim nodded once. "It's no news that you and I both had reason to dislike Matt Kowalski . . ." Her voice trailed off and I listened to the incessant ticking of the clock just for something to do.

"Disliked doesn't begin to describe it," I said finally.

Kim managed a small laugh. "Jerry thinks we lured him there to Birds and Bees." She rose and paced the small kitchen. "And while one of us distracted him"—Kim swung her arms—"the other whacked him."

"What? And we just left his body there on the floor of my storeroom waiting to be discovered?" I shook my head. "How dumb does Jerry think we are? How dumb is Jerry?!" I realized I was pacing now myself and forced myself to sit back down. "So, what *were* you doing at Birds and Bees?" I demanded.

"Well, I—"

"And why didn't you tell me you were back in Ruby Lake?" My voice and pulse were rising once more.

"I only—"

I was on my feet again and we were standing nose to nose. "And what are you doing seeing Randy Vincent? A married man!"

"Too many questions, Amy! Give me time to answer one first." Kim swayed and her legs wobbled. "Oops." Her eyes glistened. "I don't feel so good." She pressed the back of her hand against her forehead.

"When's the last time you ate?"

"That cute lawyer, Derek Harlan, had some Chinese food brought over to the police station last night."

I pointed to the stairs. "You go get cleaned up. I'll fix us some dinner." While my best friend slowly trudged up the stairs to shower, change into some clean clothes and, hopefully, brush her teeth, I scrounged around for some food.

And some answers.

By the time Kim came back down, looking if not like a million bucks, at least a hundred, which was ninety-nine more than she'd looked like earlier, I had a simple yet healthy spread laid out on the kitchen table.

"Pork chops and apple sauce." Kim smiled. "Thank you, Alice." She'd thrown on an ornate black Juicy Couture tracksuit, though I'd never known her to run a day in her life unless it was to beat out another shopper during a store sale. The back of the jacket was lavishly embellished with glittery gems and gold studs. I guess it's the style that counts. The bottoms were the matching velour-floral-jewel-boot-cut pant.

"Shut up and eat," I replied. Okay, so I'm a

Brady Bunch fan. Who isn't? The reruns never end, so it's learn to love 'em or live without TV. I jabbed at my chop while Kim destroyed hers by drowning it in ketchup.

Over coffee, Kim told me how she'd been seeing Randy Vincent for a couple of months or more. It seemed they sort of ran in the same circles, she having worked in real estate and he being in property management. Kim had handled a couple of sales for him. "I didn't want to tell you because I was afraid of what you'd think."

"I don't know what to think," I said. And I honestly didn't.

"Randy's been separated from his wife for more than a year, you know."

"So why don't they get divorced?"

She shrugged and bent at the waist, touching her fingers to the floor. "He says they haven't gotten around to it. You know they share the business."

I knew. Like I said, Vincent Properties owned a number of rentals around Ruby Lake. I'd seen several of their signs around town. "And his wife is okay with you seeing her husband? Maybe she finally got mad and decided to kill Matt Kowalski and frame you—us—for it."

Kim shook her head. "No. She's fine with it. Lynda's been seeing some guy for nearly a year now."

Lynda is Randy's wife. I didn't know what was going on with them, but at least there were no children involved. "So I ask again, what were you doing at Birds and Bees the night Matt got killed?"

She let out a low moan. "Randy had some work

to do. Taxes. It's crunch time, you know. I went to the store to get my tablet so I could read." I knew Kim liked to read novels on the electronic device. Me, I prefer paper. "I'd inadvertently left it there when I went to Florida. It was under the front counter."

Now that she'd mentioned it, I realized that it had been there before the murder and not after. "What time did you get to Birds and Bees?"

"Around seven, seven thirty, I'd say."

That was well after I'd gone. "So did you see or hear anything?"

"No, not really." Kim hesitated. I rose and re-filled our coffee. "I mean, I thought I heard noises. But in that old house, we're always hearing noises, right?"

I nodded. Old houses make old noises, old spooky noises. Squirrels and nocturnal critters make noises. And rain seeping into your walls and crumbling your foundation, no doubt, made noises. "Wait a minute," I asked. "Was the door locked when you arrived?"

"Sure."

"And you went in the front?"

Kim nodded. "Yeah, why?"

I shrugged helplessly. "I'm still trying to figure out how it got unlocked. Like I said, it was un-locked when I got back from Aaron Maddley's farm."

"Matt must have done it."

"I suppose he might have picked the lock." But I didn't think he'd had the brains for it. His motor skills seemed more in line with popping open beer cans. I couldn't quite picture Matt as a cat burglar. Then again, there was a lot I apparently didn't know about Matt Kowalski. I hadn't seen him in years. People change. I'd changed. Maybe Matt had too.

I pulled a notepad from Kim's junk drawer and fished out a half-chewed pencil.

"What are you doing?"

"We need to learn more about Matt." I drew his name in big block letters at the top of the sheet. "And then we need to come up with a list of names."

"Names?"

I nodded. "Of people who might have wanted him dead."

A small smile passed her lips. "Besides us?"

"Definitely besides us." I tapped the stubby eraser end of the pencil against the lined paper. "So, who have we got?"

Kim shrugged helplessly. Her mouth opened and closed. "Sorry, I don't have a clue, Amy."

"Well, I do." I flipped the pencil over and put tip to paper. I paused. "Damn." I bit the inside of my cheek. "I don't."

We sat in silence for several minutes. "This is nuts," I said, finally breaking the silence. "There has to be someone in this town who wanted Matt dead."

Kim raised an eyebrow.

"Otherwise, he'd still be alive!" I slammed my fist against the table and thought about everything that had happened since the murder. "What about Mayor MacDonald?"

"Mac?"

"Yeah. Remember how I said that Moire Leora had seen him peeking in the door at the shop?"

"You mean, maybe he's the killer, returning to the scene of the crime?"

I nodded. "That's what they do in the movies." Just because it was a stereotype didn't make it any less true. "We'll have to poke around, see if the good mayor might have had reason to want Matt dead."

"I suppose . . ." Kim sounded unconvinced.

"Speaking of Mac. You used to work with him. Ask him if there have been any recent house sales on Sycamore Street."

"Why on earth do you want to know that?" Kim's brow shot up. "Are you looking for another place?"

I explained about the woman with the stroller.

"I don't know," Kim said, shaking her head. "That sounds like a stretch to me. Maybe they bought the house but haven't closed on it yet. Maybe she just figured what she wanted a bird-feeder for was none of your business and told you that story to shut you up." I made a face.

"Or maybe they're only visiting and she did buy a house on Sycamore Street." Kim crossed her arms over her chest. "In another town."

I frowned. "Just ask him." Everything she'd suggested made sense, but it hadn't made it any less annoying. Maybe more so.

"Fine."

"Tiffany over at the diner also told me how her ex, Robert, was spying on her from across the street."

"The sleaze," spat Kim.

"Agreed," I said. "But what if he wasn't spying on Tiffany?"

"Huh?"

"What if he was breaking into Birds and Bees to meet up with Matt?" I speculated. "And kill him."

Kim snorted. "Why, car deal gone bad?"

I folded my arms and steamed. "Could be."

Kim laughed. "Girl, you are going off the deep end. Matt didn't have a driver's license, remember? He's not allowed to drive."

I remembered. Surrendering his driver's license had been part of Matt's deal with the court after the incident that had resulted in Kim's boyfriend's death. Then again, I had no idea whether or not that order still stood.

"Do you have any motives for all these potential killers you're inventing?"

"Somebody killed Matt Kowalski," I replied firmly. "And I'm getting tired of people around here suspecting you and me!"

"Okay, okay. Calm down, Miss Marple."

I shot daggers at her. Hey, if you can't shoot daggers at your best friend once in a while, what kind of friend would she be?

Kim shot daggers back. See? We're on the same wavelength. "So what do we do now?"

I scrubbed my face with my hands. "We need to dig around. Figure out who wanted Matt dead and who had the opportunity to do it. The sooner the better." I wasn't sure being under suspicion of murder was good for business and said so.

"At least you have an alibi," Kim said.

"The police say there's a several-hours window of time when Matt could have been killed. So I'm not so sure how tight even my alibi is. Can't Randy vouch for you?"

"Sure. Except for the little while I was gone to Birds and Bees."

And we both knew that was plenty of time to commit murder.

"I'm having dinner with Aaron Maddley tomorrow," I explained. "He went to school with Matt too. Maybe he'll have some idea who—" I stopped because Kim had a bug-eyed look on her face. "What? What is it?"

"Aaron Maddley?" Kim gasped. "You're having dinner with Aaron Maddley?"

"Yeah, what's the big deal?" Kim's mouth hung open. "He isn't married, you know." Okay, that was just mean of me.

"But, Amy, Aaron Maddley could be our killer!"

15

"Excuse me?" I wrinkled up my nose at her. "Aaron Maddley? Are you sure we're talking about the same person?" Kim said yes, but I wasn't buying it. "Mild, easygoing, laid-back guy, good-looking in an all-American way?"

Kim nodded with every descriptive I mentioned. But there had to be some mistake. Some misunderstanding. Aaron Maddley wouldn't hurt a fly. Heck, he'd probably build it a cute little red cedar fly house. "Builds birdhouses for fun?"

Kim cocked her head. "I don't know why I didn't think of this earlier."

"Think of what?"

"You do know Matt got Aaron's littler sister pregnant?"

My jaw fell.

Kim scratched the side of her head. "Must have been four or five years ago."

I confessed that I hadn't even known Aaron had a little sister. "What's her name? Where is she now?"

I was sorry about what the louse had done to her, but if what Kim said was true, it would give her a good reason to want to knock him upside the head with a piece of wrought iron. There are those who believe one knock deserves another. I'm not one of them, but I know they're out there. "Could she have killed him after all these years?"

"Her name is Grace. I believe she's working down in Atlanta." Kim cleared the supper dishes and rinsed them in the sink. "At least, that's the last I heard."

"What happened to the baby?"

"Miscarriage," explained Kim. "Aaron's sister is okay, but you can imagine Matt wasn't high on Aaron's list of friends."

"Or Grace's."

"Or Grace's," agreed Kim. She waved a dirty fork in my direction. "But we know Aaron was in town. Grace is in Atlanta."

"Maybe yes, maybe no." I decided I'd mention it to Chief Kennedy and ask him to look into Grace Maddley's whereabouts on the night in question.

"Good idea." She towel-dried the plates and slid them away in an upper cabinet. "I guess I shouldn't have said what I said about Aaron possibly being a murderer."

"Actually . . ."

Kim faced me. "What is it?"

I sighed and leaned against the kitchen counter for support. The granite was cold against my fingers. "Aaron wasn't exactly there—at his farm—when I arrived to pick up the birdhouses."

"Oh?" Kim leaned back too.

I shook my head. "I had an appointment with

him around seven. Not a firm time; I'd mentioned I'd be out that evening. He said he'd be around and to stop by whenever."

"But?"

"But when I got there"—I shook myself, not wanting to believe what I was going to say, what I was thinking—"but Aaron didn't answer the door. I waited a bit, looked around the yard." I paused for a moment, trying to scare up the memories of that evening, not realizing how important those memories might be. "I didn't see him anywhere. The house was dark. I didn't spot him in the yard or fields."

"So then what?"

I shrugged. "About fifteen or twenty minutes later he came out of that big barn of his."

Kim smiled. "Sounds pretty anticlimactic to me. He was in the barn the whole time."

I shook my head no. "We went into the barn to get the birdhouses. His pickup was inside. I remember it was making ticking noises."

"Ticking noises?" Kim's nose wrinkled like a concertina.

"The kind of noises an engine makes when it's cooling down."

"You don't think—"

"There's a rutted dirt track behind the barn that leads out to the main road and there are big sliding doors on each end of the barn." I explained how Matt could have driven in from the opposite side and I'd never have seen or heard him. "The barn's at least a hundred yards from the house. Maybe more."

"So he could have driven into town, offed Matt, and driven back home."

We both let those words sink in. Aaron Maddley had means, motive, and opportunity.

Reluctantly, I added Aaron and Grace Maddley to my list of suspects. Admittedly, our suspect list was meager, but that was a good sign. "The fewer suspects, the more our chance of catching him." A light drizzle was falling outside. I could only imagine what that was doing to my property and hoped that my contractor was on top of things.

"Or her," Kim added. I guess she meant Grace Maddley. I'd definitely be asking the police chief about her.

I left shortly after. Tomorrow was the big day. Our official grand opening. The one we'd advertised in the *Ruby Lake Weekender*. Kim and I had decided to divide and conquer. She'd find out if any houses had sold on Sycamore—I don't know why, but I still had a funny feeling about that couple— and I'd try to figure out if Robert LaChance might have had a reason to want Matt Kowalski dead. The way things were going, I wouldn't be surprised. It was beginning to seem like Matt had harmed a number of people in Ruby Lake at one time or another, either directly or indirectly. But how many of those people might have been upset enough to want him dead?

Divide and conquer. Like a pair of American white pelicans herding an unsuspecting school of bluefish into the shallows for easy hunting.

Maybe we could use the same strategy to catch a killer.

Speaking of fish, I had a bigger fish to fry at the

moment. And her name was Esther Pilaster. I wanted to know why she'd practically thrown me to the wolves, first denying that she'd seen me drive home the night of the murder, but then insisting on practically shouting to anybody who would listen that she'd seen me murder the guy.

At home, I climbed the stairs, tired and angry, sustaining myself with the knowledge that Esther's lease would one day come to an end. As I pounded up each step, I couldn't help thinking how happy I'd be when that day arrived.

The last owner of the house had lived on the top floor like me and had operated a pet shop downstairs. The pet store had failed, or so I'd been told. Maybe the shop's owner had simply grown weary of having Esther the Pester as a neighbor.

Esther had signed her lease with Gertie Hammer and there was no breaking it—at least not without spending a bundle on lawyers. A bundle I didn't have. So what I had was an impossible tenant. I smiled. She'd be out on her keister the day her lease expired. I'd even help her pack.

I knocked on Esther the Pester's door harder than necessary. Okay, I banged. Hard. I'd pay for it later with bruised knuckles, but right now it felt good.

"What do you want?" Esther glared up at me, a butter-yellow housecoat cinched tightly around her waist, fuzzy peach slippers on her feet. Her hair was up in big black curlers. Why hadn't I noticed earlier how much like Edna Turnblad from *Hairspray* the woman looked? Albeit a shorter, older, lumpier version of a dragged-up Harvey Fierstein from the original Broadway production, but still, even that distinctive voice of his was similar to Esther's.

Maybe if I asked her, she'd break out into a chorus of "You Can't Stop the Beat."

"Why didn't you tell the police that you saw me arrive home the night Matt was killed?" I planted my hands on my hips and returned her glare. Two could play that game. "You could have helped my alibi."

"Because I didn't." She pulled her collar tight.

I pulled a face. "Of course you did."

"Did not."

"I saw you."

"Impossible. I was watching the Hallmark Channel. Only came out of my room when I thought I heard someone prowling around." She smiled an evil smile. "And that someone was you." How could that smile suddenly look even more evil? "Holding the murder weapon in your hands, if I remember correctly." She tilted her head back. Taking me in or sizing me up? "And I do."

I took a deep breath. "Ms. Pilaster, it is certainly not impossible. In fact"—I dug my fists deeper into my hip bones to keep from even considering punching the old woman in the nose—"it is entirely possible. Because. I. Saw. You." I had to remove a hand from my hip to point my finger at her nose, but it was worth it.

"Did not." The door started closing in my face.

I stuck my foot out and slipped inside.

"Hey, you can't come in here!"

I sniffed tentatively, then, catching a whiff of what I was certain was nicotine, sniffed once more, taking a deep, long breath through my nostrils—a tactic designed to ferret out the truth. I whirled on her. "Have you been smoking?"

I narrowed my eyes and watched her face for telltale signs—of what, I didn't know. I was sure there were dead giveaways when it came to lying, I just didn't know what they were. If I did, I'd have known that my boyfriend of six years had been cheating on me far sooner than I had. Fool me once, shame on me. Fool me twice . . . well, I'll have an excuse to break your lease.

I wiped the sweat that had formed across my brow. The Pester kept the room warm as a Swedish sauna. Oh well, not my problem. She was responsible for her own electric bill.

I marched to the kitchen in search of an open ashtray. Nothing. A few dirty dishes in the sink and even on the tile floor, for heaven's sake. An ancient dish towel was hanging from the oven handle. An open can of Dinty Moore beef stew sat on the small kitchen table next to a bag of baby carrots. I must have interrupted the woman's dinner.

I walked quickly to the living room before she could bury the evidence of smoking that I knew I'd find. Smoking is definitely not allowed in the house. Especially by septuagenarians who might fall asleep watching *Wheel* with a lit Pall Mall wedged between their lips.

Nothing. An empty saucer and matching cup, down to the matching chips on their lips, rested on the coffee table. I felt a tickle in the nose and rubbed my nostrils with the back of my fingers. "*Achoo!*" I looked accusingly at Esther, who was standing near the window, her hand on the ledge.

"Looks like more rain," she said idly.

"Do you have—*achoo!*"

"Gesundheit."

"Thank you," I replied. What can I say? Convention forced me. "Do you have a-a—" I sneezed three times in quick succession. Loud and hard. Esther thrust a lotioned tissue at me. I wiped my nose. "Are you keeping a cat in this apartment?" I narrowed my eyes at her.

"'Course not." Esther pulled at the sleeves of her robe. "It's against the rules."

I chewed my lip. "Yes. It is." I tapped my foot on the worn carpet as she matched my stare. I headed for her bedroom.

"Hey, you can't go in there!"

"Watch me!" I pushed open the bedroom door and stepped inside. It smelled like old lady. Probably douses herself in Chanel 1 Million BC. The bed was unmade and the mattress sagged. The grip end of a baseball bat was sticking out from under the bed. I saw it, but I didn't want to know what it was doing there. Maybe she played third base for the Dodgers during the season.

The dresser was shoved beneath the front window, its matching mirror leaning on the floor in the corner. "How many windows do you have in front?"

"One." She looked puzzled. Big deal. So was I.

I pressed my face against the window and looked toward the street. The glass was cold against my forehead. I left the bedroom and stared at a wall in the living space where I thought there'd be another window, or maybe part of a bigger room. Rats. Esther couldn't have seen me the other night. Her bedroom window was in the corner of the house. I'd seen her, or who I mistakenly thought was her, at the next window, toward the middle.

But that window belonged to the empty apartment next door. I wasn't about to admit any of this to Esther the Pester. I'd never hear the end of it.

I sneezed once more and headed for the front door. I waved off Esther the Pester's offer of a fresh tissue. At the threshold, I waved my finger at her. "No pets and no smoking!"

"Next time get a warrant!" I heard Esther yell as she slammed her door shut behind me, turned the key in the lock, and pulled the chain.

Out in the dim hallway, I stared at Esther's door for a moment, then walked down the hall to the apartment next door. Maybe Esther had seen me. Maybe she'd been in the unoccupied unit and hadn't wanted to admit that she'd been somewhere she didn't belong.

I jiggled the handle. Locked. But that didn't mean anything. Except that it wasn't likely that Esther could have gotten inside. Maybe I'd imagined the whole thing and had only thought I'd seen someone. If I told Kim about this, she'd probably say I'd seen a ghost, a specter of some long-ago resident of the house who wandered room to room in search of peace.

I shivered. Probably from the temperature difference my body had experienced going from Esther's steam bath of an apartment to the relatively cool hallway. It had absolutely nothing to do with spirits.

The apartment next to Esther's was empty, and I'd been considering renting it out for some extra income. Maybe now the time had come. Better to have tenants than an empty, spook-inhabited space. Then again, I didn't need another Esther. Maybe I could find a nice elderly nun or a solitary monk who'd taken a vow of silence and enjoyed making fruitcakes in his spare time. I like fruitcake.

The key was upstairs in my apartment in a drawer somewhere. Tomorrow I'd open the apartment up and have a look around.

During the daylight.

16

Saturday went off without a hitch. Sort of.

Lance Jennings, the reporter with the *Ruby Lake Weekender*, had shown up. I wasn't surprised to see him. It was his job to cover such things around town as store openings, but I hadn't expected him to get in my face about the murder.

"Listen," I said as he pigeonholed me in the corner near the coffeepot, "I've spent the week avoiding talking to the press about Matt Kowalski's murder, so I'm not about to talk to you about it now."

"Don't be like that, Ms. Simms," wheedled the big man in the cheap black suit and white T-shirt. Lance is about forty years old and about forty pounds overweight. His wavy brown hair sweeps back over his round head. His hairline, like his welcome here at Birds & Bees, was receding. "People want to know this stuff."

I leveled a finger at his thick nose. "I paid to advertise to your readers about the store being open.

If they want to hear about our products and specials, I'll be glad to talk to you. If you want to talk"—I dropped my voice—"murder, you'll have to do your talking someplace else."

Lance pouted and tapped his right foot. He reached for the camera he always seemed to have draped around his neck. "How about a picture of you?"

"That would be fine."

"Great." He looked around the showroom. "How's about we take one over near where you found Matt's body?"

I stomped away. There was no point trying to force the man to leave. He outweighed me by a ton. Besides, I needed to stay in the good graces of the press. I needed all the positive comments I could get. And his father owned the paper. "Do me a favor," I said, sidling up to Kim.

"Sure, anything."

"Go make nice with Lance Jennings." Lance. I'd like to pop him like a bad boil.

Kim pulled a face. "Oh, come on. Anything but that, Amy. Why?"

"Because I might have been a little rough on the guy and we need all the goodwill we can get."

"Forget it."

I folded my arms. "You owe me."

"For what?" Kim huffed.

"Please, let's not even begin to go down that road."

Kim stuck her tongue out, then headed for Lance, who was busy taking shots of the children sitting around low tables near the front, scribbling in bird-themed coloring books. I'd picked up the slender

books and a couple packs of crayons at one of
those under-a-buck stores.

A boy nudged me with his elbow. I looked down.
He was holding a plastic bag. That plastic bag was
filled with water. A two-inch goldfish hung sus-
pended in the middle of the water. "Can I help
you?"

"I think he's sick." The boy extended his arm
and the bag toward me.

I bit my cheek. "How can you tell?"

"He's not moving as much as he used to." The
boy had a crewcut and wore heavy flannel-lined
jeans, a Carolina Panthers sweatshirt, and a brown
parka.

I sighed. "I'm sorry."

"I bought him here. Can't you fix him?" His
dark eyes beseeched me.

I rubbed the back of my neck. "But this is a store
for wild bird supplies, not fish." I sighed. No reply.
"I suppose you bought your fish here when this
was a pet store?"

He nodded. "Mr. Allen sold him to me."

"Follow me," I said. I led him to the kiosk where
I'd had a computer set up to assist customers with
birding questions. I googled around for a bit.
"How's your water?"

"Change it once a week."

I nodded and searched some more. "Here's
something." I tapped the screen. "It says here that
goldfish like variety in their food. What are you
feeding this little guy?"

The boy shrugged. "Flake food. Still got the big
container that came with him."

I picked the plastic bag up off the counter and

returned it to the boy. The fish seemed oblivious. "You should try another food. Maybe that will help."

A woman who'd been looking over my shoulder poked her finger at the fish. "The hardware store sells fish food."

"They do?"

"They've got everything," she gushed. "It's practically a general store." The boy disappeared, but she kept talking. "Frankly, I'm surprised to see that you're open."

I tried not to let my displeasure at where she was leading show. She was a potential customer, after all. "You mean because of the murder."

"Murder?" Her eyes lit up like they were on fire. "No, I meant because of that big blue thing dangling from your roof."

"Big blue—"

She nodded vigorously. "I thought maybe a tornado or something had damaged the building or that the whole shebang was going to be torn down."

"Excuse me." I pressed past her and headed for the door. Outside, I looked up. Yikes!

"What is that thing?"

I turned. Kim had joined me. We both stared up at the roof. "Why didn't you tell me that thing was up there?"

"I didn't know it was. I came in the back way, remember?" She craned her neck. "I didn't notice it from back there." She scrunched up her face. "Though it seems pretty hard to miss."

I nodded slowly. A ginormous blue tarp had been draped over the pitched roof, looking like a giant blue Morpho butterfly had veered horribly

off course from Latin America, ended up in North
Carolina, and landed on my roof.

And died.

I was heading back up the walkway to the door
when the boom went off. My shoulders jerked re-
flexively and I ducked. A very large and very mad-
looking peregrine falcon zoomed out the open
door and took to the sky. Its long, sharp, blue-black
wings flashed against the billowy white clouds overhead.

His keeper, a nice young man named Roland
Ibarra, came zooming after him and he didn't
look happy.

I found Cash, my contractor, standing in the
middle of the store, looking lost and apologetic.
"Sorry about the noise, folks." His hands were hidden in his pants pockets. "Just doing a little repair
work on the roof." He grinned. It wasn't helping.

"That bird pulled my hair!" shouted a young
woman, clutching her frizzy red scalp.

"He scared off Roscoe!" shouted a heavyset
woman in an olive shirt and slacks, who must have
been Roland's assistant. He ran the Raptor Rescue
Ranch near Morganton and had offered to come
in and give a demonstration today.

That might not be happening now. "I'm sure
everything will be just fine," I assured her. While
Mom ran to assist the distraught redhead who'd
had her hair rearranged by the equally distraught
falcon, I turned to Cash Calderon and whispered,
"What the devil was that racket?"

He jerked a thumb over his shoulder. "The men
were unloading some supplies for the job. I didn't
mean to cause a commotion." He pulled off his

cap and scratched his head. "I didn't realize you had such a to-do going on today."

"Don't worry about it." I patted his arm. "I'm sure everything will be fine." I figured if I kept repeating it, it would have to become true. "Why don't you and your men get all that stuff down to the basement or up to the roof or wherever it is that it all has to go?" I pointed to the stack of lumber, nails, sheetrock, and myriad other building materials that had piled up on my sales floor.

Roland threw open the front door. The lovebirds cooed madly. I covered my ears. I was tired of them already. "Quick, honey!" He pointed to a knapsack. "Grab Roscoe's food and my handling gloves!"

"Your bird attacked me!" cried the redhead. Mom had her hands full.

The woman in olive green ripped open the pack and withdrew a pair of thick, arm-length black leather gloves. Honey? I guess she wasn't only Roland's assistant. She tossed him the gloves and they both hurried out of doors. Half my customers went with them.

I couldn't blame them. That appeared to be where the big show was.

I grabbed the contractor as he headed downstairs carrying some supplies. "How long is that thing going to be on my roof?"

"The tarp?" I nodded. "Two-three days, tops. Gotta have the tarp to keep the rain out while we fix the roof. Sorry."

"Don't be," I answered with a sigh. After all, I was sorry enough for the two of us.

* * *

"Maybe you should beg off?" Kim suggested later as we closed up shop.

It had been a long, long day. We were both dead on our feet. No pun intended and apologies to Matt Kowalski. Mom had come in to help for a few hours, then retired early. She was going to be spending the next few nights at Aunt Betty's house. We both thought it best what with all the construction going on around the place. Mom thought I should stay with Aunt Betty too, but I knew there really wasn't room at my aunt's house for the both of us. Besides, I felt better sticking around. Keeping an eye on the store.

Kim and I had locked up, straightened and restocked the shelves, and sunk to the floor. We were leaning shoulder to shoulder against the front counter and peering out the windows. "No," I said in response to Kim's suggestion that I blow off my dinner with Aaron Maddley. It was a nice thought. Head upstairs, take a long bath, have a quick light meal, then sink into a year or two of oblivion. Okay, eight hours minimum. But I couldn't do it. Dinner with Aaron, murder suspect and birdhouse crafter extraordinaire, awaited.

I pushed myself up from the floor. "I can quiz him about his sister."

The Lake House was crowded, but we had a reservation. Red velvet draperies hugged the windows designed to take advantage of the lake view. There were tables outdoors as well, but in this weather they'd been kept closed to dinner service.

Even in the winter, barring rain, like we were experiencing now, diners could enjoy eating out on
the deck if they so chose. Large propane-fueled
heaters kept the area cozy despite the cold.

Most everyone dressed up at least a bit for dinner
at the Lake House. I did too. I'd opted for a form-
fitting black dress and black heels, with a string of
pearls. Nothing too showy, nothing too suggestive. I
didn't want anybody, especially Aaron, getting the
wrong idea.

A massive stone fireplace to the left blazed
brightly. We handed our coats to the check girl. I
noticed heads turn as the elegantly dressed host
led us to our table near the water. I didn't know if
they were looking at me because I was a murder
suspect or because I was on a date, but I'd decided
I wasn't going to let it get to me either way.

Aaron asked what kind of wine I liked and we settled on a domestic red from one of North Carolina's
many wineries, this one located in the Yadkin Valley.
Not everybody is aware that North Carolina is home
to over a hundred wineries and was at one time the
country's leading wine-producing region.

My stomach was nervous, so I settled on a lightly
seasoned baked fillet of sole and steamed vegetables. Aaron was stabbing at his steak when I decided to skirt my way around to the questions I
had roiling inside me. "So," I said, swirling the
wine in my glass, "terrible about Matt's murder,
isn't it?"

Aaron jerked his head back. "I'm surprised
you'd even want to talk about that."

"Why?"

"I don't know." He picked up his glass. "It did

happen in your house. We are in a nice restaurant. Having a nice meal."

"I know," I said quickly, pasting on a smile. "But that's just it. It did happen in my store, in my house. I'm curious to know what Matt was doing there and why it got him killed."

Aaron seemed to think this over. "I guess I get it."

"So, do you have any idea who might have wanted to murder him?"

He looked taken aback and grabbed for his napkin. "Me? None at all." He balled up his napkin and wiped the side of his face. An awkward silence fell over us, then he said, "I'm sorry. Do you mind if we talk about something else?"

"Sure." I sipped slowly, my mind trying to find a way to steer the conversation back toward Matt's murder without giving myself away. Then it hit me. I smiled. "Do you have any sisters or brothers, Aaron?"

He looked up from his plate. "A sister." He reached for a dinner roll and extended the basket. I declined.

"Oh," I replied. "Does she live around here? Maybe I know her. What's her name?"

Aaron tugged at the skinny black tie knotted at his collar. "I don't think so. Grace hasn't been back to Ruby Lake for years. She lives in Savannah." He chewed slowly. I watched the muscles of his mandible working back and forth. "About the birdhouses, I was thinking maybe of doing some for cardinals next. You know, some platform nest boxes. I read that cardinals prefer those to the enclosed kind."

I nodded absently. At the moment, I cared nothing about birdhouses, even if they were ostensibly why we were meeting for dinner. Savannah. Hadn't Kim said Atlanta? Not that that meant anything, except that Kim had been wrong. It wouldn't be the first time. "I'm surprised she doesn't come home to visit more often. Savannah's not that far." Not so far that a woman couldn't drive up, commit a murder, and be back home again—four hours at most each way, I reckoned.

Aaron looked at me in silence for a moment. Fluttering shadows from the candle on our table played across his clean-shaven cheeks. I wondered if I was looking into the eyes of a murderer. Finally, he shrugged. "Not everybody misses this town."

I nodded politely and pushed my carrots around on my plate.

"What about you, Amy? Any brothers or sisters?"

"Nope. Just me. Mom says I'm all any mother needs." I leaned against the back of my chair. "I'm not quite sure how she means that though."

Aaron smiled. "I'm sure it's meant as a compliment. I'd say you're all any man needs, too. I mean—" He blushed.

We both finished the wine. He signaled the waiter for a second bottle, but I begged off. "It's been a long day," I said. "If I drink any more, I just might lay my head down on the table and take a nap."

"Coffee?"

I agreed to the coffee and he ordered two. Not because I wanted some but because I wanted to keep him talking.

"So about those nest boxes—what do you think?

Is it something you could see carrying in your store?"

"Sure," I said, with a toss of the hand. "Let's start with half a dozen whenever you're ready and we'll see how they do." He agreed. I planted my elbows on the tabletop and rested my chin in my hands. "Are you and your sister close?"

He looked at me sharply. "I suppose so. Why do you ask?"

"Oh, no reason." I shoved a lock of hair behind my ear. "I guess it's just that not having any siblings makes me curious about the relationship between brothers and sisters." My finger played along the stem of my glass. "I suppose you'd do anything for her?"

Aaron nodded. He took a deep breath and his eyes scoured the dining room. "Hey, isn't that your lawyer?"

"What?"

He pointed across the table. "Over there. With that woman and little girl."

He lowered his arm and I swiveled my head. Derek Harlan occupied a table with what had to be his wife and daughter. The woman was a knockout brunette with full red lips and the whitest teeth I had ever seen. Diamond studs decorated her earlobes.

The woman said something that set Derek to laughing, and the little girl, probably seven or eight years old, was beaming too. So, the happily married man was out for a family meal. Good for him. "The jerk."

"What?"

"Oh, sorry." My hand flew to my mouth. "Did I say that out loud?"

Aaron chuckled as the waiter set down our coffees and offered us a small pitcher of cream and a bowl of sugar. "I'm afraid so. I take it Mr. Harlan's not your favorite guy."

"Not by a long shot." I added a spoonful of sugar and stirred thoughtfully. Aaron hadn't been much help at all. "How's the farm?"

He shrugged his strong shoulders. I had no trouble imagining he had the strength to kill. "So-so. It seems like there's always too much to do and too little time to do it all."

I nodded to show I understood. "I guess that's why you weren't around when I first showed up at your house the other evening."

"Pardon?"

"You know, when I first arrived at the farm to get the birdhouses," I explained. "I couldn't find you anywhere. And then, boom, suddenly there you were."

He smiled and sipped his coffee. Black and unsweetened. "I don't remember. I must have been out in the field."

"Of course." Except that he hadn't been. At least, I didn't think he had. I needed to get a look in that big barn of his. Aaron Maddley could have driven into town, murdered Matt Kowalski, and made it home within the time in question. Maybe he'd been cleaning up inside the barn, washing away blood or some other evidence of the crime. I couldn't come out and ask him and there was no way to know without taking a look in that barn myself.

"Something wrong?"

I shook my head and settled my half-empty cup down on my saucer. "No, I just saw somebody else"—actually a couple of somebodies—"that I know. Sort of."

Aaron twisted his neck. "Who?"

I pointed with my butter knife. "The mayor, Mac MacDonald, and Robert LaChance."

Aaron started to get up. "Do you want to go over and say hi?"

I said no. What I really wanted was to be a crumb on that table so I could hear whatever it was the two men seemed so engrossed in discussion about. Both had been seen in the vicinity of Birds & Bees the night Matt died. Coincidence?

17

I froze. There it was again. That banging. I lay still, taking quiet, shallow breaths. I listened to the wind howling outside. I could hear the rain pelting the roof too. A doozy of a storm was raging outside. Did that explain the noises that had wakened me?

I never should have had that coffee. Caffeine does things to me at night. It doesn't just simply keep me buzzing, it keeps me thinking. And that's not always a good thing. Letting your imagination run away with itself sometimes leads to consequences. Unthinkable consequences.

No, there they were again. These noises didn't sound like the storm. They sounded different somehow. Too regular maybe. I silently pushed back the covers and sat up. I was alone in the apartment. I was beginning to regret that Mom was staying with Aunt Betty. As I listened to the clatter above me, I was regretting my decision to stay behind all the more.

Isn't it always that fool woman who stays behind that gets killed by the ax murderer in all those movies? I felt around the floor using my toes and found my slippers. I slipped on my terry cloth robe.

I could still feel the spot on my left cheek where Aaron had gently kissed me as he dropped me off at my door. I didn't know what to think of that. I needed to keep my distance. The man could be a cold-blooded killer.

Then again, his lips had been surprisingly soft . . .

A gust of wind rocked the windows and I almost jumped back under the covers. I'd have jumped out of my skin if it hadn't been factory sealed. Maybe it's only some poor animals who've come into the attic to get out of the cold and the wet, I told myself.

As much as I hated the idea, I had to leave the safety of my apartment to check the attic. I opened the small storage closet in the third-floor hallway. To reach the attic, the home's original designer had built a steep, narrow staircase into the side of the closet. I put a tentative hand on the handle and was surprised how easily the tiny door opened. The opening was so narrow, I had to turn sideways to squeeze through. Narrow steps led to the top. The low-ceilinged space felt tight, claustrophobic. It smelled damp, and I tasted dust on my tongue. Tenebrific shadows danced on the walls as two brilliant flashes of lightning appeared in the small roof window about six paces to my right. A moment later, the muffled boom of thunder rattled the loose floorboards.

My breath caught in my throat. I wished I'd

brought a flashlight. I wished even more that I'd brought that baseball bat I'd seen under Esther the Pester's bed. All I owned was a lightweight, tapered French rolling pin. Perfect for rolling pastry dough. Not so perfect, I suspected, for fending off murderous maniacs or, possibly, vengeful ghosts.

As my eyes adjusted to the darkness, I noticed a glow of light that seemed to be coming from behind a pair of crossbeams. An untidy pile of boxes leaned up against the thick beams, preventing my seeing further. I crept toward the light, like a moth to the flame—hopefully, not like a lemming to its death . . .

I held the rolling pin out at arm's length. A floorboard squeaked underfoot and I froze. My heart thudded against my chest. The wind kicked up outside, like I'd angered some crazy elemental god, and the rain came down even harder. The basement was probably a swimming pool by now.

I crept up to the ceiling joists, bending low to avoid a strut. I thought I could discern some sort of scraping sound, but couldn't be certain. My mind could easily be playing tricks on me. Being scared half to death could do that to a person.

I lifted one slippered foot, then the other. I turned the corner. A man's hulking figure lurched toward me. He had some sort of clawlike weapon in his right hand. I stepped back and screamed.

I also dropped the rolling pin. In the process, I had learned something about myself. I'm useless at self-defense. But I was still pretty good at running. I turned and I ran.

I didn't get far. My assailant's hand reached out and caught the back of my robe by its hood and I felt it slip away. Unfortunately, my arms were stuck inside and I was trapped. Done in by my own robe. I whirled and prepared to strike.

"Ms. Simms?" I felt the arm release me.

I shouted. Unfortunately, there was no one to hear besides the two of us. Except Esther Pilaster, and I couldn't imagine her doing me any good. Besides, she was back down on the second floor. I rather doubted she'd hear my death cries way up here.

"Are you okay?" The big hulking figure bent low and turned the beam of light coming from the lantern on the floor toward me.

I gaped. "Mr. Calderon?" I sobbed. "What are you doing here?"

He must have seen my eyes go to that big claw hammer gripped tightly in his right hand. I also noticed he was dripping wet. His dark blue eyes narrowed. "I was worried about the roof. What with this big storm we're having." Thunder rumbled in the distance, as if designed to bring home his point.

I felt every inch of my skin bristling. Was this Matt's killer I was facing? Cash is a big, brawny guy. A guy who could as easily swing a birdfeeder hook as he could a hammer.

"I thought I'd check on the tarp." He used the hammer as a pointer. "A couple of the rope tie-downs came loose." He stuffed the hammer in his belt. "But don't worry, I nailed them back down."

I looked about the low space. Shadows hid most everything. I'd never been up here before and didn't care if I was ever up here again. "How did you get up here?"

"Your mom gave me the key, remember?"

I nodded slowly. I guess that was true. I really couldn't remember. I kept at arm's length from the contractor. I wasn't sure if I was buying his story or not. Better safe than sorry.

"Well—" He took a step toward me. I gasped and matched him step for step, but in the opposite direction. "Guess I'd better be going now." He picked up his lantern. "Hope I didn't disturb you any—"

"Wait!"

His brow crinkled and drips of rainwater ran down the sleeves of his jacket. "What is it?"

I pointed. "What is all that?"

Cash Calderon slowly turned the beam of his light in the direction I was pointing. "Oh yeah. That." He rubbed his forehead with his cap's visor. Even in the dim light, I discerned a smile. "I'd been meaning to mention that." He stepped toward the corner and toed the sleeping bag with his boot. "Looks like somebody'd been spending some time here."

I nodded, slack-jawed. A rumpled red sleeping bag lay in the corner. There were a couple of empty takeout containers, a half-consumed bottle of water, a bottle of Kentucky bourbon that had also been nearly depleted, and wads of stained paper napkins. And that's just the highlights. The corner was a veritable nest. But who or what had been nesting there?

In my house. Right above me. I shivered at the thought. "I-I don't understand."

"One of my workers discovered this the first day on the job. Like I said, I've been meaning to tell you about it." He zipped his jacket. "In case you weren't aware."

I shook my head in the negative. "I had been hearing noises. I thought it was squirrels. Or something." I waved my hand in the air. "An animal."

He looked surprised. "Not an animal at all. A human." He picked up the red sleeping bag. "Whoever was here probably cleared out when you moved in."

Somebody had been living in my attic? That was both extraordinary and scary. Who was he? When was he here? How long had he been here? Was he actually living here or merely a nocturnal visitor? I repeated Cash's words in my head. Cleared out . . . or been murdered? My mind spun in circles, then came to an abrupt stop. Matt! It had to be Matt! It could only be Matt.

But what did that mean? Matt had been living in my attic and had been found dead on the second floor. What had he been up to, and why had it resulted in his being murdered?

If he had been secretly living in my house, I'd be the one who wanted him out. Why would somebody else kill him?

18

"Maybe he was hiding from someone," suggested Kim. We sat in the apartment, batting around hypotheses and scenarios to explain what Matt might have been doing in my attic.

"If it was Matt," I reminded her.

"Oh, it was Matt Kowalski, all right." Jerry Kennedy marched through the door and dropped his hat on an empty chair. He hitched a thumb over the top of his belt. "Got any coffee?" I'd waited until morning to call the police station and report what Cash Calderon had discovered in my attic. So you'd think Jerry would have had breakfast and his fill of coffee by now.

"How do you know for sure it was Matt?" I ignored his plea for coffee.

"Dusted for prints. His are all over the place." The chief did a turn around my tight galley kitchen. "Now, how's about that coffee?"

"How's about telling me what you found out

about Grace Maddley?" I snatched up the coffeepot and held it out at arm's length.

"Not much to tell." He sniffed. "I telephoned the Savannah PD, like you asked. They told me they'd interview the girl." He helped himself to a mug from the mug tree beside the gas stove and nudged it toward me.

I grudgingly poured. I looked him in the eye. "Please let me know when you hear back from them."

"Fine." He blew on his coffee and took a sip. "This is good brew. But I don't expect anything to come of your lead on Grace Maddley."

I frowned and shoved the carafe back into the belly of the coffeemaker. "Why not?"

"After all this time?" Jerry raised his eyebrows. It wasn't a pleasant look. "If she was going to kill the punk because of what he put her through, why didn't she do it years ago?"

I agreed. But I wasn't going to tell him that. "That still leaves her brother, Aaron."

He nodded and helped himself to the open bag of pecan sandies I'd purloined from Kim's house. "That it does," he agreed, mouth full of cookie, shortbread crumbs spilling down his uniform.

"And there were no other fingerprints?" I asked hopefully.

"Nope." Jerry wiped his mouth with the back of his hand. "None that mattered anyhow. Yours and Matt's, of course. And some smudged prints that could have belonged to Ronald Reagan or even Santa Claus for all we could tell." The chief set his mug down on the little table beside the door where

I drop my keys and purse and screwed his cap back on. "Ladies." He nodded and left the apartment, pulling the door shut behind himself.

"Now that he's gone," Kim said eagerly as she curled her legs up under her butt, "tell me how your date with Aaron went."

"Not much to tell." I flopped down on the sofa beside her. "We ate. We chatted. I saw Robert LaChance and your buddy the mayor confabbing at another table." I refrained from mentioning Derek Harlan and family.

"Come on, Amy. Spill." She grabbed my shoulders from behind and squeezed. "I want details. Juicy details."

I pushed her hands away. "There are no details. Every time I tried to ask him about his sister, he changed the subject."

Kim rubbed her chin between thumb and forefinger. "Hmmm."

"Hmmm is right. He was downright evasive."

"Evasive, or you're just a lousy Mata Hari?" teased Kim, referencing the famed WWI spy.

I decided to evade the question. "I'm keeping Aaron's name near the top of my suspect list," I said, folding my arms over my chest. "If only I could get in that barn of his . . ."

"Why?"

I explained how I thought there just might be some evidence out there.

Kim wrinkled her nose. "Evidence? What sort of evidence could there be? The police have the murder weapon."

I shrugged. "Who knows? Bloody clothes. Something that belonged to Matt."

"I suppose . . ."

"Whether it will tie him to the murder or exonerate him, I don't know. But I'd sure like a look around."

Kim paced back and forth. "You know . . ."

"Yes?"

"Well, Aaron's a farmer, right? Grows vegetables?"

"So?"

"So don't all the farmers around here attend the weekly farmers' market Monday mornings?"

I leaped at Kim and hugged her tight. "Kim, you're a genius!"

I yawned. It was a desultory Sunday afternoon and I was alone in the store. Patchy clouds scudded across the mountains and the lake was devoid of recreationists. There was a decided lull in customers and I sat on a stool behind the counter thumbing through a copy of *Bird Watchers Monthly* when the lovebirds announced a customer. At least I thought it was a customer. Seeing who it was, I'd have been happier to see a tax collector.

"Mrs. Hammer," I exclaimed, none too happy and plenty surprised to see Gertie Hammer marching toward me. "What brings you here?" Surely she didn't want to buy a birdfeeder? She'd be more likely to buy a shotgun and blast the little birdies to smithereens if they came anywhere near her.

She braced her thick knuckles against the countertop. Her brilliant blue eyes sparked at me. Her gray-black hair was buried beneath a brown knit cap with white trim. What had started as a widow's peak had become an entire range. "I heard you've been having some troubles." She tugged down the zipper of her puffy lime-green down jacket, then peeled off her gloves and thrust them in the pockets.

I slowly closed my magazine and pushed it aside. "You could say that." I thought of the million problems with the house and the thousands of dollars those problems were going to cost me and my pitiful bank account. And while I'd have loved to blame Gertie for all those problems, I'd been the one foolish enough to buy the place in my haste to get started, without getting a proper inspection done.

Gertie nodded and reached into her black leather purse. The thing was giant. Big enough to hold a bowling ball. And a pair of size ten shoes. "And I don't mean the murder," she quipped. She waved her arms in circles. "It's all the other stuff."

I eyed her warily. What was the old battle-ax up to? It couldn't be anything good. It was never anything good.

She went on. "Roof leaks, critters invading the attic—"

"Well, it wasn't exactly—" I was about to explain how it appeared I'd actually had a human infestation rather than an animal one, but she cut me off.

"Foundation troubles."

I frowned. I suppose she'd been talking to my contractor. Oh well, my woes weren't exactly privileged contractor-contractee information.

"Of course, there's this too." She pulled a rumpled *Ruby Lake Weekender* from her inside coat pocket. She thwacked the front page.

I read the headline: "Falcon Attacks Shoppers at Birds & Things Grand Opening."

Great, Lance hadn't even gotten the name of the store right. I read on. He'd had no problem making a big deal out of Roland's falcon taking a little nip out of one of my customers' hair though. Talk about making a mountain out of a molehill. I had a good mind not to advertise with the paper again.

Besides, Roland and his assistant-slash-girlfriend had coaxed Roscoe back down from that big pin oak. Eventually.

I handed back the paper. "Was there something you wanted, Gertie?" Besides to get my goat.

She beamed a mouthful of crooked teeth. "Like I said, I feel bad for you. Real bad."

Okay, now I was really getting suspicious. And nervous. "I'm afraid I don't understand. So you came here to . . ." I hesitated, trying to come up with the right words. But with *Gertrude Hammer* and *nice* there were no words that joined the two things together. "Pay your condolences? Offer some"—dare I say it—"advice?" There, I'd said it.

Gertie harrumphed and her head wobbled side to side. "No, don't you get it?"

I shook my head no and watched in fascination as she reached into her bowling-bag purse and extracted a green vinyl checkbook. She tore out a pre-written check and handed it over.

"This ought to cover it."

My eyes went from the strange woman standing before me to the strange check with all the zeroes on it stuck between my fingers. "I don't understand," I said after a moment. And I didn't. The amount written out was all I had paid for her property and then some.

Gertie cocked her head. "I'm agreeing to buy the old place back from you. Lock, stock, and barrel."

I laid the check slowly down on the counter.

"Problems and all."

"But why?"

The little old lady shrugged her shoulders. "Like I said, I feel sorry for you. I feel sort of like I took advantage of you."

Alarms went off in my head. Gertrude Hammer never felt sorry for anybody. And the Gertrude Hammer I knew lived to take advantage of other people. In particular, unsuspecting people. If there was a sucker born every minute, then Gertrude Hammer was the suckee.

So why on earth would she now be offering to so generously buy back this money pit that I'd discovered I'd paid way too much for?

"I'm sorry," I replied. "But I'm afraid I couldn't."

Her eyes flashed with malice for only an instant and then a phony smile took over her face. It was like watching an alien clone body-snatcher in action. "Nonsense." She pushed the check toward me. "Of course you can. Don't be shy. Don't worry about how you're taking advantage of a poor old woman. Please"—she slid the heavily zeroed check ever closer—"humor an old woman. I won't rest easy if you don't let me make amends."

Amends? Was that it? Was Gertie dying? Was this her attempt to get past Heaven's gates? "Is everything okay, Mrs. Hammer?"

"Sure, fine."

"Are you—" How could I put this delicately? "Feeling well?"

She pushed out her chest. "Fit as a fiddle. Look, are you going to sell me back the house or aren't you?"

I shook my head. "I'm afraid I couldn't. I appreciate the offer, though. Really, I do."

"So take the check already. We can close tomorrow and you can cut your losses."

I sighed. "Sorry. Birds and Bees has only started. I really want to make a go of it." Having this store had been a dream of mine. I couldn't let it go so quickly.

Gertie pulled a face. "Suit yourself." She pointed a gnarled finger at my nose. "But mark my words, you'll fail just like all the other businesses. Why, the last business, that pet store, didn't last six months!"

I nodded. I'd heard all about that. "I really have high hopes."

"Hopes!" Gertie snorted. "You can't live on hopes, Simms. It takes money. And if you don't sell, this place is going to take all you've got. And more. Just ask that fool Theo Allen and all the others before him who thought they had what it took. Allen thought he had the moxie to run a pet store! The man was a retired truck driver, for heaven's sake. Didn't know the first thing about pets. I wouldn't trust him to feed my dog for a day!" She shook her head in evident disgust. "Six months!" She waggled her fingers. "Six months!"

"Did you know somebody was living in the attic, Mrs. Hammer?"

"Huh? Attic? What attic?" Gertie looked taken aback. She planted her hands on her hips and glared. "What are you going on about, Simms?"

I explained how we'd discovered evidence that someone had been living upstairs in the house's attic.

"All the more reason," Gertie said with a shake of the head, "to sell this place and get out while you can!" Gertie zipped up her jacket with a quick, sharp motion.

I promised I'd give her offer some thought. But the only thought I was going to give it was to wonder what in the world the devious old woman was up to . . .

19

I flew to the front window like an eastern wood pewee being chased by a mockingbird and pressed my nose to the glass. Gertie was hobbling down the sidewalk in front of Birds & Bees and quickly disappeared around the corner. The old woman could move.

I could move too. I raced back to the counter, snatched the bag of trash from the can and headed for the back door. The bag was only half full and I normally hated to be so wasteful, but this was an emergency. I gripped the doorknob with my free hand and slowly pushed it open. It squeaked miserably like a baby bird waiting for food. I promised the hinges some oil if they'd just shut up.

Sliding sideways out the door to keep from having to open it wide, I peered left and right. The Dumpster was ahead and to the left. I spotted Gertie Hammer at the edge of the back parking lot, standing under an elm that butted up to and buckled the sidewalk in that spot.

She was talking to some man in a tan suit, overcoat, and galoshes. And I recognized him. What
the devil was Gertie Hammer doing standing on
my sidewalk talking to Robert LaChance?

Had they simply run into each other?

The pair hadn't seen me, so I remained frozen
where I stood. Holding the big, near-empty black
trash bag in front of me like it was going to hide
me. Stupid, I know. What could Robert LaChance,
Tiffany's ex, and Gertie be talking about? Was she
in the market for a new car?

Hard to imagine. For as long as I could remember, Gertie had been driving a big old Oldsmobile
Delta 88. It had started life beige but was slowly
turning to rust. Then again, weren't we all?

The car dealer grabbed Gertie's arm. He seemed
to be pleading with her. To do what?

Robert's head swiveled my way and Gertie looked
too. I smiled and waved and sauntered over to the
Dumpster. I tossed the bag over the side and casually looked over my shoulder as I returned to the
back door.

They were both gone.

I stared up at the roof. The blue tarp seemed to
have held up, but I noticed the metal stairs attached to the back of the house appeared to have
a couple of loose supports. That could be danger-
ous. I'd have to remember to ask Cash Calderon to
take a look at that before somebody got hurt. I
considered asking Cash to pull them down, but if I
did want to rent out the other unit, I'd want the
renters to use those stairs, thus avoiding the store
completely.

Realizing I'd left the store unattended, I hurried back inside only to discover Mac MacDonald coming down from the second floor. He hesitated as he spotted me, then ambled down to ground level. "Ms. Simms." He extended a hand. "I'm Mayor MacDonald. My friends call me Mac."

"I know who you are." I forced myself to smile. What was the man doing upstairs where he didn't belong? "Can I help you with something, Mayor?" I looked pointedly up the stairs. "Come to see the scene of the crime?"

He flashed unnaturally white teeth and I noticed a slight pink color to his cheeks. "Mac." His hand was cool to the touch. He filled out a black wool suit, matching knee-length coat, and a homburg. The man was all of forty but dressed like he was eighty. "Actually, I was looking for you."

He turned and headed toward the front. I followed. A sweet odor followed him too, like apple pie and citrus. It must have been the cologne he was wearing. Either that or he was a messy eater. "I wanted to welcome you to the business community." He fiddled with a birdfeeder pole. "And wish you luck." Did he realize it was a pole similar to the murder weapon? "How's everything going?"

"Pretty good," I replied. "Considering."

The mayor nodded. "The murder. Yes, that was a terrible thing." He shook his head. "Just terrible. Not good for the town. Tourism suffers." He ran his tongue over his upper lip. "Not good for business."

Mayor Mac MacDonald slid the birdfeeder pole back into its slot. "I do hope it doesn't jeopardize your fledgling business." His gray eyes bored into me. "So many businesses seem to fail these days."

There was a sadness to his voice. Real or induced? I couldn't tell.

I shifted uneasily side to side. This guy came to offer a welcome and wish me luck? "I'm hoping the police will solve this horrible crime soon. Tell me, do the police have any news?"

The mayor shook his head. He watched the monitor for a moment. I had a bird identification DVD playing at the moment. He rubbed his sharp nose. "Chief Kennedy says he has several leads. I'm confident we'll have this little matter solved before you know it."

Little matter? A murdered man in my house was a little matter? I shadowed the mayor to the sales counter, where he extracted one of the locally designed postcards from the rack.

"I'll take this one. I like to support our local businesses," he said as I rang up the big spender for the two seventy-five he was shelling out. He adjusted his hat. "You might consider joining the Ruby Lake Chamber of Commerce, Ms. Simms. They're always looking for new members." He stood, holding his postcard, staring out at the lake for a moment, then departed.

I couldn't remember the last time I'd been so happy to see somebody leave. And that was saying a lot. I'd had Jerry Kennedy in my apartment just that morning, after all.

I was pushing some extra chairs in front of the stairs to keep people like our dear mayor from going upstairs, when the lovebirds cooed. I'd been meaning to do as Kim suggested and get some rope or chain, preferably with a sign attached, asking folks to stay off the stairs, but hadn't had the time yet.

I hurried to greet my customer. It was the stroller couple, although they didn't have a stroller or any children at all with them this time.

I smiled. "Hello, it's good to see you again!" I had some questions and hopefully the two of them had some answers. I didn't know if it would clear up Matt Kowalski's murder or not, but I don't like unanswered questions.

The young woman approached, loosened her pale blue scarf and took off her cap. Straight blond hair spilled to her shoulders. "Can you believe it?" I arched my brows. She smiled. "We forgot to buy birdseed." Her hand lightly slapped her forehead and she glanced at her husband, who laughed too.

"I don't know why I didn't think of that myself." Amy Simms, ace salesperson. Not.

He shook his head. "Not much good having a feeder and no food to put in it. We were glad to see you were open today. It being Sunday and all."

"Only afternoons."

He looked toward the ceiling. "What's going on with the roof?"

I couldn't help looking too. "Oh, I'm having some minor repairs done. Roof leak."

"That can be serious," the woman said. "We had a roof leak in our last place, didn't we, honey?"

"Sure did."

"Tell me about it. Water had run all the way down to the basement. The contractor's got to patch things up from top to bottom."

"Bummer," replied the man.

"Yeah, bummer," agreed his wife.

"I hope your contractor knows what he's doing. An old place like this needs to be properly restored."

"Oh, please, Ted." She turned to me, a twinkle in her eye. "You do not want to get my husband started."

"Hey, c'mon, Sally!" laughed her husband. He spread his arms in placating fashion. "What can I say? I'm sort of a history buff. I like old places. And yours is a beauty."

I laughed with them. "Yeah, well. This beauty needs some serious cosmetic surgery."

"We're the Nickersons, by the way."

I held out my hand. "Amy Simms. Welcome." I asked them if they'd like some special blend, but Sally suggested they start with one of the prepackaged bags of seed.

Ted set a ten-pound bag of the black sunflower seed I'd recommended on the counter. I rang him up.

"From my alma mater, I see," I said.

"Excuse me?"

"Your beanie. UNC-Chapel Hill. I went to school there too."

Ted looked at his wife. "Oh yeah. Go Devils." He shoved a strand of brown hair up under the knitted cap.

I tilted my head and handed him change for a twenty.

"Renovations can be a bear. I'm a bit of a DIYer myself. How long does your contractor expect all your renovations to take?" asked Ted.

"I don't know." I glanced out the window. "But you can ask him yourself." A battered red pickup had pulled up to the curb. Cash Calderon unfolded himself from the interior and stepped inside the shop.

"Good afternoon, Ms. Simms." Cash wiped his feet carefully on the mat. He was dressed in his Sunday best and I barely recognized him. He'd even shaved.

"Hi, Mr. Calderon." I extended my palm toward the young couple. "This is Ted and Sally Nickerson. They've just moved into a house on Sycamore."

"Welcome," the contractor said, giving Ted's hand a brisk shake. "I was passing by and thought I'd ask how the roof held up. Any more trouble?" He turned his gaze to the spot in the corner where the ceiling tile had come crashing down the other day.

I couldn't help but look too. "No, nothing. Nothing new at least."

"Don't worry, Ms. Simms." I'd asked him a dozen times to call me Amy, but he said he thought it was more respectful of his customers to use their surnames. "We ought to be finished with the roof in the next day or two." He paused a moment. "If the weather holds up and we don't get any more rain, that is."

"That would be wonderful."

"After that, we'll get to repairing any areas with water damage, check for mold, fix the foundation, and seal the basement." I knew he was trying to be helpful, but all I was hearing were dollar signs.

He rubbed the back of his neck. "I'll need to get in that empty front unit. All that water." He nodded sagely. "It has to go somewhere, and it seems to be following a path down the front of the building. I'd like to make sure there's no damage in there."

I agreed. "I've been meaning to take a look inside, myself." I told the contractor that as soon as I found the key, I'd be sure to give it to him.

"Nice guy," Ted said, balancing the birdseed on his left shoulder. He shared a look with his wife. "Guess we ought to be heading back to the house."

"Speaking of houses," I started, stepping quickly around the counter, "which one is yours?"

"Pardon?" Sally asked.

"I mean, on Sycamore. You see, I, ah, have a friend on Sycamore and when I mentioned I'd met this *lovely* young couple, she said she was unaware of any recent sales on the street."

Sally and Ted shared a look again. What was with these two? Were they telepaths or something?

I went on. "And then when I saw you going into that cabin at the motor inn—"

"Excuse me?" Ted tugged at his ear.

"You what?" Sally's forehead reddened. "Were you *spying* on us?"

"No, I—" I held up my hands defensively.

She turned to her husband. "Can you believe this?"

He shook his head, a look of disgust on his face. "Is this what everybody in this town is like? Sticking their noses into everybody else's business?"

"No, of course not!"

Sally planted her fists on her hips. "If you must know, it was my aunt's house. She recently passed and left it to us."

"We're having it fumigated," barked Ted.

"Termites." Sally practically spat the word out. "Let's go, Ted."

I propped my back against the counter. The sound of the slamming door was still ringing in my ears. Oh well, at least it blocked out that ceaseless cooing of the lovebirds . . .

20

I telephoned Kim and we agreed to meet at Ruby's for dinner. I filled her in on what I'd learned over the course of the afternoon.

"Of course," I said, stuffing a plump, hot onion ring in my mouth and chewing for a moment, "it all raises more questions than it does answers."

Kim glommed a ring off my plate and twirled it round her finger before biting into it. "Something's fishy, all right. But it's not this sandwich." She pushed her plate to the edge of the table and waved for our waitress.

Tiffany came quickly. "What's up?"

"I ordered the chicken patty with slaw." She lifted the lid of the bun with her fingernail. "But this baby's all beef."

"Sorry." Tiffany sighed and rolled her eyes. "That Len. You'd think he could keep his orders straight." Len was one of Moire Leora's longtime short-order cooks. His memory was a little short though, too. "Give me a couple of minutes."

"No hurry," Kim said, reaching for her soda.

"So now I've probably lost a customer for life and have no idea what Mac was doing in the place."

"I called his cell, but he hasn't gotten back to me." Kim sucked at her drink. "I think you're barking up the wrong tree about the mayor. Why would he care what's going on at Birds and Bees? Why would he murder Matt?"

"I don't have a clue," I admitted. I folded my arms. "You want to tell me why Gertie Hammer came in acting all sweet as tea and offering to buy the place back from me, and then had a powwow with Robert LaChance?"

A blue plate clattered to the tabletop. "Robert?" Tiffany straightened the plate in front of Kim. "Sorry about that."

"No problem."

"What about Robert?"

I explained how I'd spotted her ex behind Birds & Bees moments after Gertie had been in, offering to buy the old place back from me. "Are Robert and Gertie friends?" I knew it was a stupid question even as I asked it. Gertie's friends with no one.

Tiffany shook her head. "I can't imagine what the two of them could have had to talk about. Maybe she has a problem with her car?"

"Yeah, that could be it," Kim replied. "The old clunker is bound to have a problem or two. The car, not the woman. Well, both."

The three of us laughed.

I told Tiffany about my troubled days. I knew the poor woman had troubles of her own and figured that nothing would cheer her up more than to see she wasn't alone. "I still can't figure those Nickersons though."

"How's that?" inquired Tiff.

"Well, he was wearing a UNC-Chapel Hill beanie. When I mentioned I'd gone to school there too, he said 'Go, Devils.' "

Both women gave me blank looks.

"The Devils are Duke—the Blue Devils, to be precise. We're the Tar Heels."

"That is odd," admitted Kim.

"Were you able to find out anything about that house on Sycamore?"

"House on Sycamore?" Tiffany scooched in beside Kim.

I explained about the Nickersons' claim to be moving into a new house.

Kim waved her hand. "You heard what the lady said. Her aunt left her the house. End of story."

"I suppose." Though I wasn't ready to let go of the Nickersons just yet. The two were slippery as a pair of greased pigs.

"I could find out," Tiffany offered. She pushed her pen behind her right ear.

"Oh?" I asked hopefully.

She nodded as she rose from the booth. "I have a friend. A neighbor, really. Anyway, her daughter works afternoons at the motel, part-time, as a housekeeper. I can ask her if she knows anything about them." She hesitated. "If you like?"

I grinned. "I like."

Monday morning it rained. Or to be more precise, it hadn't stopped raining since Sunday evening.

North Carolina can be like that. Some days are beautiful, Carolina blue skies—the kind James Taylor likes to croon about—other times . . . well, your roof leaks. The contractor had called to say he was sorry but there was nothing he could do about the rain and that it would be impossible to finish the roof until it dried out.

"Cheer up," Kim told me. "The ceiling hasn't caved in." She glanced nervously at the plastic sheet duct-taped to the ceiling in the far corner. "Not yet, anyway."

I grabbed my coat from a hanger on a nail near the back door. "Thanks for coming in to open."

"No problem. I guess I could hardly say no."

I flashed a wicked smile. "Especially since this was your big idea."

"Hey," Kim replied. "I only said that farmers normally go to the farmers' market Monday mornings. I didn't tell you to go break into a man's barn." She crossed her arms. "And that's exactly what I'm going to tell Jerry Kennedy if he or one of his officers catches you at it."

I zipped up my coat and tucked my hair under my wool hat. "Sure you don't want to come?"

"I have to open, remember?"

"I could call Mom. I'm sure she'd be happy to come in." Mom had a low tolerance level for her twin sister and was probably near her limits already.

Kim's mouth turned down. "Just go." She unlocked the back door. "Somebody's got to be available to bail you out later."

* * *

The sky was leaden, and it was so dark and the rain so heavy that I needed my headlights on for the drive to the farm. The windshield wipers thwacked to the beat of "There Are Worse Things I Could Do" from the musical *Grease.* I felt a little that way myself. I felt *a lot* that way. For a frightening five minutes, tiny hailstones bombarded the Kia.

I pulled into the long dirt drive leading to Aaron's house, relieved to be off the messy roads. Unfortunately, the dirt had long turned to thick, oozy red mud. The near-bald tires spun as I pulled up to the house, and the back of the minivan broke to the right before coming to a stop. I cut off the engine, listening to the unsettling sound of rain pelting the metal roof of the van as I gathered up my courage. I knew I had it around there someplace.

The drapes were pulled open but there was no sign of life inside Aaron's house. Not even a glowing lightbulb. I knew he had a big German shepherd, but the old boy must have been dozing; otherwise I'd have expected to see his big, hairy paws up on the window ledge as he gazed out at me with those penetrating and predatory chocolate-brown eyes of his.

There was no sign of Aaron's battered old blue Toyota Tacoma. So that meant that, indeed, Aaron was at the farmers' market. Either that or the pickup was tucked safely away in the barn.

Not a pleasant thought.

The rain kept beating down on the thin roof of the Kia, as if trying to drive me and the van into the ground. My fingers drummed an accompaniment on the dash. Lightning created a show against the backdrop of the mountains. I was slowly going mad.

Sloughing off my shoes, I grabbed my boots from the backseat and slid into them. I glanced at my watch. I'd been here five minutes or more and still no sign of life. It was time to get off my butt and search the barn or turn around with my tail between my legs and head back to Birds & Bees.

I squeezed the door handle and pushed open the door. Cold, hard rain lashed against my face and hands as I ran to the relative safety of the barn. I pulled at the big barn door and opened it a crack. Thank goodness it wasn't locked. I'd brought no tools and wouldn't know how to pick a lock anyway.

I heard a horse whinny and froze before continuing. "Hello?" I called tentatively. "Aaron? Are you here? It's me, Amy Simms. I thought I'd come talk to you about those birdhouses . . ."

Nothing, thank heavens—only the rain hitting the roof above, echoing madly. I pressed on.

Inside, the mingled scent of hay and a mix of earthy odors that only life on a farm could create greeted my nostrils. I also smelled fear. I seemed to have carried that in with me.

What I didn't find was a light switch. When was I going to learn to carry a flashlight?

I slid across the floor, my boots heavily caked with mud growing heavier as the straw clung to the bottoms, adding another five pounds to me. A crack of light, not much, outlined the gap in the back barn doors. From my last time here, I knew there was a workbench to the left and some stalls to the right. I headed to the workbench.

I discovered a strip light attached to a shelf above the bench and flipped it on. It wasn't much, but the glow allowed me to see dimly around the barn. I quietly and carefully searched the workbench, checking all the bins and the bottom drawers. I saw nothing out of the ordinary. No obvious murder weapons, instruments of torture, or trophy body parts.

For the first time, I wondered if I dared search his house. Assuming I could break in. Assuming that German shepherd didn't eat me for lunch.

I noticed a simple wood ladder in the far corner, leading to a loft. I'd save that for last. Not having any portable light, I wasn't sure what I'd be able to see anyway, assuming I didn't break my neck trying to climb up and down in the near darkness.

I approached the horse, not much more than a black shadow, and rubbed his nose. "How are you, boy?" He could have been a she—either way the animal replied with a gentle whinny. I patted his side and continued my search.

Going on the premise that Aaron Maddley and/or his sister, Grace, had murdered Matt Kowalski and then Aaron had driven back here to the barn—this was where I'd seen the pickup that night with its engine still ticking, after all—where would he hide the evidence?

Whatever evidence that might be. I turned slowly around the big, quiet barn. My eyes had grown accustomed to the low light and I now noticed a ragged stack of hay bales to the right, beneath the loft. A glint of something shiny caught my eye.

I crept to the corner. The edge of a trunk of some sort stuck from behind several bales. It rested on a black oilcloth. The trunk was closed but unlocked.

I lifted the lid. My eyes grew wide and my mouth went dry. A rumpled pair of dungarees and a torn and bloody shirt lay inside. A wood-handled knife lay atop them. I bristled.

"Amy?"

I jumped and screamed. The lid of the trunk slammed down on my knee, then shut with a bang. As I spun around, I slipped and tumbled against the rough wallboards of the barn. I felt a splinter jab into my palm and winced in pain.

I scrambled to get off my knees. Hands grabbed me.

"Are you all right?" Aaron grabbed me by the elbow and lifted me easily.

I nodded as I tried to balance myself on two feet once again. Kind of hard when you've been frightened to death. And caught in a barn by a vicious killer.

"Let me hit the lights." Aaron released me and I watched his shadowy figure fade. A moment later big overhead fluorescents sprang to life.

I hobbled over, hoping to make my escape, but he stepped in front of me and held out his arms. "What are you doing here, Amy?" He wore a black rain poncho, slick with water, over a pair of sturdy dungarees and work boots.

"I, uh . . ." My eyes swung madly around the barn. There had to be some way out of here. Maybe if I climbed to the loft I could hold him off until the police arrived. But why would the police arrive? I hadn't told them I was coming. I couldn't telephone them because, like an idiot, I'd left my purse in the Kia.

"Why don't we go inside and I'll make us some coffee?" he suggested. "You're shivering." Aaron turned toward the open barn door. "Are you all right? Did you hurt your hand?"

I realized I'd been holding my open hand up like a stop sign, feeling the sharp and no doubt germ-filled splinter under my skin. "It's nothing." I pulled my hand away from his grasping fingers.

I thought about jumping him right then but knew it would be futile. He was a lot bigger and stronger than I was. I didn't even have a weapon of any sort. I hadn't realized I was shivering and didn't know if it was from being drenched with cold rain or from fear of being murdered out there in that desolate barn. But I was definitely shivering now. Uncontrollably.

"N-no, that's okay," I said. "I really should be going. Sorry. I only stopped by to ask if you'd started on those birdhouses." I made a large circle around Aaron and headed awkwardly to the exit.

"You came all the way out here for that?"

"Sorry," I said over my shoulder. "I should have called first."

"No problem." He'd caught up to me and laid a hand on my damp shoulder. I flinched. My heart beat against my chest. "Are you sure you're okay?"

I nodded. "I'd better get back to the store."

Aaron walked me out, flicking off the lights and shutting the barn doors behind us.

I felt his eyes on me as I backed up the minivan and headed quickly toward town.

* * *

"Why didn't you warn me?" I gasped, throwing off my wet coat and hat and tossing them recklessly on the front counter regardless of the mess it would create. I'd already stomped in with my mud-caked boots on, leaving a messy trail in my wake; how much bigger a mess could I make? Besides, I was rattled. The entire way back to the store, I'd driven with one eye on the rearview mirror, trying to be certain Aaron Maddley wasn't following me in his pickup truck.

"I couldn't," replied Kim. "I tried, but you weren't answering your phone." The customer she'd been assisting over at the seed bins eyed us suspiciously.

Mom stood behind the counter. "Amy Hester Simms, what have you been up to?"

Uh-oh. All three names. Spoken in a clipped staccato cadence. Never a good sign with my mother. I shot Kim a searching look. Hopefully, she hadn't told my mother about my little breaking-and-entering adventure. Technically, I wasn't sure it was breaking, since the barn doors weren't locked. If I'd had time to get into Aaron Maddley's house, that would have been another story. Probably one ending in my incarceration. Or being swallowed whole by an unnaturally large German shepherd. What did he feed that thing, anyway? Magic, gigantism-inducing beans?

I wiped drops of cold rain from my nose with the back of my sleeve. "Nothing, Mom." I'd blasted the van's heater all the way home and was still chilled to the bone. I'd heard fear could do that to a person. I'd been experiencing it a lot lately, so I knew it had to be true.

Mom stepped out from behind the counter and began refilling the seed bins. Kim led her customer to the register and rang her up. "That's not what Kim's been telling me." Mom tapped her foot.

I gulped. "You told her? It was supposed to be a secret!" The customer left hurriedly. I guess she didn't care much for family squabbles in the middle of her shopping experience. I grabbed a small pair of tweezers from my purse and gingerly yanked a mile-long pine splinter from my right palm. I winced.

"What's wrong with your hand?" Mom asked.

"Splinter." I held up my palm. "Gone now." I flicked the splinter into the trash can.

Kim folded her arms. "I didn't tell your mother anything. What do you think I am? A snitch?" She pulled the apron from around her waist and placed it on a hook on the wall behind the counter. "You may as well tell her now, though."

"Well . . ." I wasn't sure this was a share-with-Mom kind of story.

Mom's eyes bored into me more effectively than any harsh police-interrogation-room overhead light, and my resolve failed me. I told my mother about our suspicions and how I'd gone to Aaron Maddley's farm to have a look around.

Mom shook her head in disbelief. "You really think he or his sister might have had something to do with Matt's death? I mean, I remember hearing what Matt had done to Grace, about the baby and all—and it was an awful thing—but still." Mom pushed her shoulders back and wagged her finger at me. "And to go out to Mr. Maddley's barn and snoop around like that!" She gripped my arm. "What were you thinking? What if he'd caught you?" I lowered my eyes. "You could have gone to jail, Amy!"

I felt my face flush. "Actually"—I cleared my throat and admired my toes—"he sort of did."

"What?!" gasped Mom, waving a hand in front of her nose.

I stuck my arm out at Kim. "She should have warned me! Besides, it was her idea!"

"Hey!" exclaimed Kim. She punched me in the arm. "Don't go blaming me for this. And I'll have you know, I did try to warn you, like I said earlier. It's not my fault you didn't answer. When Aaron came in here and—"

"What?" I was confused. And my arm hurt. The girl packed a good punch. "Aaron came here? To the store?" I massaged my upper arm.

She nodded. "That's what I'm trying to tell you. It was just before you arrived, Mrs. Simms."

"What did he want?" I asked.

Kim heaved a shoulder. "Said he was in the area and wanted to say hi. To you, that is." Kim smirked. "I think he's smitten." She fluttered her eyelashes and propped her hands under her chin. "He said the two of you had a lovely date Saturday night."

"It wasn't a date." It was an interrogation. Sort of. I had seemed to be the only one of us interested in talking about the murder that night.

Mom arched her right brow and faced me. "Smitten? Isn't that lovely, Amy?"

I pulled a face. "Oh yeah, nothing like having a cold-blooded murder suspect smitten with me to make my day."

Mom rolled her eyes. "Suddenly you're Miss Choosy?"

Mom's been watching too much of the Kardashians—thinks bizarre is the new normal. I waved at Kim to continue. "Go on. What else did he say?"

"Nothing much. Said the farmers' market was cancelled due to rain." I should have expected that—it is an outdoor market. "He said the parking lot was flooded and all the merchants agreed to reschedule."

I sank down on the stool behind the register and pulled off my boots. I really needed to be smarter about this whole investigating thing before something went seriously wrong. I didn't want Mom reading about my murder in the *Ruby Lake Weekender*. Besides, Lance would probably get my name wrong. Then Mom would truly have a conniption fit.

"I tried to phone you, but you didn't pick up."

"I left my phone in my purse in the van," I said. I rubbed my feet through my stockings.

Kim nodded. "I even suggested he might want to stop at the diner and get something to eat. You know, trying to slow him down from going back to his place. But he said he wanted to get home and catch up on some chores. He also said he might get started on those cardinal houses for you."

Maybe. But I wondered if I'd ever be seeing those birdhouses or even Aaron Maddley ever again. Something told me our business relationship might be over. Especially after I turn him in.

Of course, I might be asked to testify against

him at his trial. What would it be like, having to face him in the courtroom?

"I hope this serves as a lesson to you," Mom said. She returned the feed scoop to its holder and straightened the bags. "Snooping around on private property."

"Mom."

"Spying on people."

"Mom!"

She turned to face me. "Yes, dear?"

I sighed. "Don't you want to know what I found?"

Kim's eyes sparked. "You found something?"

I nodded and explained about the torn and bloody clothes and the knife. When I was done, there was stunned silence.

Mom looked suddenly pale and troubled. "I don't like this at all," she said quietly. I rose from the stool and urged her to sit. "What is happening to our nice little town?"

I dug my phone out of my purse and dialed. Anita Brown, police dispatcher and pinochle champ, answered.

"Hello, may I speak to Chief Kennedy, please?"

"What are you doing?" Kim asked.

"Hopefully, exposing a killer."

21

A squat man with tight black curls, bushy brows, and a crooked nose smiled at me. "I've got hives," he said, his face animated. "What can you do for me?"

I squinted one eye at him. He didn't look too bad. No facial swelling. No wheals. "Calamine lotion?" I mean, what do you treat hives with?

He bent over double, slapping his hands against his calves, and guffawed. "Calamine lotion, that's rich." He straightened, flashing black eyes and white teeth. "I like you, lady. You're all right." He wore a baggy blue raincoat over a nondescript, even baggier gray sweat suit.

"Thanks," I said rather nervously. Was it take-a-day-off-from-the-asylum day?

He stuck out his hand. "Mitch Quiles. I own Quiles Apiary." He looked like he'd make a perfect Sancho Panza if they ever did a remake of the musical *Man of La Mancha.*

I looked at him blankly.

"Over on Hillsborough?"

Hillsborough. That wasn't far from where Aaron Maddley lived. "Sorry," I said, shaking my head. "I'm afraid I haven't heard of it. I'm sure it's lovely though," I hastened to add.

He beamed. "Yeah, it's lovely all right. I saw in the paper that you've got apiary supplies. It's about time I was able to buy local." He rubbed his hands together. "So, what have you got?"

Finally, I understood what he was going on about. "Ohh," I said, drawing the word out. "Hives." I smiled. "I get it now."

I waved for him to follow me to the alcove under the back stairs where I had a small selection of beekeeping supplies and gear.

"Nice," the man said, taking it all in. "You have bees?" There was hope in his voice. Maybe he was wishing to find a fellow bee enthusiast.

"No. Not yet. I hope to, though."

Mitch Quiles bobbed his head. "It's a great hobby. Of course, for me, it's a business." He fondled an inexpensive cotton/poly blend bee-keeper's suit hanging from a hook.

"I don't have much in bee inventory," I explained. "I wasn't sure how much demand there'd be for any of it. Compared to the birds, that is." I had a few basic starter kits, bottles for honey, screens, protective clothing, feed, and an assortment of hive accessories.

"Bees are important, miss. Mighty important."

"Oh, I agree completely. I'll have to stop by your place some time."

He beamed like a proud peacock. "I'd be happy to show you around."

"You know, I have a friend"—boy, that was sure using the word loosely, considering I'd ratted the guy out to the police—"who lives out your way. Aaron Maddley. Perhaps you know him?"

"Sure, I know him," Mitch replied loudly. "Neighbor of mine. We share a property line."

"Is that so?" Maybe Mitch Quiles had noticed something or someone out of the ordinary, like Aaron's sister, Grace, out at the farm. "Did you happen to notice—"

"Kim!" Randy Vincent stood in the doorway. He was dressed in black leather pants and a black leather jacket. He held a motorcycle helmet under his arm. I was no detective, but I knew he hadn't ridden here on the bus. Was he auditioning for the role of Danny Zuko in the local dinner theater's revival of *Grease, the Musical?* All he needed was a pompadour and he'd be a shoo-in. If he could sing and dance, that is.

"Randy!" I heard Kim shout from the other end of the store. "What are you doing here?"

He trounced across the floor, his motorcycle boots pounding against the floorboards. "I got your message." He held out his cell phone. "What's going on?"

"Speaking of floorboards"—Mitch lightly tugged my sleeve—"have you got any screened bottom boards?"

I pushed my tongue against the inside of my cheek—torn between watching the nascent drama unfolding between my best friend and her boyfriend, and my new customer. My eyes scanned the alcove. "I'm pretty sure I ordered some." I tapped a finger of my left hand against the splinter wound of my right palm. Sometimes it takes a little pain to get one focused. "I don't see them here. I may not have had time to unpack them yet. Let me check for you." I hurried to the storeroom, looking over my shoulder at Kim and Randy having words in the far corner near the coffee machine.

Bottom boards, bottom boards. My eyes flitted around the space. Finally, I found an unopened case of bottom boards from my supplier up in Minnesota. Bottom boards are just what they sound like, the floor of the hive upon which all other components are built. Often, as temperatures rise in the spring, bees collect there. Screened bottom boards help produce better broods, increase airflow and reduce varroa mite infestations, and are part of a good integrated pest management system. The varroa mite is a parasite that only reproduces in honeybee colonies and, if gone unchecked, can destroy an entire colony.

I slit open the case with a box knife and took a stack of boards to the front. "Here you go." I handed several to Mr. Quiles.

He turned one over in his hand. "Looks good." He ran one under his nose and took a whiff. "Cedar. I like that."

Kim and Randy had disappeared by the time I'd rung up Mitch Quiles's purchase. Before he left, he promised to drop me off a free jar of his honey.

The remainder of the afternoon flew by. No bird puns intended. Kim never did come back to the store. Mom left when Aunt Betty came by around three to give her a ride back to her house. I was just about to lock the door when it pushed toward me.

I leaped back. "Aaron!" I looked madly around for a weapon but came up empty-handed. I retreated behind the counter and he dogged me. "What are you doing here?" Why wasn't he in jail?

He glared at me, his hands buried deep in the pockets of his heavy dark coat. "Surprised to see me?" His eyes danced. "Why? Because you thought the police had arrested me?"

"Well, I—" I glanced over his shoulder out the window. Where were the police when you needed them?

"I thought we were friends, Amy." He shook his head. "Maybe more than friends."

"I'm sorry, Aaron." I fiddled with the register to keep my hands busy, but I kept one eye on him. "I don't know what you're talking about."

He raised his brow. "Are you trying to tell me that you didn't telephone the police and report to that lamebrain Jerry Kennedy that you'd found some kind of crazy evidence out at my place?"

Silence but for the ticking of the clock on the wall behind me. Finally, I spoke. "If you're innocent, you have nothing to hide."

"If you're smart," Aaron huffed, "you'll stay out of things that don't concern you." He spun on his heels and headed for the door.

"Matt Kowalski's murder is my business!" I shouted angrily. "And I'll stick my nose wherever I damn well feel like it!"

He stopped in the open door and shook his head slowly. "Do you always think the worst of everybody, Amy? Because if you do"—he paused as Kim, finally, came pushing past him—"I feel sorry for you."

He let the door close behind him.

"Well, at least he didn't slam it," I quipped.

Kim raised an inquisitive eyebrow. "Want to tell me what that was all about?"

I frowned and folded my arms across my chest. "You first."

"What's that supposed to mean?" Kim's eyes were red and puffy and she looked completely worn-out. Her clothes were rumpled and her makeup, well, let's just say she's looked better.

"Let's see, Randy comes in here dressed like the Fonz and the two of you disappear. You show no sign of life for hours." She hadn't even answered my texts or phone calls. "Want to tell me what *that* was all about?"

Kim said nothing, her focus out the window.

I blew out a breath. The woman could be so annoying. "Then you return, looking like somebody with a story to tell. And a sad one at that." I tapped her on the shoulder. "Are you even listening to me?"

"Huh." She twisted her head to one side.

I pulled a face. "What?"

She pointed. "That pickup."

I saw Aaron Maddley climbing into his Tacoma at the curb. "What about it?"

"It looks sort of familiar." She turned to face me. "I feel like I've seen it before."

I wasn't sure that mattered. "Ruby Lake is a small town. You're bound to have seen it at least once in a while."

"No." Kim shook her head. "I think I saw it here."

My brows shot up.

"At the store."

I felt my pulse quicken. "When?"

"The night I came here," she said softly, "to pick up my tablet."

The night Matt Kowalski was murdered . . .

22

"You broke up with him?!" I thumped the cushion of the sofa in my apartment and leaned back. "Why?"

"Because of you," cried Kim. "Because of what you said!"

"What did I say?!" I was practically shrieking. "I didn't say a thing." And I did not want to be the reason that any two people broke up.

Kim sniffled and I tossed her a tissue from the box I'd carried over from the bathroom. She'd gone through half a box of the things already. "Maybe not in so many words, but your eyes did."

I rolled my unfairly blamed eyes. "Oh brother." I poured us each a second glass of wine, or maybe it was the third. Zinfandel goes down fast and doesn't leave a tally. The buzzer sounded and I raced downstairs to let the pizza deliveryman from I Heart NC Pizza inside.

We drowned our respective sorrows in pizza and wine. The alcohol spilled freely into our glasses while Kim's sorrows spilled out from her heart. It seemed somehow she'd gotten the idea that I disapproved of her relationship with Randy and so had broken things off with him. That's why he'd come into Birds & Bees all upset.

"I meant no such thing," I said for the umpteenth time. "And if I implied it," I said, taking her two hands in mine and squeezing, "I'm sorry."

Kim wiped her eyes with a pizza-shop napkin.

"If you keep crying like that your eyes are going to turn permanently red."

Kim chuckled. A trace of a smile lit her face.

"It's true," I continued. "I read it online someplace."

Kim wiped her pink-tipped nose. "Thanks."

"Feel better?"

Kim blew out a breath and propped her elbows on her knees. We sat on the sofa. The TV was on. The Food Network is a great go-to when you want to take your mind off other things. Like murders and breakups. You could kill an entire evening just debating the wisdom and merits of Anne Burrell's latest hairdo. "Yeah."

"Good," I said. I waved the empty wine bottle in front of her nose. "Because tomorrow you're going to have one hell of a headache." I bit my cheek. "We both are." Not to mention I'd eaten half a large pizza.

We moved from the couch to the bedroom. "Speaking of tomorrow," I said, arranging a clean set of sheets on Mom's bed—Kim was going to be staying over—"why don't you call Randy tomorrow and have a real heart-to-heart?"

Kim agreed. "You know, Amy," Kim said as she

lay in freshly made bed, her head against the pillow and hands pulling at the comforter, "I've been thinking."

I grinned. "Haven't we both been doing a little too much of that lately?" I knew I had. Still, I had to ask. It's part of the friendship code. "What about?"

"What about Dwayne?" She arranged the blue-gray comforter around her legs and now looked like a tightly wrapped, bedridden mummy.

I scrunched up my nose. "You like Dwayne?"

"No!" She giggled. "Do you suppose he could be the murderer?"

My hand rested on the doorknob. "He got here *after* the murder, remember?"

"Did he?" Kim's eyes bored into mine. "Or did he murder Matt and then *conveniently* show up at the back door?"

OMG! Why hadn't I thought of that?!

I said goodnight and headed to my room. I was still thinking about Kim's last words when I heard the strange banging in the middle of the night. Why hadn't I considered Dwayne Rogers? I'd considered Aaron Maddley, Mac MacDonald, and Robert LaChance . . . heck, at this point, I was even mildly considering Gertie Hammer after her weird appearance in the store and her offer to buy me out—but why not the burly trucker?

What if he'd been lying all along? How convenient would it be to show up after the murder and act all surprised? Did he know Matt? They were about the same age, so that was entirely possible.

I'd have to ask Chief Kennedy if he'd investigated Dwayne's whereabouts at the time of the murder. I also wanted to know what he'd learned after interrogating Aaron. The man was walking around loose instead of locked up behind bars. What about those bloody clothes? That knife?

There was that noise again.

I rolled over onto my side, held my breath, and listened. Nothing. Sure, it only happens when I'm not trying to hear. I threw back the sheets and stuffed my feet into my slippers. I glanced at the clock. One freaking thirty. Lovely.

I was going to get to the bottom of this. Strong winds howled outside. That meant the storm was blowing out and cool, dry air was blowing in. Cash Calderon was right. Tomorrow would be bright and sunny. He'd telephoned me earlier and announced that, if all went well weather-wise, he'd be able to finish up the roof and start on the downstairs ceiling tomorrow morning—this morning, I realized dolefully.

I felt around for my robe and knotted it around my waist. I heard thumping upstairs. Either the tarp had come loose or Cash was up there fiddling with things to make sure nothing else got ruined. I'd find out soon enough.

Then I heard the scream.

I threw open my bedroom door and ran into the living room. I slammed into a soft body and heard another scream.

"Amy!" cried Kim. "Did you hear that? What was that?!"

I raced to the side table beside the sofa and flicked on the table lamp. Kim stood shivering in a baby-blue teddy. "I-I'm not sure," I said. I glanced upward. "But I'm pretty sure it came from up there."

We looked at the ceiling, then one another.

"Should we call Jerry?"

I grimaced. "Jerry? Really?"

"He is the police."

I tossed her Mom's robe. "Put that on," I said. "It's probably Mr. Calderon checking on things."

Kim appeared hesitant, though she wrapped the too-large peacock-blue robe around herself.

"What are you doing?" Kim asked as she followed me out of the apartment and I pushed aside some spare summer outfits from the side of the closet in the hall.

"This is the way up."

Kim pouted. "I'm not so sure I want to go up." She looked over her shoulder. "Couldn't we go down instead? Like to a motel?"

"It's nothing," I said, trying to sound convincing. I looked up the narrow stairs. There was no sign of any lights. "Mr. Calderon? Is that you? Are you up there?"

I grabbed Kim's hand and dragged her up with me.

"Amy, I don't think—"

"Shh!" I held my finger to my lips and mouthed, "I think I hear something." Or someone. "Listen."

Kim nodded silently.

Suddenly, we heard the sound of pounding—footsteps coming our way. I started to back up. This was no time to march bravely forward. This was time to run!

Unfortunately, the stairway was narrow and Kim hadn't gotten the orders to run. She stood frozen in place. Blocking me.

"Go! Go!" I cried, giving her a push to get

started. The pounding grew louder. Whatever it was, it was coming our way. A white shape appeared at the top of the steep stairs and came barreling toward us. A ghost?

Kim screamed, and because—and only because—I was raised to be polite, I let out a bloodcurdling scream myself. The white figure bowled us over and we crashed to the floor of the dark closet.

I felt bruised in more places than I thought I had. I pushed myself off the floor. "Are you okay?" I asked Kim, who was tangled in Mom's robe and the half dozen articles of clothing in the closet that had somehow managed to wrap themselves around her.

She nodded. "I'm fine."

"Good." I leapt to my feet.

"Where are you going?" shrieked Kim.

"I'm not letting whoever that was"—or whatever that was—"get away!"

Kim groaned and followed.

I heard something downstairs. Whoever it was, they had a head start. I half tumbled down the stairs just as I heard the back door slam.

I spilled out into the night. The sky was starfilled, clear and windy. A running, all-white figure turned the corner at the edge of the parking lot. I raced to follow, splashing through icy puddles of rainwater.

But when I got to the sidewalk at the edge of the street, there was no sign of my unwanted visitor. I stood at the edge of the silent road, listening for telltale evidence of somebody lurking.

The wind howled but the night was otherwise quiet. All was still on the roads and walkways.

A hand grabbed me from behind. I screamed.

"Amy!" Kim puffed, her hand falling from my shoulder. "Are you okay?"

"Let's go inside," I said. I was cold and wet and felt terribly exposed and vulnerable out there in the dark in the middle of the night. "And call the police."

"Already done," replied Kim.

I smiled. "Tell me something. Do you believe in ghosts?"

Kim took a moment. "No."

"Neither do I." I opened the back door and headed for the small kitchen at the rear of the store. I knew there were some tea bags in the cupboard. And I knew we could both use a cup. "Neither do I."

23

Chief Kennedy slowly worked his flashlight along the floor and walls of the attic. "I don't see a darn thing." His face was pale and his cheeks sagged. He wasn't responding well to being wakened in the middle of the night.

He toe kicked some loose insulation back against the wall. "Maybe it was that nighttime squatter of yours, come back for his things."

That was an unsettling thought considering Matt was dead. "All his stuff is still there."

The police chief worked his light over the sleeping bag and pile of junk the occupier of the attic had left behind. "Appears so."

We went back down to my apartment and I put on some more tea. "Quit leering, Jerry," I snapped. Kim's robe was riding high on her legs and Jerry was taking it all in.

Jerry turned red and made a point of focusing on his tea. Poor guy had probably never had herbal tea in his life.

The phone rang. "Who could be calling at this hour?" It was nearly 3:00 a.m.

"The killer?" Kim said. She pulled her robe down to her ankles.

"Answer it," said Jerry Kennedy.

I did. "Hello?"

"Amy!"

"Mom? What are you doing calling me in the middle of the night?"

"Anita called me."

Uh-oh. The police dispatcher and my mother were friends. I should have known better . . .

"Chasing a burglar in your attic? What exactly were you going to do if you caught him?" demanded my mother. "Did you even think about that?"

"Nothing happened, Mother."

"Nothing happened? A maniacal killer is on the loose and you try to catch him?" She took a quick breath. "You could have ended up like poor Mr. Withers. You could have been killed even."

"Mom," I said firmly. "Nothing happened. I'm okay. Kim's okay. Chief Kennedy is here now—" I came to a sudden stop. "Wait. What? Back up. Mr. Withers?" The little guy who'd come into Birds & Bees because he couldn't figure out how to load his birdfeeder? "What about him?"

"Mugged," Mom answered. "And if another couple hadn't stepped into the alley, who knows what might have happened? His attacker hit him and then ran off when the other people showed up."

"Ohmigod."

"That's right. He'd been at the Coffee and Tea House. I heard he was walking back to his car, through the alley there on Parker Street, you know?"

I nodded, though I knew she couldn't see me. There's a narrow alley between the coffee shop and the hardware store leading to a gravel parking lot in back. "Is he okay?"

"Yes, thank goodness. He's on bed rest. Doctor's orders. But at least he's okay. In broad daylight too!"

I told Mom that I'd try to stop by one day soon and check up on him. I said goodnight to Mom and relayed the news to Kim.

Jerry nodded. "We took the report earlier today. Not much to go on. Probably some punk passing through from out of town who thought he'd take advantage of the situation and rob the old man."

"What about Dwayne?" I asked Jerry Kennedy as I walked him out to the front door. I was going to make sure I locked it up tight after he left too. Kim and I had already decided to sleep with our doors locked and barricaded.

"What about him?" The chief yawned and put his hand to his mouth.

"He might have murdered Matt."

Jerry snorted. "Not a chance."

"How do you know that?"

"Because he got to your store after the murder. You said so yourself."

"But what's his alibi? Does he have one?" My arms flew wildly. "What about fingerprints? Have you even fingerprinted him?"

He smiled sardonically. "Yeah, we fingerprinted him, all right. Standard procedure. But so what?"

"So his fingerprints could be all over"—my eyes

lit around the room—"I don't know." I crossed my arms over my chest. "Something incriminating."

Jerry shook his head. "Of course his prints are going to be on stuff around here. He delivered most of it!"

I squinted angrily at him. "You should still check and see if the man has an alibi. You are the chief of police. Can't you at least do that one simple thing?"

"He has an alibi, Simms."

"So?" I demanded. "What is it?"

Jerry thumped his hat against his leg. "It's you!"

I turned red with anger. "What about Aaron Maddley?" If I wasn't getting anywhere nailing Dwayne Rogers for the murder, then surely Aaron Maddley made a prime suspect.

He frowned. "We searched all over the barn. And the house. Boy, was Mr. Maddley unhappy about that." He grinned. "Especially when it came out that you were the reason we were there."

I narrowed my eyes at him. "And I'll bet you were the one who told him."

Jerry shrugged. "Couldn't see any harm in it. Anyway, he explained about the clothes, though we took them to have them analyzed anyway. Some folks don't always tell the truth." He yawned once more and glanced at his wristwatch. "But in this case, I'm inclined to believe him."

I bit my lower lip. "So? What's his explanation for the bloody clothes?"

"Says he was birthing a foal."

I squeezed my eyes shut. Had I been wrong about Aaron?

"And as for Mr. Rogers, Simms, I'll have you

know I checked on Dwayne. He was making a delivery in Ethelberg at the time of the murder. And do you know what that means?"

I quickly calculated the distance and time in my head. My heart sank. "It means he couldn't have been in two places at once."

Kennedy smiled victoriously. "That's right. The man could not have been in two"—he held up two fat fingers—"places at once." He popped on his hat. "Stay out of police business, Amy. Stick to doing what you do best." His arms swept the room. "Birds and bees."

He snorted, his eyes landing on the pile of debris in the corner that had been caused by all the water damage. "And frankly," he said, turning the door handle and setting off the lovebirds, "I don't think you're all too good at that either."

I watched the arrogant jerk swagger to his police cruiser. Stepping on the mat, I'd set off those damn lovebirds again. I stepped aside, picked up the mat, and hurled it across the room.

I'd had to do something to let off some steam. I leaned against the doorjamb and shut my eyes. I could hear the perky cooing of the lovebirds from over in aisle three . . .

24

I yanked the covers off the bed.

"Hey!" shouted Kim. "What'd you do that for? I was still sleeping."

"I've made an executive decision," I declared.

"What sort of executive decision?" She eyed me warily.

"Birds and Bees is closed for the day." What with all the construction due to happen today, I figured the best thing we could all do was to stay out of Cash Calderon's way. The sooner he and his crew got their job done, the sooner things could get back to normal around here. And having us and customers out of the way would definitely make the job go all the faster. "Hit the showers, girlfriend. We'll grab breakfast at Ruby's."

We grabbed a couple spots at the diner and Tiffany rushed to greet us. "I'm so glad you're here, Amy." She laid down her order pad and leaned closer. "I did like I said. I asked my friend's daughter about"—she looked around the room like a nervous spy—"those people."

I smiled. Moire Leora swept over with the coffee-pot and filled our cups, then quickly flew off. During the busiest hours, the woman flitted around the dining room like a ruby-throated humming-bird.

"Linda, that's my friend's daughter, said they seem okay. Keep to themselves."

"Does she happen to know how long they've been staying there?"

Tiff nodded. "About a week or so."

"Does she know how much longer they are planning on staying?" asked Kim. "Supposedly, they're moving into a house in town."

Tiffany shook her head. "She doesn't know anything about that. At least, she didn't say. She did say they were into hiking and rock hunting—stuff like that."

"Rock hunting?" I knew there were people into the hobby. I didn't get it myself. The Carolinas are full of rock. Who'd want to waste their time hunting for more of them?

"Oh yeah." Tiffany snatched her pad. "She said the room is full of hiking and outdoor gear."

Kim shook her head and ordered the breakfast special: one egg, one biscuit, and homemade chunky cinnamon applesauce. I went for the same. "I don't understand hiking or camping," Kim said with a yawn. "If I want to rough it, I'll stay in a two-star motel."

There were bags under her eyes. It had been a late night and an early morning. I'm sure I looked no better. Cash and his crew had arrived at seven thirty. We'd spent the night with our bedroom doors locked and the sofa pushed up against the door to the apartment.

Tiffany headed for the order window, then turned back. "Oh, and guess what?"

"What?"

"Robert came by last night. He'd had Jimmy for the day. Anyway, when he dropped him off, he happened to mention Matt."

The hairs on the back of my neck rose. "Your husband mentioned Matt?" Kim and I shared a look. "What exactly did he say?"

"Not much," bubbled Tiff, rubbing her ball-point pen against her teeth. "Mostly he wanted to boast about some mysterious big business deal"— she wiggled her fingers—"he was working on. Like I could care." She rolled her eyes.

"But what did he say about Matt?"

"Huh?" Tiff tugged her earlobe. "Just that Matt was always shooting his mouth off when he shouldn't. Bragging. Stuff like that. If you know what I mean?"

I watched Tiffany's backside as she scooted to the order window—as did nearly every pair of male eyes in the joint. Not that I'm jealous or anything. I'm just saying.

I didn't know what Tiff or her ex, Robert, had meant. But I knew someone who did. The man himself. I added checking out LaChance Motors to my list of things to do.

"Want to go down to Charlotte and hit the mall?" Kim asked, breaking my train of thought.

I explained how I wanted to take advantage of

the store being closed to take care of a few errands and Kim and I parted ways, agreeing that we'd meet up at the store in the evening to see how the contractor's work had turned out. Hopefully, the roof and ground floor would be done and there'd only be the basement and any other random areas left to work on.

I walked into Olde Towne Hardware and it was something like stepping into the Old West. Rosario and Pedro Flores had bought the place from Old Man Riley when he retired. I was certain Mr. Riley had a first name besides Old Man, but that's all I'd ever known him as.

I approached the pine-board-faced counter and told Pedro what I needed.

Pedro is a squat man with a leathery complexion and a perpetual smile. Rosario, on the other hand, could be a bit sharp, wore a frilly red and white apron, and spent most of her workday cleaning up after the customers. She liked to run a neat and tidy store and resented all the dust and dirt the customers brought in and the way they manhandled and disarranged her goods. She was busily reorganizing some nuts and bolts even now.

"You could use rope, of course, Amy." Pedro rubbed his hands together. He had lustrous black hair. If it were an inch or two longer, he could have had a pompadour. "But I've got some very nice chain." He led me over to the wall near the front. "And we have these eyebolts that you could attach to your newel posts."

He grabbed a couple. "Like so," he said, pressing an eyebolt to the side of the shelf and looping a link of the steel chain over it. He grabbed a carabiner from a small gray plastic tray and secured it to the chain at the opposite end. "Then use one of these as a clasp."

"Perfect. I'll take one of those too." I'd spotted a PRIVATE—NO ADMITTANCE sign on a rack of assorted plastic signs. While the DANGER—KEEP OUT and POSTED—PRIVATE PROPERTY signs might be more effective, they were definitely less customer friendly. "This should keep unwanted guests from climbing to the private living quarters." I hoped. If this failed, there was the option of adding an electric charge to the steel chain. I was growing tired of having so many people wandering around my house in places they didn't belong.

"How's the construction coming? I've driven by a couple of times and noticed several trucks."

"Slowly but surely."

He looked at me over the top of his thick-rimmed black glasses. "Find anything interesting?"

"What do you mean?"

"That's an old house. Once you start opening up the walls, you never know what you'll find."

"The only thing I've found so far," I said with a frown, "is a house in a sad state of disrepair and that somebody has apparently been squatting in my attic." That somebody being Matt Kowalski.

"How interesting." He scooped up a couple of hanging hooks and jiggled them in his open palm. "You can use these to attach the sign to your chain."

"Thanks."

As Mr. Flores rang me up, I said, "I heard about your robbery the other day."

He shrugged and ran my credit card. "It was nothing," he said lightly. "Someone broke in through the back after hours."

"Did they get much?"

"Only some little things. A shovel, a mattock, a couple of buckets, and some nylon rope. Maybe more." That jibed with what Jerry had said. He swept his hand through the air. "In a place like this, it's not always possible to tell what is here and what isn't."

I looked around the cluttered space. "It would be hard to discern if one more nut or bolt went missing."

He laughed at my small joke. "We got off easy."

Rosario snorted. I guess she didn't agree.

The shopkeeper continued. "Nothing compared to what happened to that man in the alley." Rosario moaned loudly but continued sweeping.

I nodded. "My mother told me about that."

He nodded somberly. "Nasty business." Mr. Flores handed me back my credit card. "Nothing like your murder, *ciertamente.*" The bell above the door rang and two middle-aged men entered and headed for the power tools. Rosario scooted after them with her broom.

I threw my purchase on the passenger seat and headed across town, past the town square, past the lake, which looked like a jewel in the clear blue sky, and turned up Airport Road. Maybe Jerry

Kennedy was certain about Dwayne's innocence, but I hadn't made my mind up.

I turned off onto a lonely rural side street with crumbling blacktop and stopped outside a dreary redbrick house on a large hilly lot. It wasn't much to look at. But this had to be where Theodore Allen, Dwayne's uncle, lived. The big Cole's Trucking semitrailer and cab were parked a short distance from the house.

I parked my Kia at the bottom of the driveway. My feet crunched up the gravel drive as I approached. The back doors of the trailer hung open. Nothing but a few empty pallets, a pallet mover, an old broom with half its bristles missing, a crumpled old bottle of bleach, a few tarps, and some rope. A battered and muddy blue pickup rested under a tin-roofed, freestanding carport to the right and behind the house.

What had probably once been a lawn was now a yard of weeds. The nearest neighbors were about six or seven hundred feet away on each side.

A dog barked halfheartedly as I trudged up the brick steps and rang the bell. I rang again. "Hello?" I tapped on the glass storm door.

Peeling burgundy paint curled up around the edges of the front door. It opened a crack and a face peered out. "Yeah?" the man rasped. He smelled of tobacco and beer.

I smiled and met his eyes through the dirty storm door glass. "Mr. Allen?"

His brow furrowed. He had a dark complexion and his square chin was dotted with gray stubble. "Yeah. Who are you?"

"Amy Simms. I was looking for Dwayne. Is he here?"

The old man shook his head.

"His truck's here." I turned my head in the direction of the big vehicle.

"He's taking a nap." A gnarled hand gripped a walnut cane with a metal tip.

I pouted. "Oh, I see." A fat black Labrador pushed his way between Theo Allen's legs. "Would you mind if I come in for a minute? I'd like to talk to you."

He squinted and I thought I detected mistrust in his eyes, though I couldn't imagine what made me appear so suspicious.

"I'm harmless, really."

The door pulled open. "You'd better come in, then."

"Thank you." I was hit by a blast of warm air. A compact woodstove burned in the tiny living room. A small, tattered sofa and two navy chairs draped with quilts filled the stifling space. A row of books, mostly old North Carolina history books, rested on a simple wood shelf above the stove. It seemed a bit of a fire hazard, but who was I to mention it?

I noticed Theo Allen leaned heavily on the cane as he walked to the heater and tossed some pellets in its feeder. "Have a seat."

The big dog had flopped down on the sofa, so I settled for one of the chairs.

"You want something to drink?"

I hesitated. "I wouldn't say no to a cup of tea, I suppose."

"Be right back." He rose rather spryly and disappeared around the corner.

Dwayne's uncle was gone several minutes. I considered getting up and exploring, maybe finding which room Dwayne was dozing in and waking him, but the way that big dog kept looking at me told me I'd better remain seated. I love dogs—I'm not sure if they love me.

Mr. Allen returned with a glass of tea on a tiny saucer for me, then returned to the kitchen for his. "What did you want to talk to Dwayne about?" he asked, settling into his chair and setting his cup on a TV tray to his left.

"I was wondering if there was anything else he might have remembered or might have seen the night Matt was murdered." I looked toward the hall where no doubt the bedrooms were. "Do you think he'll be asleep long?"

A wan smile passed over the old man's face. "You never know. The boy keeps all hours. Heard him come in late last night."

I nodded. "Tell me, did Dwayne and Matt know one another?"

Mr. Allen said nothing for a moment. He turned away and sipped his tea.

As he did, I tried mine. It tasted like dishwater. I settled my cup between my knees. Suddenly, I wasn't thirsty.

"I heard they went to school together." Okay, I was making that part up, but now that I'd thought about it, I'd have to have Mom check into it for me.

"Maybe. I wouldn't know." His fingers wrapped around the handle of the cane. "What's it matter?"

I shrugged. "It doesn't, I suppose." I smiled. "I guess I'm just nosy."

The old man's jaw worked side to side.

I cleared my throat. "I hear you had a pet store in the house I bought from Gertie. Quite a coincidence, isn't it?"

He shrugged.

Dwayne's uncle wasn't much of a conversationalist. "Do you know," I began, "Gertie came by the other day and offered to buy the place back from me. Can you believe it?"

He leaned closer. "You don't say?"

I nodded. "Offered me what I paid for it and then some."

Mr. Allen's lips curled up. "Greedy old biddy. Charged me way too much rent."

"Was Esther Pilaster your tenant too?"

He shook his head. "She moved in after the place was empty."

Lucky him. Unlucky me.

"I'm sorry things didn't work out for you. Do you like pets? Is that why you'd gone into the business?"

"Nah. I mean, I've got a dog." He pointed his cane at the beast, then grabbed a cold pipe from the TV tray and stuffed a wad of tobacco in its bowl. "Drove a truck all my life," he boasted, "until they retired me." He sighed. "A man's got to have something to keep himself busy. No kids. Wife's dead. Tried joining the town council but realized pretty quick that politics wasn't for me."

"I know what you mean. At least you have your nephew, Dwayne, to help you."

"He's a good boy." He looked at my cup. "You want me to warm you up?"

"No, thanks," I replied hastily. One cup of dishwater was plenty. "I see you're a history buff too."

He looked perplexed. I nodded to the bookshelf. "I noticed your choice of reading material."

He frowned. "That was my wife," he said gruffly. "She liked all that stuff."

I set my tea down beside the stove and got up to run my finger along the books. They were all old hardcovers, probably all published before I was born—all related to North Carolina's history. I pulled down a thick volume covered in charcoal cloth, called *North Carolina's Gold Rush* and another titled *The Story of North Carolina, Its People and Places*.

He grunted. "Wife was a history teacher."

"So was my mother." I slid the book back in its place. "I guess I'd better be leaving." I buttoned up my coat. "When Dwayne gets up, would you ask him to give me a call? Or better yet, come by the store if he gets a chance?"

Mr. Allen pushed himself up from his chair with the aid of his cane. The dog raised his head, then let it fall back down to the sofa cushion. I couldn't blame him. I was dog tired too.

I grinned. "So, Mr. Allen, as someone who's been there and done that, do you have any advice for somebody trying to run a new business in Ruby Lake?"

He smiled sardonically as I pushed my hands into my mittens. "Yeah." His tongue darted in and out. "Try another town."

25

I warmed up the van and headed back toward town. The sun was shining and, despite my woes, I couldn't help but feel good. Until the van lurched to the left toward the cliff, that is. Airport Road is treacherous at the best of times, and now my Kia was acting like it was trying to kill me. I pulled the wheel hard to the right as a sedan whizzed by me going the other direction.

The van jumped to the left again, as if determined to plunge over the steep embankment. "No!" I screamed. "What are you trying to do?"

I know it's crazy to try to talk a van out of killing itself, but if you'd been in my position, you might have done the same thing yourself.

The van shook. I was having trouble steering. I spotted a small turnout up ahead. Putting my entire body weight into the effort, I managed to wrestle the wildly swinging steering wheel. The van skidded sideways across the bumpy surface. I screamed some more and didn't stop until the Kia came to a halt mere inches from the cliff's edge.

My breath caught in my throat. I looked down. And down was a long way down.

A hand rapped at the passenger window. I jumped and the van shook. "You okay in there?" A young woman in a navy parka and a ski cap eyed me anxiously.

I gulped and nodded. I moved over to the passenger side and climbed down. I assured the young woman once again that I was okay. "I don't know what happened," I said. Together, we walked around the vehicle. My left rear tire was completely flat. Worse than flat. It was shredded.

I groaned. "That's gonna cost me."

The young brunette patted my back. "Be grateful." I arched my right eyebrow. "It could have cost you your life."

The young brunette—her name was Pam—stayed with me until the tow truck arrived.

"Where to?" the tow operator asked. "Nesmith's gas station?"

"Yes." Zander Nesmith runs the nearest service station, so that made sense. I'd used him before and knew he did good work.

"No, wait." I climbed up into the passenger seat of his tow truck. "Take it to LaChance Motors." They had a service center and could fix me up. And I could do a little snooping.

The tow truck driver drove me to my destination, unhitched my Kia, and I paid him off. I left the vehicle in the capable hands of the service manager, who told me he'd have a mechanic take a look at the van as soon as he could. I'd explained what had happened and he said it would be best to check the vehicle out for any other damage not visible. "That kind of accident," he said, scratching the side of his jaw, "you might have messed up your axle or something. We'll probably need to keep your car overnight. We're sort of backed up today."

Great, I thought as I wandered between rows of used vehicles. More money.

"Can I help you, miss?"

My eyebrows rose with glee. I was in luck. The big man himself was in. I explained about the accident.

"At least you weren't hurt." Robert LaChance flashed bleached white teeth, a sharp contrast to his tanning-booth-darkened skin. "That's what counts. You're going to be needing a rental car, right?" I swear I saw dollar signs flash in his pupils.

LaChance Motor's business operations are run out of a doublewide trailer. A wooden stairway led up to a small porch with a couple of those cheap white outdoor chairs you pick up at the local big box. Robert LaChance deftly threw open the sliding glass door and ushered me inside.

He waved to a redhead occupying a cheap laminate desk near the door. "Any calls?"

"Just Mac. He wants you to call him back soon as you can."

Robert nodded. "Come this way," he said, "Ms. . . . ?"

"Amy Simms."

I followed him into a small, cramped office with a large oak desk. The desktop was cluttered with pa-

pers. "Mac?" I said. "Mac MacDonald, the mayor?"
A bottle of red wine sat beside a small flat-screen
TV on a narrow table behind the desk.

He nodded distractedly, his fingers sifting
through papers as he leaned back in his chair. "I'll
be right back."

Robert LaChance rose and left me alone in his
office. Over my shoulder, I noticed him whisper-
ing in the secretary's ear. Her tight V-neck white
sweater pushed out in all the right directions and a
gold sheath skirt rode up over her knees. Were
they an item too? She was young enough and
pretty enough to be his type. The jerk. I'd have to
introduce him to Derek Harlan. They could phi-
lander together.

My eyes drifted over the papers on Robert
LaChance's desk. Mostly car-related things like in-
voices and warranties, a couple of car-enthusiast
magazines—I'd seen Robert driving around town
in his flashy old red Ferrari, so I knew he was into
cars—and a brochure from one of those quick service food chains.

"Got it," Robert said, falling back into his chair,
waving a yellow folder. "Tommy tells me you're
going to be needing a vehicle for at least a day?"
He raised his brow in question. "Said your tire's
shot and your lug nuts were loose. A couple of the
lug bolts were even bent. That's not good." He
made commiserating sounds, but I was seeing
those dollar signs in his eyes again.

I nodded. Tommy was his service manager.
"Hopefully, that's all I'll need it for."

"Of course." He wet his thumb, selected some
papers, and handed them to me to sign. He picked

up a pen and pointed to two lines for initials and one for a signature, then handed me the pen. "A lot of work being done on your store, huh?"

"Yes, you could say that." Funny, he didn't know my name a minute ago but now he knew about my store.

Robert nodded. "As a fellow business owner," he replied, leaning back in his chair and folding his hands behind his head, "I know what that's like. Seems like I'm always pouring money into this business."

Yeah, and into his flashy clothes, cars, and expensive wine. While Tiffany, his ex and mother of his child, waited tables in a diner.

"Have you ever considered selling the place?" He looked at me eagerly.

"The house?" What kind of a question was that? "No, I mean, I just bought it." And I couldn't imagine who'd want it. Except that Gertie Hammer suddenly did.

The car dealer shrugged. "Still, most businesses fail in their first year, you know."

This guy was definitely no Mr. Sunshine. I thought about Dwayne's uncle, Theodore Allen; he'd only lasted six months. "I'm hoping things pick up in spring and summer."

He snatched up a plump cigar from a humidor at the edge of his desk and rolled it between the palms of his hands. "That's the spirit." His words sounded phony, but that could simply have been the used-car salesman in him coming out.

I pushed back the signed papers. "You must be a fan of Bella Bologna." Bella Bologna was one of

those popular upscale Italian restaurant chains
that cost a million bucks or more to franchise.

"Huh?" Robert leaned forward.

"I couldn't help noticing the brochure."

"Oh, that." His eyes darted around the desk.
When he spotted the glossy brochure, he tapped it
with his fingers, then slid it under a pile of paper-
work. "A buddy of mine is trying to get me to in-
vest in a place over in Raleigh."

"Are you going to?" It was none of my business,
but I was curious. Besides, if he could afford to in-
vest in a friend's business, he could afford to give
Tiffany and their child more support.

Robert LaChance evaded my question as elegantly as any toreador could hope to slip past an
angry bull's horns. "I've got a sweet little Corolla
for you. Only forty-nine ninety-nine a day."

To paraphrase the character Elphaba Thropp
from *Wicked*, I was tired of playing by the rules of
somebody else's game. I parked behind Ruby Lake
Town Library and ran inside. John Moytoy sat at
the reference desk assisting a young woman and
child with selecting some early readers. He smiled
and winked my way to let me know he'd be with
me as soon as he could.

I worked my way over to the history section. I
wanted to learn more about Ruby Lake; specifi-
cally, more about the house at 3225 Lake Shore
Drive.

My house.

Why was Matt Kowalski found dead there? Why

had Gertie Hammer sold me the place? Well, I knew the answer to that. It was a piece of junk. A death trap. No pun intended, Matt Kowalski. Why was it attracting squirrels and squatters and midnight ghosts?

"Hey, Amy. What's with the history book?" John looked at the book in my hand. "I'd have expected to find you in the nature section." The librarian dressed casually, yet impeccably, in tan pants and a canary-yellow shirt buttoned up to the collar. The slenderest of silver chains wrapped loosely around his neck. He said it was a good luck charm.

"Hi, John." John Moytoy is a Native American, Cherokee to be precise. He's cherubic in body and disposition. He's also an old classmate of mine. "Moving into a historic old house, I thought I'd try to learn more about it." I closed the book, returned it to the shelf, and plucked another. "Are you aware of anything interesting or unusual about the old place?"

John thought for a minute, rubbing his thumbs together like he always did when considering a problem. "Sorry," he said, giving his head a shake. A lock of jet-black hair spilled over his right eye and he pushed it back into place. "Nothing comes to mind."

"Too bad." I patted his arm, then pulled off my hat. He smelled of library books and Old Spice, making me feel all warm and cozy. John Moytoy is comfortable with himself and with others. He's as laid-back as they come and sharper than most.

He perused the shelves, selected a couple of heavy volumes, and led me over to one of the study alcoves where we sat. "Is there something in particular you're looking for, Amy?" he asked, keeping his voice low.

I picked up a book on the history of North Carolina and thumbed the pages. The tome included several sections containing old black-and-white photos of buildings and cabins from earlier days.

"Do you know anything at all about the history of the house? Like who owned it before you?" He peered at me over his glasses. "Who built it?"

"Gertie Hammer owned it before me," I said, and I couldn't help making a sour face as I said it. "I'm not sure who owned it before that." I thought a moment. "I do remember hearing that the place was nearly a hundred and fifty years old." Mom said she'd remembered hearing that the house had been built at the end of the Civil War.

John started rubbing his fingers together again. "You know . . ." He looked off into the distance. His eyes were the color of a brown-headed nuthatch's crown.

"Yes?"

"There might be something on the old place in the archives. Perhaps some stories in the old *Ruby Lake Weekender,* or even one of the larger papers making mention of when the house was constructed, who the architect was—that sort of thing." He blinked at me.

"That would be perfect," I replied. "Where do we begin?"

John smiled at me and rested his hand on my shoulder. "*We* don't begin." He pointed at me. "You do." He checked his watch. "I have work to do." He rose from the chair at the study carrel and waved for me to follow him.

John pulled a key from his key ring and unlocked a warped oak door leading to a back room.
He flicked on a light switch. Metal shelving ran up
and down the long, narrow, and windowless room.
Row after row of boxes covered each shelf.

"What is this place?" I whispered.

"Archive room." Dust rose from the floor as he
worked his way toward the back. "Goes all the way
back to eighteen-something." He tapped a sagging
old box with his open hand. "I'd suggest you start
here."

I pulled a face and coughed as dust hit me in
the nose, mouth, and eyes. "Don't you have all this
on computer, or microfilm, or microfiche," I said
hopefully, "or something?"

John smiled. "No, but if you're volunteering to
perform the task for us?" He arched a playful brow.
"The library is always looking for volunteers."

I scowled and pulled down the box he'd
pointed me to. "I'm afraid my plate is pretty full
these days, John. Otherwise, I'd be delighted."

John laughed, filling the small space with joy.
"Yeah, I'll bet you would!"

He left me to my task and I lugged the first box
over to a long walnut table against the far wall.
There was no chair, so I sat on the tabletop and
gingerly started removing the box's contents, one
by one.

I yawned. And coughed up more hundred-year-
old dust.

It was going to be a long afternoon.

John came in later with coffee. "How's it going?"
He handed me an old Kiwanis mug. "I brought you
this."

"You're a life saver," I replied, drinking greedily.

"So," he said, jumping up beside me on the table. It rocked back and forth for a moment but held.

"I'm not sure." I hadn't found out who'd built the house, but after searching several boxes—and there were only a million or two more to go—I had found a few stories that mentioned my house. "What do you think of this?" I held up a copy of the *Weekender* from 1892.

"Ghosts?" A look of bemusement crossed my friend's face.

"Hey!" I gave him a friendly shove. "I'm not saying I believe, I'm just asking what you think."

I went to shove him again, but he held up his mug of coffee. "Uh-uh," he said, "don't want to spill any coffee on library property."

I drank while he read. The article told the story of a Heather Sampson who had run a boarding house out of my current home. That is, until she was murdered in her bedroom, stabbed multiple times. She'd only been in her early forties and her killer had never been caught. Her ghost was said to haunt the old place ever since. I found several other references to Heather's ghosts in further editions of the paper strung out over the years.

"The stories sort of dried up in the twenties," I told John.

John grunted. "After a while, a lot of these stories sort of fade away. What are you trying to say, Amy?" He handed back the paper. "You think Heather Sampson has returned?" He wiggled his fingers in the air. "Woooo-wooo! Haunting your place?" He raised an eyebrow playfully. "Do you think she's resorted to murder herself?"

I shook my head and rolled my eyes. "Of course not." At least not that I'd ever admit. I certainly hoped she hadn't been stabbed in what was now my bedroom. "But something strange is going on in that house." I slapped the paper against the table. "And I want to get to the bottom of it."

"Easy with that," John said, gently taking the paper from my fist before I did any damage. "Library property, remember?" John folded his hands. "When you say strange"—he hesitated— "you mean the murder?"

I blew out a breath. "I mean the murder and all the other weird things that have been going on in that house ever since I bought the place, including the fact that Gertie suddenly wants to buy it back for more money than I even paid her."

John's brow shot up. "Strange doings, indeed."

"You don't know the half of it." And he didn't, so I filled him in on all the craziness, from the noises, to the murder, to the squatters, to the screams, and to the mysterious white figure in the night.

John took it all in with the patience of a saint. Like I said, the man is cherub material. When he saw that I was finished venting, he placed the dry, yellowed newspaper back in the carton and returned the carton to the shelf. "Follow me."

"Where are we going?"

"Follow me," John repeated in lilting tones. He guided me back to the freestanding shoulder-high shelf of books near the checkout counter. This was where all the recent additions to the collection were kept. His fingers played over his lips as his eyes scanned the shelves. "Here it is." He lifted a trade paperback from the bottom shelf.

"What's this supposed to be?" If I sounded dubious, it's because I was.

John smiled. "If you're into ghosts and things that go bump in the night—"

I read the title aloud: "*Crazy Carolina: Stories of the Misfits, Misadventures, and Mysteries of the Tar Heel State.* What am I supposed to do with this?"

"Read it," replied John. "At the very least you'll have some fun." He patted my back. "I think you could use it. I've been wanting to read it myself ever since we got it in. But it's been so popular, we can hardly keep it on the shelf. I've been telling Luann we may need to order more than just the two copies." Luann Wiggins is the head librarian. "The author's local, from over in Winston-Salem." John led me to the front desk and checked me out. "Maybe it will give you some ideas."

"Ideas I don't need," I quipped. "I've got plenty of ideas." He walked me to the door and held it open for me. "What I need are answers. Tell me, John, can you think of any reason Gertie would want to buy my house?"

"Senile?"

We both laughed. "Sure, there's that. But why would she be talking to Robert LaChance?"

"The car guy?" John looked perplexed. "Not a clue."

"Me either." I hesitated. "What about Bella Bologna?"

His right eyebrow arched. "I hear the orecchiette with chicken is quite good."

"Ha-ha. No, I mean how much do you think it costs to open a franchise?"

John looked bemused. "More than you or I have

got, that's for sure." When he saw I was expecting a real answer, he gave it some thought, then said, "A million bucks? Maybe more. Why?"

I told him how Robert LaChance was considering investing in one down in Raleigh.

John whistled. "That's a lot of money. I didn't know his pockets were that deep."

I added how I had a hunch the mayor might be an investor too.

John laughed. "Never happen. You know how little the town pays Mac?" I didn't. "Not enough to live on. That's why he keeps the real estate gig."

"I suppose . . ."

"Look, Amy, as your friend, you want my advice?" His arm draped over my shoulder.

The corners of my mouth turned down and I looked at him sideways. "Maybe."

"Stop looking for conspiracies. It's Birds and Bees you ought to be worried about."

I waved goodbye to John and sighed as I climbed into the rental car. John didn't understand. It was Birds & Bees that I was worried the most about.

26

Cash Calderon stuffed his hammer in the leather tool belt around his reasonably trim waist. He wore loose dungarees and a red-and-black checked flannel shirt. He and his men were wrapping up work for the day.

I took a look around the store. The ceiling had been patched and painted. There were no telltale signs of water damage. They'd made a lot of progress. "Looks great."

"Are you sure?"

"Yes." I patted his arm. "You've done an excellent job."

"I know it's taking a bit longer than I said it would." There was an apologetic tone to Mr. Calderon's voice. "But with this weather—"

"Really," I said, cutting him off, "I'm very happy." I patted his arm once again. "Why do you ask?"

"Well"—he shuffled his boots along the floor—

"I wanted to be sure you're satisfied with the quality of the work."

"Very. I couldn't have done better myself," I teased.

"I'm glad to hear it. I was concerned what with that other contractor sniffing around." He looked sheepish. "I thought maybe you were unhappy with the work and looking to replace me."

"No!" I gasped. "Wait. What other contractor?"

Cash described a man who'd been by less than an hour ago, come in, taken a look around, and then left again. "When I asked him if I could help him in any way, he said he was asked to come by."

"Well, I certainly didn't ask him to come by," I said, puzzled. I crossed my arms over my chest. "How do you know he was a contractor?"

Cash touched the side of his nose. "I've got a nose for them. I can sniff them out," he said slyly. "Besides, I should know. I'm one myself."

I rubbed my chin thoughtfully. "I wonder who the devil he is."

"I don't know," Cash said. "He's not from around here, that's for sure. I'd know him if he was."

One of Cash's men joined the conversation, a young kid with bouncy black bangs and a rail-thin frame. "Whoever he is, I saw him cross the street." The young man pointed with the screwdriver in his hand.

"The diner?"

"Yep."

I shrugged. "That's it, then. He was probably meeting someone at the diner and wandered into

Birds and Bees. Maybe he's a potential customer."
A girl could hope.

I locked up behind the men and headed over to
Ruby's, figuring I might as well see this guy for myself. There was a good-sized dinner crowd and
Moire Leora waved to me from behind the register. "Sit anywhere you like!"

I nodded and searched the dining room. Mayor
Mac MacDonald, Robert LaChance, and a third
man, who looked vaguely familiar, occupied the
far corner booth. A fourth man, whom I knew
slightly better, rose from the table and teetered my
way.

I intercepted him in the alcove leading to the
restrooms. "Mr. Withers," I said. "Remember me,
Amy Simms, from Birds and Bees?" I tilted my
head toward the shop. He wore the same well-
worn tan wool suit he'd had on when I first met
him.

"Oh, of course." He smiled and his moustache
twitched. "I remember you." He rubbed the side
of his neck, which was bandaged, reminding me of
a white-banded killdeer.

"Are you all right? I heard what happened. A
mugging, how terrible!" My fingers flew to my
chin. "I thought you were supposed to be on bed
rest?"

Mr. Withers tossed his hand. "Bed rest! I don't
know what the doctor was on about. A man goes
stir-crazy lying around in bed all day. Thought I'd
come out and grab some grub that didn't come
out of the freezer."

"Good for you. I see you were having dinner
with the mayor and Robert LaChance."

He nodded. "Yeah, bumped into the guys and they asked me to join them." He smiled wistfully. "Talked about the old days, like when your place used to be a bank and a man could walk around this town without getting himself attacked." He looked at me somberly. "Or killed." He smiled once more. "Probably bored them to death, listening to an old man ramble on."

"Nonsense. I think you're adorable."

He blushed and scratched his hair. "In fact, I told them about the time that armored car got robbed right outside the bank. Your shop, Birds and Bees, used to be a bank at one time, you know."

I nodded absently. I knew. He'd told me so more than once, including not half a minute earlier.

"Happened a long, long time ago." He chuckled, then rambled on. "The only reason I remember at all is because I ran into that feller at your store the other day and it got me to thinking, and—"

I couldn't take my eyes off the action at the corner table. The man with Mac and Robert had picked up his coat and laid it across his lap. "I'm sorry," I interrupted. I leaned closer, rested my hand on Mr. Withers's and whispered in his ear. "But who's that other man with them?"

My eyes darted to the broad-shouldered stranger across from Mac and Robert. Definitely the guy I'd remembered from the store. He had a large, lumpy nose I'd never forget—in fact, it looked more like the prow of a ship than a nose.

Mr. Withers glanced back. "Some buddy of theirs." He scratched his stubbly chin. "From Raleigh, I think." He smiled. "Got a free meal out of them, so I can't complain!"

As Mr. Withers said goodbye and headed off, I approached the men's table, but all three had disappeared. A busboy was clearing their plates and glasses.

I plunked down on the still warm vinyl bench seat and sighed. I suddenly realized that the man with Mac MacDonald and Robert LaChance was the same burly, pasty-faced man I'd noticed come into Birds & Bees on opening day. I remembered because I'd seen him come in, but I had not seen him depart. And that was around the time that the Nickersons had come in . . .

What did it all mean?

"Mind if I join you?"

I looked up slowly. "Mr. Harlan." I pulled myself together, straightened my sagging shoulders.

He smiled. "It's Derek, remember? Mind if I join you?"

I slid to the far back of the booth. "Oh, I remember, all right."

He slipped off a heavy black leather jacket and laid it on the bench across from us as he sat next to me. Beneath, he wore a black turtleneck sweater and a pair of jeans. I guess he wasn't in lawyer mode. "So, I had a word with your Chief Kennedy today."

"Oh?" I grabbed a plastic menu and looked it over. I guessed wrong. He was in lawyer mode. "So? Any news?"

Derek shook his head. Our waitress bustled over and we ordered drinks. "Nothing concrete. There's a two-hour window, at least, during which Mr.

Kowalski was likely murdered. But no evidence linking anyone to that crime." His eyes twinkled. "Except for you, of course."

I frowned and sipped my tea. "Of course."

When the waitress returned to take our orders, I chose the baked mac and cheese with a panko and parmesan crust. Comfort food. And comfort was just what I needed. Derek Harlan ordered the fish and chips. We made small talk until our dinners arrived.

"What about you?" he said, pushing the chips my way. "Find out anything?" I couldn't resist grabbing a few despite my best intentions. I was looking for comfort food, remember? The lawyer sprinkled some pepper over his cod. Who does that? "I hear you've been nosing around?"

I frowned once again. I seemed to do that a lot around this guy. "Who told you that?" I stuffed three fries in my mouth and chewed vigorously.

"Chief Kennedy, for one." He broke off some fillet, aimed his fork at me. "He seems quite annoyed with you."

"Yeah, well, I'm not exactly thrilled with him these days." I snatched another handful of the jerk's potatoes and pushed them in my mouth. "I mean, why hasn't he solved this case yet? It's not like he's got a million other murder cases to work on."

Derek shrugged and reached for his fries, probably worried that I was going to gobble them all up before he'd gotten any. "It's a process of elimination and a search for clues," he pontificated. "Give him time. I'm sure he'll uncover the truth."

"I'm not sure how much more time I've got."

"What do you mean?"

"It means I think somebody is trying to kill me."
I huffed out a breath. "Or at least scare me." And
they were doing a pretty good job of it.

Derek nodded and finished his plate. "I heard
about the midnight intruder." A busboy quickly
took the empty dish away. "Dessert?"

I really shouldn't. I still hadn't taken that walk
around the lake I'd promised myself. "I'll have the
apple turnover." I could see them up at the
counter, under the glass lid, beckoning, practically
calling my name. Derek ordered the same.

Okay, I'm weak. Who isn't?

"It's not only that," I said. "I think somebody's
trying to kill me next."

Derek's brow shot up. I'd noticed that his right
arm had settled on the top of the bench seat and
had been working its way slowly yet inevitably
closer to me. I slid out of reach as the waitress
brought dessert.

I explained about my near demise over the side
of Airport Road. Derek toyed with his dessert fork
and eyed me somberly. "That does sound serious.
Have you told the police?"

I shook my head.

"Well, you should. And make sure they look
over your vehicle."

I promised I would. "I'm not sure what good it
will do though."

Derek looked at his gold watch. "I'd better be
going."

Sure, he had a wife and child to go home to.

He rose and placed a couple of twenties on the
table. "Dinner's on me." The lawyer grabbed his

jacket and winked at me. "Looks like we finally got a chance to have dinner together. We should do this again sometime."

"Speaking of dinner," I said, ignoring his lecherous intent, "I saw you the other night at the Lake House with your wife and daughter."

"Yes," he answered, without hesitation. "And I saw you too. With that Aaron Maddley fellow. How was your date?"

"It wasn't a date," I replied automatically.

"Oh?" His right eyebrow formed a question mark.

I backpedaled quickly. "I mean, it was a date. But—" I was blushing, more from anger at having nearly been caught in a white lie than from embarrassment.

"But what?" He zipped his jacket up to his neck. He looked like a cat toying with a mouse. The big jerk.

I'd boxed myself into a corner. Before I could come up with something clever to say or even a halfway clever lie, the lawyer's face turned serious and he said, "You know that Chief Kennedy considers him a suspect in the murder of Mr. Kowalski?"

I nodded. "But he let him go." How amusing. Was Derek actually trying to warn me about Aaron? He should have been warning me about himself instead.

Derek nodded. "It doesn't make him any less a suspect. I hear there's some talk that he and his sister may have had reason to want the victim dead. So," he said, stopping to check a text that had just come in on his cell phone—probably his wife wondering why he was late— "even if the blood on those clothes does turn out to be something as mundane as your boyfriend claims, it doesn't prove he's innocent."

"You know about that?"

He nodded. "Chief Kennedy told me about what happened. I am your lawyer, remember?"

Not much longer, I hoped.

"I'll bet your boyfriend was pretty mad at you after that." The lawyer chuckled. "Can't say I blame him."

"What did Aaron say was the reason for the blood on those clothes in the trunk?"

"He says it was from birthing a foal. The chief's waiting for the tests to come back."

I sighed. That matched what Jerry had told me. That meant he was innocent. No, Kim had seen his truck near Birds & Bees around the time of the murder. He and his sister didn't have plenty of reasons to want him dead, but they had one. And it was a doozy.

Aaron had been late meeting me at the farm. And his sister had no alibi, just said she was home alone. That didn't prove her innocence either. They still had motive and opportunity.

Or, I thought suddenly, the back of my neck bristling . . . what if Grace Maddley hadn't miscarried? What if she had given birth to that child? What if that child had grown up to learn the truth about his or her father?

No. I'd gone down a dead end. I smothered a sigh. Even if the child had survived, he or she would be in elementary school.

I felt a throbbing in my temples.

"You okay?"

I nodded. No point telling him my whacko theories and having him scoff.

Derek turned to the waitress who'd returned with his change. "Keep it." She nodded and left. "Even if he has an alibi of some sort, it doesn't mean he and his sister—" He snapped his fingers several times in quick succession. "Grace, I think?" I nodded. "Weren't in it together."

I glared at him. Why couldn't Derek Harlan be the murderer? I played with various scenarios in my mind but, sadly, none added up. Too bad, it would have made for a neat and happy ending. I could still kick myself for having had any romantic thoughts about this guy for even one second.

He smiled suddenly. "Not that I'm saying they're guilty." He leaned over the table and patted my hand. "I'm just saying, be careful." He turned to leave, then looked over his shoulder. "And have the police check out your van."

Once again, I promised I would. Though by now, the Kia could have been repaired and there'd be nothing left to look at. "Give my regards to your wife!" Half the people in the diner were looking at me now, but I couldn't resist.

"Amy?"

"What?"

"Amy," the lawyer repeated.

I was baffled and it must have showed. Out of the corner of my eye, I noticed my mother getting out of Aunt Betty's husband's car across the street.

"That's her name," Derek said. "Amy."

My mouth fell open. Amy was his wife's name

too? Oh brother. What, so the guy had a thing for Amys?

I waited until I'd seen Derek pull out of the lot before leaving.

"Mom," I said, giving her a squeeze. "What are you doing back?" I held her at arm's length. "I thought we agreed you'd be staying at Aunt Betty's for the week?"

Mom hung up her coat on the rack I'd set up near the front of the store and did a turn around the place. "I heard that the roof had been repaired. I thought I'd come home. You don't mind, do you?"

"No, of course not!" I said quickly. "I only want you to be comfortable." The truth was that I was glad to see her. I'd had a text message earlier from Kim, announcing that she and Randy had patched things up. She'd be spending the evening with him and then returning to her own place. That meant I'd been facing having to spend a night alone in the house. Well, alone with Esther the Pester, and that would have been little consolation.

She yawned. "Well, I'll be a lot more comfortable in my own bed. And if you don't mind, that's just where I'm going." I followed her up the stairs. "You know, Amy, I love my sister dearly, but she can be quite exhausting."

I felt the same way. Aunt Betty has her quirks and then some. Then again, the seven housecats, named after the seven dwarves, of course; a springer spaniel; and two house box turtles she kept as her personal menagerie, didn't make living with her any easier. Her third husband was turning out to be a real saint.

I got Mom to bed. I'd been meaning to install the chain across the bottom of the back stairs but was too tired to deal with it. Besides, I didn't own any tools. I'd ask Mr. Calderon to take care of it for me tomorrow.

27

"Well?" I tapped my foot impatiently against the asphalt. The clouds were back and it was raining lightly. We stood on the side lot at LaChance Motors. I'd asked Jerry to look at my van like Derek suggested. "You see?" I pointed at the rear end. I was in luck; the mechanics hadn't had a chance to work on my van yet. "I think somebody's trying to kill me."

The chief squatted and peered at my wheel. "This old thing? Driving this"—he thumped the side of the van with his open hand—"I'd say you might be contemplating suicide." He shook his head. "But why would somebody else be trying to kill you? And when would they have had the chance?"

"That valve doohickey has been cut." I kicked it with my toe.

He frowned and stood back up. "Looks split to me. Your valve stem could have been leaking for a while. It's ancient." He spat and glanced at the mechanic who stood silently by, watching the show, listening to the exchange. "When's the last time you *checked* the air in your tires?"

"Well . . ."

Jerry scowled. "When's the last time you put air *in* your tires?" He folded his arms over his chest. "Or had the brakes checked or tightened the lug nuts?"

"Well . . ."

"Hell, Amy, when's the last time you washed this thing?!" He waved his arms.

I got in the Corolla and sped off. If Jerry Kennedy wanted to give me a speeding ticket, so be it. I was in no mood to stick around. A woman can only take so much.

Besides, I had to open Birds & Bees in ten minutes. If I hurried, I just might make it. As I pulled onto the main road, I turned my head to look for oncoming traffic. A beige Delta 88 sat at an angle outside the office trailer. Was that Gertie Hammer's big old car? If so, what was she doing here? Was she finally going to trade in the old rust bucket?

As much as I wanted to know, I had no time to spare if I was going to open on time. I swerved around the corner of Elm Street where it intersects Lake Shore Drive. The Ruby Lake Motor Lodge was on my left. I chewed my lip for a moment, glanced at the time on the dashboard clock, and turned down the narrow alley behind the lodge, which led to the cabins.

So I'd open the store a few minutes late. It wasn't like I had customers beating down the doors to get in. I pulled the rental car between two of the small log cabins and cut the engine. I went straight to the Nickerson's cabin and knocked.

Sally Nickerson answered, all red eyed and puffy faced. "What do you want?" she said rather sullenly.

"I was hoping to have a word with you and your husband." I peered into the dark cabin. Clothes and toys were scattered everywhere. The youngest, dressed in a diaper and a white T-shirt, was crying in a narrow yellow playpen on the floor between the two double beds. The older child lay stretched out on one bed on her stomach, watching cartoons with the sound turned down low. Empty food containers and dirty glasses were lying around, cluttering the dresser and bathroom counter. Had they been avoiding housekeeping?

"This is not a good time. Besides," Sally said after some hesitation, "he isn't here."

"Oh?" I looked over her shoulder for signs of Ted Nickerson. Maybe he was hiding in the bathroom. The tiny cabin smelled of baby powder and stale pizza.

"No. He's gone out. Rock hunting." She started to close the door once more.

I held out my hand to stop it. "In the rain?" I looked pointedly at a pile of hiking items on the floor in front of the nightstand. These included a coil of rope, a shovel, a small ax, and a plastic bucket. "Without his gear?" Several history books lay stacked on their sides, pushed up against the lamp on the night table.

The toddler cried and she yelled for him to be quiet. When he wouldn't stop, she snapped at her daughter to give him his bottle. Sally Nickerson returned her attention to me. "Look, if you must know," she whispered harshly, "Ted's left me." She sniffled. "He-he didn't come home last night. Now, please leave!"

"I'm so sorry," I said, my hand flying to my mouth. "I had no idea."

"Well, you do now," she said, reasserting herself. "So get lost!" She slammed the door in my face and this time there was no stopping it. Not if I wanted to keep all my fingers intact.

From the other side of the door, I heard a cacophony of her yelling at the crying toddler, the daughter wailing now too, and SpongeBob singing something in his high-pitched warble about catching jellyfish with his butterfly net. Ah, the sounds of domestic life.

I remained on the cabin porch a moment, pondering my next move. Catching sight of a housekeeper pushing a cart up to the cabin next door, I raced over. "Excuse me," I began. I pointed. "Do you know the people staying in that cabin?"

She eyed me warily.

"The Nickersons?"

The housekeeper swiped her arm across the side of her face. "What about them?" She looked frazzled and smelled of cigarette smoke.

"Have you seen the husband, Ted Nickerson, around this morning?" Maybe he hadn't left his wife at all. Maybe it was just her way of trying to keep me from talking to them. Then again, why had Sally been crying? And she definitely had been. Those weren't fake tears, and she'd started long before I'd arrived. Still, maybe they'd had a spat and Ted had checked into another room at the inn. That would have been the simplest, most convenient thing to do.

The housekeeper shrugged and grabbed an upright vacuum from the end of the cart. "I've got rooms to clean and I haven't got all day to do it."

I went to the lobby and checked with my good friend Dick Feller, the front desk manager. "Hi. Remember me? Amy Simms from Birds and Bees?"

He frowned. I guess that meant he did. "Can I assist you?"

"I'm looking for Ted Nickerson." I batted my eyelashes. "Can you tell me what room he's staying in?"

"Sorry," he said, "I'm afraid I can't give out that information." Lord, the man was annoying. Consistent, but annoying.

I drove back to Birds & Bees. I wasn't more than twenty minutes late and two customers stood waiting at the door. The wind was picking up again and their coats flapped. They were clearly tourists, judging by the colorful matching *See Ruby Lake Naked* T-shirts underneath. Ruby Lake Naked is a local tour operation.

"Sorry," I said, twisting the key in the lock. The air was coming in cold off the lake. I couldn't wait for the weather to warm. In the middle of summer, the relatively cooler breeze swooping across from the lake would provide welcome relief. Right now, it was a pain. A cold pain.

While the tourists shopped, I set up the register and began straightening things around the sales floor. The contractor's crew had had to move some things around in order to finish their work on the ceiling and wall along the side of the store. I pushed two shelves back into place and returned the rockers to the coffee nook. My two customers were at the register and waved for me to check them out. That's when I noticed the missing bee suit. I didn't have time to give it much thought. One of the workers may have moved it for some reason. I'd find it later.

Gertie Hammer flew through the door like a barn swallow in pursuit of a moth. She unzipped her parka and stood tapping her feet impatiently while I rang up my customers. What was all the foot tapping about? Was she planning to audition for the role Ann Miller made famous, in a community production of *Sugar Babies*? Shave her head and she might pass for Mickey Rooney—but Ann Miller? Never. She's too short.

I have to admit, I took my time, knowing that she was stewing the way she was. I caught a glimpse of her Delta 88 parked illegally at the curb and hoped Chief Kennedy or one of his officers would cruise by and write her up.

No such luck. Sure, swerve to avoid one crazed squirrel and the cops practically jump out from behind the bushes to give you a ticket. Park illegally in front of a fire hydrant and there's not a cop in sight.

"It's about time," she cackled.

"Can I help you, Gertie?" Maybe I should suggest she might like to take up beekeeping? No, she'd probably train the hive to attack anybody who approached within fifty yards of her house. I had too much compassion for mail carriers and newspaper deliverers to inflict that kind of pain on them.

I shot a look over her shoulder. That was definitely the car I'd spotted at LaChance Motors. I didn't know what it meant. If anything.

She lifted her purse onto the counter and threw down a check, and it was huge. "That's my final offer." She placed her index finger on the check and turned it my way.

My eyes widened and I think I started to drool.

"It's good," she barked. "It's a cashier's check."

"I'm sure it is." My pulse had quickened. I took a deep breath. "That's a lot of zeroes." Love it or list it, love it or list it . . . like a mantra, the words played through my mind. What can I say? I'm addicted to that show on TV where couples have to make up their minds whether they want to keep the house they've renovated or move to another.

"Are you going to take it or not?" She twisted up her lower lip.

I held my breath for a moment. I couldn't give up. I'd put too much work into making a go of Birds & Bees. "Or not." I pushed the check toward Gertie.

"What?!" Her voice rose and cracked with indignity. "Are you crazy?"

"Maybe." I shrugged. "I guess we'll find out."

Her hand hovered over the cashier's check. A woman could fulfill a lot of dreams with that check. "Last chance . . ."

"Goodbye, Gertie."

She snarled, crumpled the check up in her hand, and stuffed it back in her huge purse. "You'll be sorry!" she shouted and stormed out.

Mom came down with a fresh batch of chocolate brownies for the customers and helped out for a little while. I told her about Gertie's little visit. And very large check.

Mom whistled. "Are you sure that's the right decision, Amy? You could really start a new life with money like that."

"I have started a new life, Mom." I spread my arms. "And it's here. With you." She smiled and I kissed her cheek.

Mom worried her hands. "I had a call from Ben Harlan. He said he'd be back in town today."

"Can we not talk about the Harlans, Mom?"

She gave me a funny look. "Why ever not?"

I didn't want to share my suspicions with her—no point giving her even more worries—so I merely said, "I'd like to stick to thinking happy thoughts today."

Mom agreed. "I'm going to walk down to the market. We're out of eggs." She stopped, one arm in her knee-length coat. "Where's Mr. Calderon?"

I explained that he'd had an emergency and he and the crew were on another job. "He expects to be in this afternoon though." I raised a finger. "Grab some chicken. I'll make my enchiladas tonight."

At noon, Randy Vincent dropped Kim off for work. "I'm glad to see you two worked things out," I remarked as she hung her coat and settled in.

Kim nodded appreciatively at Cash Calderon's handiwork. "Looking good." I agreed, though there was still a slight whiff of paint in the air.

I cornered Kim in the alcove. "So, do you want to tell me about it?"

Kim smiled and added some sugar and cream to her coffee. "There's not much to tell." She tossed her head. "We kissed and made up." She blew across her mug and batted her lashes. "He's still pretty mad at you though."

"Me?" My right hand flew to my heart. "What did I do?"

Kim pulled a face.

"Wait." I held my hand up like a stop sign. "Did you pin your breaking up with him on me? Because of what you quote-unquote thought my eyes were telling you?"

Kim nodded. "So you can see why he's upset."

"He's upset? I'm upset!"

Kim scanned the counter. "No cookies?" I shook my head. She scrounged in the cupboards. "No treats?" When I said no again—apparently, the brownies had been a big hit—she plopped herself down in one of the rockers, somehow without managing to spill a drop of coffee. Neat trick. I'd have been wearing most of mine if I'd tried the same stunt.

Kim patted the empty chair beside her. "Did Jerry ever catch the guy"—she jiggled her eyebrows—"or spook who was wandering around upstairs?"

"No." I settled into the chair and started rocking. "But let me tell you what else has been going on." I filled Kim in on the possible attempt to sabotage my van.

"Huh." Kim rested her empty mug on her knee.

"Huh, what?"

I saw Derek bending over looking at your tire the other day."

"You did?" I leaned forward. "Why didn't you say something?"

Kim shrugged. "Because I didn't think anything. He said he saw something shiny. Thought it was a nail, but when he took a closer look it was only a pebble."

Was he doing something to sabotage my van? Was this the missing piece? Was I finally going to be able to blame Derek Harlan for Matt Kowalski's murder? My fingers drummed against my thigh.

"What?" said Kim, shooting a look at my hand.

It all made sense now. Well, sort of . . . "All we've got to do is figure out his motive."

Kim narrowed her eyes. "Whose motive?"

I jumped up. "Derek Harlan's, of course!"

28

I was alone in bed watching a *Love It or List It* marathon. I couldn't help wondering if I had been wrong to refuse Gertie Hammer's offer. I could buy another house, a bigger house. A house without foundation, roof, and other structural problems. A house without ghosts. More importantly, a house without the stigma of murder.

I flicked off the TV and set the remote on the nightstand. My stomach roiled. The enchiladas I'd prepared for dinner weren't sitting well. I think I'd overdone the peppers. I'd also overeaten. What can I say? It's hard to resist eating handfuls of nachos when you've got fresh salsa to go with them. Mom had brought home a pint of the stuff, complete with artichoke hearts, my favorite.

I punched my pillow, looked at the two books lying there, *Birds of Western Carolina* and the book John Moytoy had given me on North Carolina's quirky history. I really should be reading up on birds, but somehow the tufted titmouse just wasn't doing it for me tonight. I dozed off, then awoke with my nose in the book. I yawned and rubbed my eyes.

I lay still and listened to the wind howling outside. I could hear the rain pelting the roof too. A doozy of a storm was raging outside. Did that explain the noises that had wakened me?

Maybe John was right, maybe I needed to lighten up, and reading about some of North Carolina's misfits and their misadventures and misdeeds just might do the trick.

I unclipped my reading light from the bird book and hooked it to the back cover of the history book. The preface was well written, lighthearted, and not pedantic at all. I skimmed through the table of contents and flipped to a tale about Blackbeard's ghost. Apparently the pirate had been run to ground by the British navy off Ocracoke Island on the North Carolina coast. They'd cut off his head, hung it on the bowsprit, and tossed his body to the sharks. Sailors to this day say Blackbeard's spirit body circles just below the surface of the water, forever searching for his head . . .

I chuckled. I didn't believe in ghosts. But I didn't believe in reading spooky tales in bed, alone on a decidedly dark and stormy night. I mean, why tempt nature, let alone the supernatural? The TV weather report had predicted an ugly storm and it had been right. I was letting it get to me.

I stopped the tale halfway and thumbed through the table of contents once more. Thunder crashed overhead, shaking the wood-framed house. The banging had stopped—probably a branch from one of the overhanging trees that had fallen on the roof and then to the ground. It was a relief to know that Cash had finished repairs on the roof. I'd have no more water damage to worry about and he'd promised he'd plug any holes that critters might be finding their way in through.

I was settling into an interesting Indian legend about some giant serpent god at the bottom of a gap in the Blue Ridge Mountains when an inordinately loud boom of thunder rattled the windows, followed quickly by a flash of harsh white lightning. The book dropped from my hands to the floor, but with the little book light attached I had no trouble retrieving it in the dark.

I grabbed the book by the back cover. It fell open on my lap to the index in the back. I was about to try to find my spot when my eyes fell on the name Ruby Lake. "How about that," I muttered. "We made the book." John hadn't mentioned that. I wondered if he was aware of it. There were two notations for Ruby Lake.

I turned the pages to the first. It was the tale about the original owner of my house, Heather Sampson. Interesting. She was the very woman I'd been reading about earlier. I read quickly but didn't learn much new. The author had probably gleaned most of his information from the *Ruby Lake Weekender* newspaper archives.

I shivered. The former proprietress, according to the account, had been stabbed in the chest twenty-two times! Who counts these things? How do they count these things? It also mentioned she'd been stabbed to death in her upstairs bedroom. Was that bedroom now my bedroom . . . ?

I felt a sympathetic tingle in my chest and

thought I heard a light scratching or scraping sound coming from somewhere—behind the wall maybe, or outside. I paused a moment and listened. I heard nothing but the pounding of the rain against the house and against the windows. I chalked it up to an overactive imagination and lack of sleep.

I read some more. The second notation concerned a shootout in the boardinghouse that was operated out of my home, which had occurred in 1899. A trio of thieves had robbed a nearby mine and holed up in the boardinghouse. After two days of hunting, the authorities had tracked them to Ruby Lake. There had been a standoff for several days with the thieves barricaded inside the boardinghouse, holding several guests prisoner. Then a shootout ensued that left all three of the thieves and one law officer dead. The corundum, purported to be worth several hundred thousand dollars, had never been recovered.

I heard the sound of scraping again from the wall. "Probably that big old elm," I said to myself. I'd have to get some of those branches cut; they kept rubbing against the siding. Who knew what damage that might cause if left unchecked? I added it to my list of projects for the contractor.

Corundum? What the devil was corundum? As if reading my mind, the author explained. Corundum was another name for rubies. In this case, deep red rubies from the Elixir Mine ten miles northwest of . . . Ruby Lake.

I sat up straight. Rubies! Of course! At one time, this whole area was noted for its ruby deposits. That's how the town had gotten its name.

There had to be rubies hidden in this house somewhere!

I flew from the bed. "And that's what everybody is after," I muttered, fishing under the bed for my slippers. I tossed my robe over my shoulders and tiptoed out of my room. There was no light on under Mom's door. Good, she was sound asleep. Sometimes she read late into the night.

The rubies probably weren't in the attic. After all, Matt had camped out there—Jerry had found his prints all over everything—and would likely have discovered them. Then again, Matt might have found them and then been killed by whoever else was after them.

If not Matt, then Cash Calderon or one of his workers. Surely Cash or one of his crew would have mentioned if they'd found a stash, wouldn't they? Or would one of them try to keep it for him- or herself?

There was the basement. And somebody had been digging there. It was a likely spot. Though I didn't particularly feel like going down in the deep, dank hole alone in the dark.

I stepped out into the hall, locking the apartment door behind me. I headed for the basement but stopped at the second floor landing, certain that I had heard that scraping sound again. It seemed to be coming from behind the door of the empty apartment. There had been a rhythmic sound to the noise too. Unnatural. I'd never given the contractor the key, so nobody had been inside that apartment in who knew how long . . .

Maybe it was another intruder, like the one the other night. And maybe I should have called the police. But I was tired of Jerry mocking me. If this turned out to be a false alarm, a tree instead of a killer, I'd never hear the end of it.

Besides, at this hour, the station would be closed and by the time the night operator got through to Jerry or one of his underlings, whoever was prowling around my place could be long gone.

I tiptoed back upstairs to my apartment, fished around in the kitchen junk drawer, and came up with the key to the empty apartment. If there was a branch banging against one of the panes, maybe the least I could do was pull the shutters closed to keep the limb from breaking the glass.

I also found a small pencil-sized flashlight. I twisted the rim. Bingo! It worked. I thrust it and the key in the pocket of my robe.

Back on the second floor, I turned the key in the lock but it seemed frozen. Probably needed some lubricating spray. I jiggled the key and the knob up and down, pushing my shoulder against the door. I glanced nervously next door, hoping I didn't wake Esther the Pester. She would not react well to having her beauty sleep interrupted.

Finally, the door popped open. Fetid odor filled my nostrils and my eyes watered up. I felt like puking. "First thing tomorrow," I muttered, "I'm going to air out this apartment."

I groped around for the light switch and gave it a flick. Nothing. I flicked it again a couple of times. Still nothing. The corners of my mouth turned down.

I retrieved the small flashlight from my pocket and twisted. Its thin, weak light played against the floor. At least the wood was dry. Except for the pounding of the rain, I didn't hear a sound.

I crept forward, the boards creaking under my weight. I didn't know if they were trying to tell me something or simply old and in need of repair.

A flash of lightning lit the room. I could see a dark tree limb near the glass, shaking madly. I sighed with relief. The rumble of thunder passed overhead. I couldn't get used to the smell, but I wasn't about to open that window in all this rain.

I'd let it wait until morning. As I turned, the small beam from my penlight played along the wall.

I gasped and stepped back. Ted Nickerson was folded up inside an open dumbwaiter, a rope twisted around his neck, a small pickax in his bloodless, rigid hand. I'd seen a tool just like it on the floor beside the nightstand in the Nickersons' cabin at the Ruby Lake Motor Inn. His cold, dead eyes looked at me accusingly.

My mouth went dry and I swallowed hard.

So this was why Ted Nickerson hadn't returned home. He was dead! By the looks of him, he'd been dead for a day or more. I felt bile rise in my throat. My hand shook uncontrollably as I studied the corpse.

A dumbwaiter? I hadn't even known there was a dumbwaiter. I looked upward and judged where the dumbwaiter would pass in my apartment. I concluded it would be the wall in my bedroom. But since I didn't have a dumbwaiter there, someone had to have boarded it up years before.

The Nickersons must have been looking for the rubies. That explained the history obsession and the rock-hunting gear.

Had Ted Nickerson's wife murdered him and

left him here? She couldn't possibly have thought his body would go undiscovered here for long. She was probably planning to come back and move him out, dispose of his body. Perhaps in the lake. Something must have spooked her when she killed him. Probably me.

Why had she been crying when I went to speak with her then? Was she regretting what she'd done?

I hurried from the apartment and locked the door behind me. I wished Kim was there, but she was home. There was Mom, but I couldn't risk anything happening to her. I bit my lip and scurried to Esther's door. I took a deep breath and knocked.

It was several moments before I heard a sleepy reply. "Who's there?" Esther snapped from behind her door.

"Esther," I whispered, "it's me, Amy. Call the police."

"Darn right I will!" she screamed. "You banging on my door in the middle of the night. Now, go away!"

"Esther," I whispered harshly. "Somebody is dead. Now you call the police while I check the rest of the house." No reply. "Esther?"

I cursed her out and hurried back to my apartment. I'd call myself. Before I could get the door open, I heard a clatter outside. I ran to the window looking out over the back parking lot. A gust of wind had thrown the lid of the Dumpster wide open.

I turned away, then stopped. I approached the window once more. The front end of a dark pickup truck stuck out from behind the Dumpster.

It was too dark to tell for certain, but I thought it was blue.

Aaron was here! Was he involved in this with the Nickersons? Was he after the rubies too? Were he and his sister lurking nearby? Were they in the house?

My head throbbed. Too many things were happening at once. I unlocked my apartment door, found my phone, and waited for the night operator at the police station to pick up. "This is Amy Simms," I whispered. "There's been a murder and I think they might still be in the house!" I waited for a reply. "Hello?" I stared at my phone. The connection had failed. I had zero bars. I tried again. Still no signal. I shook the phone. Of course, it did no good.

I heard those noises emanating from the wall again. What the devil was going on?

Was it the ghost of Heather Sampson coming to haunt me? Looking for her killer? Looking for revenge?

Locking the door behind me, I raced out into the hall. My heart beat madly against my rib cage. I noticed the foyer storage closet was ajar and the hairs on the back of my neck bristled. I was certain it had been shut earlier. I tiptoed closer, pressing my ear to the door.

Not a sound.

If I was smart, I'd go hide under the covers and wait for the police to arrive. If they arrived . . .

I pushed aside the rack of clothes and started up the stairs to the attic.

29

The first step squeaked madly as I put my weight on the old pine plank. I squeezed my eyes shut and held my breath. All I could hear were some unfamiliar sounds, scraping and grunting maybe.

I thought I detected a flapping noise. Bats? I shivered. Did I have bats? I did not want to have bats. Birds I like. Birds I love.

But bats? Those things give me the heebie-jee-bies. They also turn into vampires that suck out all your blood, leaving nothing but your withered car-cass for the turkey vultures to nibble on the next morning. I'd seen a special on it on cable TV.

I took a long, quiet breath and resumed my climb, this time crawling on hands and knees to lessen the weight on each step. Slowly, I pushed my head up above the level of the attic floor. The last thing I needed was some crazed killer with an ax to chop it off. I did not want to be the next Black-beard. I liked my head just where it was.

A dark, hulking figure in the far corner breathed

heavily. It wore a heavy coat and baggy trousers. A hunting cap covered its head. Its back was to me. I could not see a face.

But I could see what he or she was doing. The intruder had removed some old boards, now lying against the wall and scattered at their feet, and was working with a tangle of rope inside a three-foot hole in the wall that could only be the dumbwaiter shaft.

The intruder heaved, grunted, and coughed, wiping an arm along the side of that unseen face. My skin crawled with fear and excitement. Was this Sally Nickerson, come back for her dead husband?

Whoever it was, they were trying to pull Ted Nickerson's body back out from the dumbwaiter, probably so they could dispose of it forever.

But what could I do about it? The figure turned. I ducked back down and held my breath. I counted to ten, then peeked out once more.

The figure was leaning over the shaft now. If I was quiet, I should be able to work my way around the furnace on the left. I'd be able to see the intruder better from there, at least in profile. Maybe I'd then see who I was dealing with. Was it Aaron, Grace, Sally? Derek Harlan?

I tiptoed quickly to the side of the metal furnace. It was warm to the touch, but even it couldn't stop my shivering. After a moment, to be sure I was safe, I stuck my head around the corner.

The intruder stood there, apparently deep in thought. Probably frustrated by how much trouble removing Ted Nickerson's body had become.

I saw a four-foot-long sawn-off remnant of a two-by-four lying loose on the floor. It had probably

been left there by Cash or one of his crew. I bent
and picked it up. The treated pine felt substantial
in my hands. Almost as good as a baseball bat. The
corners of my mouth turned down. I'd recently
been reminded just what a lousy hitter I was.

Still . . . I bit my lip. I'd only have to hit him or
her once.

I hoped. I fingered the board. When the figure
leaned into the shaft again, I lunged!

"Hiiyaa!" I screamed as I attacked. The intruder
turned and I realized I should have kept my big
mouth shut.

"What the—"

I skidded to a halt as the dark intruder stepped
from the shadows and aimed a flashlight in my
face. I held the board in front of my eyes. There
was something eerily familiar about that shape.
"A-Aaron, is that you?"

The figure stepped closer. "You!" he huffed.
"You just couldn't keep out of it, could you?" His
right hand was clutched tightly around the long,
black, solid-looking flashlight. His left hand was
clenched in a fist.

I swallowed, keeping the board in front of me
for protection. "Dwayne!" I said madly. "What are
you doing here?"

The deliveryman frowned and shook his head.
"You just couldn't stop nosing around, could you?"
He took a step closer.

"Stay back!" I warned. I took a mad swing. I didn't
come close to hitting the jerk, but at least I got the
reaction I wanted. He retreated a step. I swung
again and he retreated another.

My mind was racing in circles and my heart was

running an uphill marathon. Dwayne Rogers was the killer? "You killed Matt!" I said, incredulous as it seemed. I mean, why else would he be up here trying to remove yet another dead body from my house?

Dwayne smirked. "Accidents happen. Me and Matt were having a little disagreement." He shrugged. "Things got out of hand." He took a measured step toward me. "Like they're about to do again." There was an ominous and quite sociopathic tone to his voice that set my teeth on edge.

Despite the cold, sweat dripped down my face, stinging my eyes. Dwayne was a blurry dark shadow. I swung again, listening to the whoosh of air as I hit nothing.

"Strike two." Dwayne chuckled. He took another step and I retreated.

The sound of banging and awkward thumping caused us both to glance back at the attic stairs. Dwayne's uncle Theo stepped into the attic. "What the devil is going on here?" He took two steps forward, his cane thumping the boards.

"Theo!" I cried with relief. "It's Dwayne! I'm sorry, but he's our killer." I twirled toward Theo. "He murdered Matt!"

Theo's brow shot up. He leaned heavily against his cane and reached into his coat pocket. "Lord," he sighed wearily. "I never thought it would come to this."

I nodded and turned to Dwayne. "It's over now, Dwayne," I said firmly. "You'll have to come with us. You've got a lot to answer for."

Dwayne smiled. "I don't think so." He pointed at his uncle.

My brow furrowed and I slowly turned my head. Uncle Theo was pointing a revolver at me.

"Is there anybody else in the house?" Theo asked his nephew, his voice steady.

"Just a couple old ladies."

Mom and Esther. It was a good thing my mother hadn't heard that "old" crack. What would happen to them? "Please," I begged, "do what you have to do, but don't hurt them. They don't know anything. Besides, they're asleep. Do what you want— take what you want, but don't harm them." The board hung at my side.

"You get him up yet?" Theo barked to his nephew.

"It ain't easy," Dwayne whined. "The guy's all tangled up in there."

"Well, untangle him so we can get out of here!" ordered Theo.

Dwayne's lips curled downward and he turned toward the dumbwaiter. As he did, a bloodcurdling yell startled us all. I turned first. Esther was sprinting across the attic floor, baseball bat in hand. Dwayne was leaning over the dumbwaiter shaft. That was my chance!

I leapt forward, hitting him in the middle of the back with my board. "Ooomph." Dwayne let out an explosion of breath and fell into the yawning gap.

Theo turned but it was too late. Esther brought her baseball bat down on his hand and the revolver skidded across the floor. She moved in and he fought her off with his cane. It was really a sight to see.

Dwayne's moans echoed upward. His flashlight lay on the floor beneath the dumbwaiter. I grabbed it and searched wildly for the revolver, but it was nowhere to be found.

"Give me a hand here, moron!" shrieked Esther. "I can't hold him all night!"

I looked up to see Esther locked in mortal combat with Theo. I bolted toward them and slammed into Theo's side. I clobbered him with the flashlight. He kept fighting, his one good hand locked around Esther's neck.

"Stop!" I shrieked. I struck him again.

Esther had recovered her bat as we all three sprawled on the ground in a tangle of arms and legs. I watched in horror as the bat swung my way. Fortunately, Theo's head was there to stop the blow that I thought surely was going to land squarely between my eyes.

Theo twitched once, stopped moving. A large knot grew in the center of his forehead.

"Nice shot," I said, huffing and rolling over onto my back. Wow, she had a better swing than I ever did, even in my high school softball-playing prime.

Esther coughed. "I need a drink."

I grinned. "As soon as I can get up, I'll get you some water."

She frowned at me. "Water?" she scoffed. "That's no drink."

I raised my brows. "I've got a bottle of Tennessee whiskey in the apartment." Dwayne's groans had become faint and less frequent.

A glint came to her eyes. "The one above your fridge?"

Huh? I lifted my head from the floor. "Wait, you know about—" I stopped. I heard sirens in the distance. "You called the police."

"Darn right, I did." She coughed some more and shook her head. "I'm too old for this. Too much noise, too much commotion." She pointed an arthritic finger at me. "You banging on my door in the middle of the night." She let out a breath and crawled to her knees. She retrieved her baseball bat from where it lay beside Theo—who still wasn't moving—using it as a cane. "What kind of apartment house are you running here, anyway?"

"Help!" wailed Dwayne. "Hey, somebody, help!" I made my way slowly to the dumbwaiter shaft. The deliveryman was stuck upside down in the narrow hole.

"Don't worry," I called. "Somebody will get you out . . . eventually." I wiped my hands. "And then they'll lock you up and throw away the key," I said under my breath.

Pounding feet came our way and bouncing beams of flashlights spilled into the low-ceilinged attic.

"It's the fuzz," Esther said, pointing her bat at Chief Jerry Kennedy and Officer Dan Sutton. Both men had their guns drawn.

I pushed the tip of the bat toward the ground. "Careful, Esther. Jerry might think that thing is loaded and shoot you."

Esther smiled broadly, took a glance at the comatose Theo Allen, and said, "This baby's always loaded, Simms. And don't you forget it."

I returned her smile. I didn't think I would.

30

"I ran into the postman," Kim announced, wiping her feet at the door on the coco mat. I'd removed the lovebirds, at least temporarily, exiling them to the rear entrance. Too many people tramping in and out and the birds were driving everybody batty. "Grabbed your mail." Kim tossed a handful of mail—catalogs and envelopes—on the counter.

"Thanks," I said, yawning. Kim knew all about last night's events. I'd phoned her first thing in the morning. Birds & Bees would be closed for a couple of days while the police did their thing. Plus, I wanted to keep the treasure- and thrill-seekers away. Lance Jennings from the *Ruby Lake Weekender* had come by, sniffing around for the big scoop. I only let him have it after he promised to make it very clear in his article that there were no rubies in my house. The last thing I needed was for even more people to get the idea that there was a fortune in gems hidden somewhere in the old house.

I'd never get any rest and my house would be rid-
dled with holes.

I also made him promise to get the name of the
store right. "It's Birds and Bees," I'd said, firmly.
"Not Birds and Things, not Babies and Bonnets . . .
If you don't get it right this time, I'll sic Esther on
you with her baseball bat!"

Jerry Kennedy helped himself to his second
roast beef sandwich. The police had been there all
night. Moire Leora, bless her heart, had brought
breakfast and later sandwiches from the diner.

"I'm just glad everyone is all right and those
men are behind bars," Mom said.

Dwayne and Theo were actually in the hospital
under the watchful eyes of medical professionals
and armed police officers. Sally Nickerson was behind bars.

Mom hadn't been happy when she'd learned
that Dwayne had tampered with my van's rear
wheel in an attempt to kill me, or at least put me
out of commission for a while so he and his uncle
could search the house unhindered. Theo had
sent Dwayne out to sabotage the Kia while he'd
kept me busy in the living room sipping tepid,
worse-than-tasteless tea.

I, on the other hand, had been thrilled to learn
he'd been mucking around with my Kia. Why? Because I got to rub Jerry's nose in it, of course.
Maybe he'll think twice before scoffing the next
time I tell him somebody is trying to kill me.

Wait. Scratch that. There would be no next
time.

Jerry nodded and stuffed a couple of peanut

butter cookies in his pocket. "You all are lucky we arrived when we did."

The corner of my mouth went up. "I'd say Esther and I had things pretty well under control."

The chief looked at me with uncloaked disdain. "Please, if we hadn't—"

"So what about the gems?" Kim demanded. "Who's got the rubies?" She rubbed her hands together. "Do we get to keep them?" She sidled up beside me and jiggled her brow. "Partner?"

I shook my head. "Sorry. There are no rubies. At least, according to Gertie Hammer."

"That's right," Jerry said, apparently not averse to speaking with his mouth full.

Gertie had laughed when the police questioned her about the hidden stash of rubies, I explained to Kim and my mother, who was sitting in one of the rockers with a throw over her knees. I had brought the chair up near the front counter so she would be more comfortable.

Gertie had said that if there ever were rubies they were long gone or she'd have found them. She might have been lying. Still, if she had found them, I suspected she wouldn't still be driving that clunker.

"She owned the house for nearly fifty years," put in Chief Kennedy. "So if anybody should know about those rubies, it would be her."

I nodded, deep in thought. Gertie had refused to say why she wanted to buy the house back and neither were the mayor or Robert LaChance willing to talk about it. Because Dwayne and Sally Nickerson had admitted their own—at odds—involvement in their hunt for the treasure, there was nothing the police could do to make Gertie Hammer, Mac MacDonald or Robert LaChance talk about their reasons for trying to get my house.

Theo was in a coma but expected to recover. Dwayne, however, was alert and talking. And he'd talked plenty. It seems he and his uncle had read about the rubies in that new book that had come out, the one John Moytoy had suggested I read. Theo had checked it out from the Ruby Lake Town Library. So had the Nickersons. And they all wanted the rubies. With me moving into the house and all the construction going on, and knowing they were each after the same prize, things between them had heated up.

Things were moving fast. Plus they were worried that the more people who read the book, the more competition there'd be for the rubies.

Dwayne still insisted he hadn't meant to murder Matt Kowalski. "I only hit him because we were arguing. He'd been in the house for weeks and still claimed he hadn't found anything. Me and Uncle Theo were starting to get annoyed. Thought maybe Matt was holding out on us." Dwayne and Matt had been friends. Police learned afterward that Dwayne was known to have visited Matt down in Myrtle Beach during his delivery runs. Dwayne and Theo recruited Matt to help them in their scheme. Who knew if they'd intended to kill him from the start, once he'd found the rubies for them. Neither was confessing to that.

So the two men had argued, and Dwayne had whacked Matt into the next world. He'd been intending to dispose of the body, but I'd returned and stumbled on it first.

"I still don't understand how Dwayne got here in time to commit murder." Kim plucked a scrunchie from her handbag and pulled her hair into a loose ponytail. "I thought you said he was on a delivery in Ethelberg." She shook her head. "He couldn't have done it."

A sour expression appeared on Jerry's face. "We wondered the same thing. On further questioning of the staff at the store he'd delivered to, it turns out that it was Dwayne's uncle Theo who'd made the delivery. Dwayne arrived here in the pickup." The same pickup I'd seen last night from my window. The one I thought belonged to Aaron Maddley. It turned out both men drove similar models. I'd sure botched things up with Aaron . . .

"The first time we called to verify Dwayne's alibi, we just asked if Cole's Trucking had made a delivery. They had." Jerry Kennedy paused and scooped up a forkful of coleslaw. "Turns out," he said, waving his plastic fork, "the description of the driver matches Theodore Allen, not Dwayne Rogers."

So Dwayne had been in Ruby Lake getting rid of Matt Kowalski. A frisson ran up my arms as I remembered what Jerry told me after they searched Theo's house and Dwayne's truck. He explained the bleach and tarp were probably for disposing of Matt's body. Supposedly, the items help cover the odor of decay. "Dwayne's uncle is a retired truck driver," I added. "So it would have been easy for him to make that delivery instead."

"If they arranged that, it seems to me the crime

might have been premeditated," Mom said, her mouth forming a straight line. I was thinking the same thing. She sighed sadly. "I can't believe little Dwayne Rogers is a murderer."

"It happens, Mom." I patted her shoulder. Actually, I explained, he was a double murderer. He'd confessed to finding Ted Nickerson in the house searching for the rubies too. The two men fought and Ted lost. That was the commotion Kim and I had heard. Dwayne had taken the beekeeper suit and worn it as some sort of weird disguise. He'd murdered Ted Nickerson, then when he'd heard us coming up, he stuffed his victim in the dumbwaiter and barreled past us, intending to return later to dispose of the body. "He might have gotten away with it too, if the dumbwaiter hadn't become stuck."

"I think you should have that thing permanently sealed up," suggested Mom. I agreed.

"If there *were* rubies, who would they belong to?" Kim apparently couldn't let go of the idea of instant riches. Not that I could blame her.

Officer Sutton came down the stairs, all slack-jawed and sagging. "They need you upstairs, Chief." I'd never noticed what a long neck he had. And with those big eyes of his, he was practically ostrich-like.

Chief Kennedy nodded. "Search me," he replied to Kim's question, grabbing a handful of home-made barbecue potato chips and heading for the back stairs.

"Who's taking care of Sally Nickerson's poor children?" Mom asked.

"The motor inn staff have sort of adopted them

until a relative arrives. Sally's sister is coming over from Nashville," I explained. There never had been a house on Sycamore.

Mom rose and gazed out the front window. "I think we should rename the store Birds & Bees & Blooms," she quipped. She'd been out front gardening earlier while the police worked inside, and her clothes were covered with grass and dirt stains.

I smiled contentedly. The garden was beginning to shape up and spring was just around the corner.

There was a rap on the front door. Mom looked at me. "It's John Moytoy, from the library."

I waved to him. "It's okay," I told Mom. "Let him in."

"Good to see you, John." I squeezed him. "As you can see"—I spread my arms—"everything is back to normal. The murders are solved and I've got you to thank."

"Oh?"

I explained how I'd read the tale about the missing rubies in the book he'd lent me.

John beamed.

I blanched. Over John's shoulder, a well-dressed woman in heels stomped toward me. Unfortunately, I hadn't told Mom to lock the door behind John. They say bad things happen when you don't lock the door behind you. This was one of those times.

Her hair was pulled back in a tight knot and her eyes were aflame. The woman was clearly agitated. And I recognized her right away. I gulped and braced myself. It was Derek Harlan's wife, Amy. I shot a look at the back stairs. It was good to know the police were here in case I needed backup.

"Stay away from my husband!" she cried.

"I don't want anything to do with him!" I said. I felt color coming to my cheeks. Mom, Kim, and John were all staring at me. "He was my lawyer. Nothing more." I rubbed my hands together. "And he's not even that any longer." Thank goodness.

She narrowed her eyes and glared at me darkly. "I heard you had dinner with him!"

Uh-oh. She must have heard about us sharing a booth at the diner the other night. One of the perks of living in a small town. "I *did not* have dinner with him," I replied with indignation. "*He* had dinner with *me*. And it wasn't really dinner," I added quickly, seeing the storm clouds gathering in her eyes. "It was more a consultation!"

Amy Harlan pointed her finger at me. Her nail was pink and brightly polished. "Just stay away from him or, I swear, I'll kill you!"

She stormed out.

John chuckled. "Who was that?"

"Derek Harlan's wife," I said sourly. "Amy."

"His wife's name is Amy?" Kim snickered and brought her hand to her mouth. I glowered at her. Best friends can be such a pain.

John's brow furrowed. "Derek isn't married."

"Tell that to his wife."

"No, really." John ran a hand along the countertop. "I've met Derek. He's come into the library a few times doing research for cases he's working on. We've chatted." He rapped the counter with his knuckles. "I'm telling you—the man isn't married. He's been divorced for over a year. He moved here to be closer to his daughter. His wife has custody, at least during the school year."

I narrowed my eyes, studying John's face for signs of subterfuge. Was he pulling my leg? Yanking my chain? Trying to get my goat? I'd get even with him, if he was.

Still, I did see the beginnings of a beautiful beach wedding starting to make itself known again. I shook myself. Nope. Never in a million years. Not with a nut job like that for an ex-wife. I'd steer clear of Derek Harlan. Too bad I'd blown it with Aaron Maddley. To take my mind off things like dead bodies, hidden treasures, and—perhaps most annoyingly—men, I rummaged through the mail Kim had dumped on the counter, picked up the letter opener, and slit open an official-looking letter from town hall. My jaw fell.

"What is it now?" A worried look crossed John's face. Mom turned and studied me.

"Yeah, what is it, Amy?" interjected Kim. I felt her come up behind me and lay a hand on my shoulder. She read. "Can they do that?"

"I-I don't know."

"What?" John said, clearly annoyed at being kept in the dark.

I held out the official notice from the town's planning commission. John's eyes darted across the page. "They want to widen the street? Demolish your house through eminent domain?"

I felt Kim's hand tighten around my upper arm. "They can't do that," she said. "Can they?" She was beginning to sound like a parrot with a new favorite phrase.

I sighed, rested my elbows on the counter and my head on my fists. I was thinking of renaming the store: Birds & Bees . . . and Blues.

Two state police officers trooped through the front, asked for the chief. I pointed up the stairs. "Did I really go through all this effort and all this"—I waved my arms uselessly in the air—"mayhem, only to lose it all now?" I asked no one in particular.

Kim's mouth flattened. "You were almost killed."

"You should have wakened me," scolded Mom for about the, oh, I don't know, umpteenth time.

"And possibly get us both killed?" I couldn't help retorting. "Sorry," I said, instantly regretting my tone if not my words.

Mom shrugged.

"I'm only sorry I wasn't here to help," Kim said. "Just think, if it hadn't been for Esther . . ."

"I know." I sighed. My arms fell to my sides. "I still haven't thanked her properly." I glanced up the back stairs. "I suppose I should," I said hesitantly. My eyebrow rose. I was hoping Kim or my mother would talk me out of it. But no such luck.

Kim gave me a shove. "Yes," she said firmly, "you should. Don't worry about everything else. We'll figure it out, girlfriend!"

I climbed the steps like a woman on her way to her own hanging. I knocked on Esther the Pester's door. I really was very grateful for Esther's help. If it hadn't been for her, I might not be alive today.

The door creaked open. "Yeah?" She wore a pink, lime-green- and-white-striped housecoat and fuzzy pink slippers. Esther and her amazing Technicolor housecoat. Her hair was wrapped in a threadbare bath towel.

"Hi, Esther." I played with my fingers. "I wanted to check on you. Everything all right?"

"Fine." She held the door open a crack.

I sniffed. "You're not smoking, are you?"

The old woman pulled a face. "Had some hickory-smoked bacon for breakfast. You want some?"

"No, thank you." This wasn't going the way I'd planned. I told myself to be nice. This woman had saved my life, after all.

"See you around." Esther started to swing the door shut.

I pressed my palm against it. "I want to thank you again for all your help. Without you . . ." I sighed. "I don't know what might have happened." I glanced meaningfully toward the attic. "Or if I'd even be standing here today."

"Yeah, well . . ." She placed her hand over the doorknob, glanced over her shoulder.

"I want you to know," I hurried on, "that you're welcome to stay here"—I gestured with my chin—"in this apartment for as long as you like."

Her eyes narrowed with suspicion. "I've got a lease."

"I know, I know," I said quickly, throwing up my hands. I took a deep breath and started again. "What I'm trying to say is forget the lease. You will always be welcome in my home." I gave her my biggest, most warmhearted smile.

Esther slanted her eyes at me and chewed her lower lip. She kicked her feet behind her, one then the other. "Okay, well, gotta go."

She swung the door toward me and I turned. Then I heard what sounded like a meow and spun on my heels. I threw up my hand. The apartment door slammed against my palm. I winced but ignored the pain. My pupils narrowed. "Did I just hear a cat?"

Esther's lips turned down. "Nope." She shuffled her feet oddly behind her.

I tilted my head to one side and eyed her dubiously. "Well, I heard something." A tickle crept up my nose. I rubbed my index finger under the tip of my nose. "You know I don't allow cats."

The old woman stroked her throat. "Phlegm. When you get to be old like me, the stuff seems to collect in there." She made exaggerated throat-clearing noises but I wasn't sure that I was buying them.

I'd be keeping an eye on Esther the Pester.